Return to Bakeoven Road

Sandy Cereghino

Return to Bakeoven Road

A Novel

Bakeoven Series
Book Two

Sandy Cereghino

Sandy Cereghino

Copyright © 2020 by Author.
Cover by Sandy Cereghino

Printed in the United States of America at
Gorham Printing, Inc
Printed in the United States of America

ISBN978-1-7342467-0-1

All rights reserved. No part of this publication may be reproduced, stored in a retrieval system, or transmitted by any form or by means – for example, electronic, photocopies, recording – without the written permission of the author. The only exception is brief quotations in printed reviews or articles.

Return to Bakeoven Road: a novel/Sandy Cereghino
1.Title 2. Fiction 3. Romance 4. Road 5. Angels 6. Wishes

Return to Bakeoven Road

...can wishes come true?

Sandy Cereghino

Sandy Cereghino

Return to Bakeoven Road

Chapter One

Lou relaxed her head against the leather headrest of her office chair, mindlessly twisting the engagement ring on her finger. Three months had passed since the paper published her feature story, *Angel on Bakeoven Road*, and it still surprised her the number of readers who called the paper daily asking for copies.

In the beginning, it was a story of survival, but turned into so much more after interviewing the six cross holders. Each person had survived different accidents along that country road, to be comforted by the same young woman for nearly eighty years. The brief encounter had sent their lives on a new path.

Lou never realized how important the power of hope and second chances had resonated with others. It wasn't until after her wreck on Bakeoven Road, where she underwent a life changing experience of her own, that Lou felt compelled to search for this woman and learn her story.

Along the way, she re-examined her life, and opens her heart again. Forgiving her father was the first step. He disappeared when she was young and reappeared when she needed him most. Second, was coming to terms with the loss of her mother, who died the year before. The biggest surprise was finding love when she least expected it.

What seemed like a lifetime, had only been about eighteen months since Jason arrived in town. Lou remembered how the sparks flew from their first meeting, and not in a good-way and it made her chuckle. She was trying to prove to her boss she had what it took to fill the position of investigative reporter, until he informed her, she would have a partner.

Jason hadn't been excited about coming to the west coast either. How would this help him to get his life together after losing his family in a car wreck? He definitely did not want to do a story about survivors, but God had a way of changing people's lives. Before either of them could admit it, life was worth living and love was worth taking a chance on.

Lou glanced at the ring around her finger and sighed. They were still navigating their long-distance engagement as they pursued their careers. Jason returned to work at his paper, and Lou was working on her newest assignment to find Kelly's family.

She felt she owed it to her.

Hitting the save button, Lou logged off her computer and gathered her things. Jason would be in town for the weekend and though eager to pick his brain about her new project, she focused on him and nothing more, until once again it was time to say goodbye.

Jason brushed the tears dripping down her cheek. "Now Lou, what are those all about?"

Lou lowered her head, ashamed of her weakness. They had been repeating this scene more times than she could count over the last six months, but today felt different.

"I'm sorry, Jason. I don't know what came over me. I only get to see you once a month and I miss you."

Jason lifted her chin and kissed her lips, drawing her close to him.

"I miss you too. I talked to David and he agreed I need

more time off. So, next month I'm here for two entire weeks. Do you think you can stand me for that long?"

Lou threw her arms around his neck and buried her face in his chest, drawing in his musky scent.

"That's wonderful. Maybe we can talk about setting a wedding date." Lou bit her lip, watching for a reaction to her question. Neither had mentioned the wedding for months.

Jason held her away from him. "I was wondering when we would discuss that. I thought you might have changed your mind."

Lou gasped. "You can't be serious. I thought you were the one with cold feet."

"Me? Wasn't I the one who asked you to marry me twice, even at the expense of getting another leg cramp?"

He had a wide grin and his eyes sparkled with mischief. Lou swatted his arm and couldn't help but laugh remembering that special night.

"If you had thought of the ring the first time, it would have saved you a second trip to the floor. And my father standing over us like we were nuts."

Jason surrounded her in his arms again, burying his face into her hair.

"That was quite a sight. I couldn't go another day not knowing if you would be my wife." He kissed the top of her head. "I realize we've been busy with work, but I want us together forever and soon. How about you?"

Lou could feel Jason's heart pounding, keeping rhythm with her own. If she was truthful, she had been worried, but hearing him now, relief flooded over her.

"Any day, any place," she whispered.

Jason released her once again and checked his watch.

"I'm sorry Lou, but I have to get going if I want to make it back to Portland in time for my flight. Pick two dates. We can choose one when I come back and start planning. I would like Fred and Joan to come, and Fred as my best man, if that's all right with you?"

"Of course, it is. I love Fred. Are you sure you don't want to talk about this some more?"

"Why? You want to marry me, don't you?"

"Yes."

"Then pick a date and I will be there with bells on. Well, not bells, but you know what I mean." Jason picked up his bag and started down the steps. Stopping at the bottom, he turned to her. "When I get back, you can let me know. I love you Lou."

Lou stood watching from the top step as he tossed his bag into the rental car.

"I love you, Jason!" she yelled as he backed out of the driveway.

Watching him drive away the realization finally hit her.

She was getting married!

Giddy with excitement and trying to wrap her head around the idea, Lou hurried into the house to call Julie.

***

Jason smiled as he drove towards Portland, then a frown crossed his face. They have never discussed what to do about their jobs since getting engaged and their long distant relationship was wearing on him.

Could he live and work in The Dalles?

Could Lou move to New York City?

He loved his job and being back to work made him feel alive, but he loved Lou more. Somehow, they would have to decide where they would live together. Questions continued to niggle at his brain all the way to Portland and his flight home.

***

Lou grabbed a cup of coffee and snuggled against the cushions on the couch, trying to gather her thoughts before she called Julie.

Jason wanted her to pick a date.

Really? What if she chose the wrong one?

Did she want a church wedding like Julie's, with the whole bridal party or something simple? Then there was Dad's upcoming wedding to Mary, and she didn't want to overshadow their big day.

A million thoughts buzzed through her head and she felt like she was still in a fog when Julie answered.

"Hey Lou. It's so good to hear from you. What's going on girlfriend?"

"Hey yourself. How's the married life going for you? You ready to leave that bum and come home? Oh, that's right, he knocked you up."

She could hear Julie laughing on the other end.

"Lou, what a terrible thing to say, but I'm glad you called. I was thinking about you and realized we haven't talked about your wedding or when it will be. Did you and Jason decide on a date yet?"

Silence.

"Lou? You still there?"

"I'm sorry, I dropped the phone." She was lying. To tell the truth, she was scared.

"Jason just left, and we talked a little about setting a date. He wants me to pick a couple, so we can choose one when he gets here in three weeks."

Her voice trailed off and she was picking at her fingernail.

"You don't sound too excited about it."

"I think he wants to get married soon. What if I pick the wrong date? What if nothing is available for the day I choose? What about Dad and Mary? I can't get married before they do, and their wedding isn't until September. That's another two months away."

"Whoa, slow down. I'm sure Jason will love any day you pick. And I'm sure your dad wouldn't mind if you got married first if you wanted to."

Lou let out a heavy sigh. She was letting her mind run wild and needed to rein it in.

"Your right, I'm making this a bigger deal than I should. So, what do I do?"

Lou hoped Julie would have the answers she needed.

"Well, first you decide if you want a church wedding or not. Once you have that figured out, find a church if it's available, and book your date. Churches book up early, though probably not as much in the winter, but still. Talk to the minister, decide on the flowers, choose a maid of honor, bridesmaids, the ring bearer, and flower girl."

Julie paused for a moment then continued.

"Next is the cake and food, while Jason picks his best man, groomsmen, tuxedos. Then the most important final decision for you is to find a bridal gown. Oh, and don't forget comfortable shoes, and if it's during the day or evening."

Lou's head was spinning, and she would have fallen over if she weren't already sitting.

"Oh my God! Are you serious? Is that what you went through for your wedding?"

Julie laughed. "Yes silly. Did you think weddings just happen when the bride walks down the aisle? There's a lot of planning to do and it can take a minimum of three months to get it together."

Lou let out another heavy sigh. She couldn't do this; it was too much.

"I don't know Julie. Even if I start now, that will put us into December. Do people get married in the winter? I think I will be sick." Lou flopped her head back.

"Listen to me. You will not be sick. Pull yourself together and snap out of this pity party. Yes, people get married in the winter. Haven't you ever seen a Christmas wedding? But that's not the point. If you don't want a church wedding, get married at City Hall by the Justice of the Peace. Pick a dress. Something that fits your personality and call it good. Afterwards, have a simple reception at the house. Jason loves you. He won't care, as long as he marries you."

Lou could feel her heartbeat slowing. Thank God she had Julie to calm her.

"You're right, I'm making this too complicated. I'm just a simple girl with simple tastes. I can't do the big production like yours. I'm not saying it wasn't beautiful, but it's just not for me. Do you understand what I'm saying?"

Lou hoped she hadn't hurt her friends' feelings.

"Don't worry Lou, no offense taken. To tell the truth, I would have loved a smaller wedding, but my parents had other plans. So, what's a girl to do?" Julie paused and caught her breath. "I'm sorry, I didn't mean it the way it sounded. I'm sure your mom would have given you a beautiful wedding."

The mention of her mother made her sad. Lou realized she would miss another milestone in her life without her mom.

"Thanks, but enough of that. I only have three weeks to decide what kind of wedding we want and when to have it. I wish you were here."

"I wish I was too, but the doctors don't want me traveling."

Lou picked up on the concern in her voice.

"Why what's happening? Is the baby okay? Are you okay?"

Julie was struggling to speak, and Lou could tell she was crying now.

"You can tell me. I'm here for you."

"Oh, Lou, I'm so worried. I know I'm only four months along, but I've been spotting. The doctor doesn't know if I will make it to term. I might lose the baby."

Lou was sitting straight on the sofa.

"Does John know?"

"Yes, he's so supportive, but I know he's anxious too. We just found out it's a boy."

The thought of Julie's son dying got her thinking of what happened to her own baby brother and how it had destroyed her mother. She forced herself to keep it together.

"Listen, you do what the doctors tell you. You know I will figure out this silly wedding stuff. Your health is the most important thing to me. Do you have help? Is your mom there? Do you want me to come and take care of you?"

Lou knew she was rambling but couldn't help herself. This was her best friend. Truly her only friend, and it worried her. Lou could hear Julie sniff then blow her nose.

"Thank you, but my mom is coming. I think that's all John can manage, though I would have preferred you." She gave a weak laugh. "Never repeat that to my mother."

Lou smiled. "You know I won't. But I mean it. I'll come if you want me to."

"I know, but let's see how things go. The doctor said if I could make it to six months, I have a better chance of making it full term. Say a prayer for me if you would."

Lou cringed. She had only recently asked God back into her life, but she would not let her friend down.

"I'll do the best I can."

"I think I'll go. I'm getting a little tired." Julie said.

"You call me, otherwise I will be in the car and on my way to you."

"Quit worrying about me and decide on a date. I want to witness my best friend marrying the man of her dreams."

Lou gave a little chuckle. "Okay, I guess we both have some homework to do. You take care of the little one and I will figure out this wedding stuff. I'll call you on Thursday."

Julie said goodbye and Lou closed her eyes and prayed to God to spare this baby.

Chapter Two

Thursday morning, Lou called Julie and so far, so good. She sounded so depressed, Lou tried to cheer her up with silly jokes, and had managed to get her to laugh. They said goodbye and Lou knew all they could do was wait and pray.

And she needed to get back to work.

Brad's approval for a second story, along with the curiosity of her readers, was pushing Lou to search for Kelly's beginnings. But there was a big problem. The journal she found in the wrecked truck, supplied little information to go on.

Kelly wrote she was leaving the orphanage where she had grown up, though she never named it, to start her journey as a circuit nurse for the local area. She wrote about breaking down and a farmer came upon her standing in the road. The farmer was headed to town in search of a doctor for his family. It was a lucky day for both and for the next two weeks, she nursed his wife and children through a bad case of food poisoning before it was time to resume her travels.

Unfortunately, she never made it and Lou wondered what Kelly would have been like if she had survived. Mostly she never expected the little story she started with, to turn into such an integral part of her life and realized the entire experience had transformed her. It gave her a newfound confidence and the power of forgiveness.

Lou pledged to be nicer to the people she worked with and those around her, understanding it wouldn't happen overnight.

After six hours doing research on the computer, and two pots of coffee, Lou needed a break and went to the ladies' room. When she pushed the door open, Karol, the receptionist, was talking on her phone. Lou didn't want to intrude until what she hears compels her to enter the bathroom and comfort the girl. This is a stretch for Lou as she hadn't been over friendly to Karol since she came to work at the paper a year ago. Karol seemed nice enough, Lou just didn't think she had anything in common with her.

Truthfully, she didn't want to make another friend who might leave her. Not that Julie left on purpose. She got married and her husband had a job in Portland. It was only an hour and a half away, but Lou missed having girl time with her.

***

Karol shook with anger, shocked that Tommy, who just broke up with her, wants her to get rid of their baby. She couldn't do that. It would be a sin, one worse than having sex in the first place before marriage. She hadn't planned to do it, but she got caught in the moment, and made a poor decision.

Worse, Karol couldn't believe she had been so stupid to believe him when he told her she wouldn't get pregnant the first time. They didn't teach that stuff in high school, where she came from, and her mother never talked to her about it either. At nineteen, she was as dumb as a box of rocks when it came to sex.

Life was so fast here, compared to the small town of Lyle, across the river in Washington. She'd never been serious about a boy until she moved to The Dalles and started working at the paper and met Tommy. He worked in the warehouse and she fell madly in love with him.

Suddenly his words flashed across her mind again. Tommy said they were through if she kept the baby and she knew he meant it. She didn't know what she would do.

Going home wasn't a possibility. Slowly sinking to the

floor, she had her face buried in her hands when she sensed someone was standing next to her.

***

Lou wanted to turn and leave but knew she couldn't. Karol was sobbing her heart out in a heap against the bathroom wall. Grabbing a fist full of paper towels, Lou cringed as she slid down next to her, fearing the floor was crawling with germs. Offering the towels without a word she waited. When Karol stopped crying, Lou asked what the problem was, but it only sent Karol into another crying fit.

Ten minutes passed and Lou was getting a cramp in her leg and had to stand. Holding out her hand, she pulled Karol up off the floor, steering her towards the sink and gently prodding her to wash her face while Lou dashed to the nearest stall. Relieved, she washed her hands, then silently guided Karol out of the bathroom, down the hall towards her office.

Once inside, Lou locked the door and placed Karol in the chair by the wall, who appeared to have finally cried herself out. When Karol looked up and seemed to realize she was in Lou's office, with Lou sitting across the desk staring at her, she acted like she wanted to jump up and run but flopped back against the seat cushion instead.

Lou watched the pained look on the girl's face and felt her heart break for her.

"Is there anything I can do for you?"

Karol gave her a look of shock. "Why are you being so nice to me? You never have before." She buried her face in her hands again.

Lou took the words as a much-deserved slap in the face. Though they stung, they were true.

"You're right, but I want to help now, if you will let me."

"Thanks, but I'll have to think about it." Karol gasped. "You can't tell anyone what you heard."

Lou saw the desperation in the girl's eyes.

"You have my word. Just know that whatever you need, I'm here for you."

Lou was shocked by the words coming out of her mouth. Why in the world was she getting involved? This was none of her business but now she had offered to help.

Karol gave her a half smile, then unlocked the door and left.

Flustered at herself, Lou straightened the notes on her desk and reached for her phone to call Jason, but remembered she promised she wouldn't tell anyone.

Setting the phone down, she leaned back in her chair, trying to understand the scene in the bathroom and in her office. Had she really offered to stand by this girl who she barely knew? Hanging her head, she pulled at her hair as if it would stretch her brain to accommodate all the problems she was stirring up.

Lou tried to think of ways she could be of help to Karol but kept coming up blank until Pastor Bill Owens, one of the Bakeoven Road survivors, came to mind. He was a youth pastor and hopefully he would know what to do in these situations. Tomorrow she would suggest Karol talk to him thus releasing her from her promise. It all sounded great in theory, but she had made a promise and would have to see it through.

***

Karol returned to her desk, unsure what to do next. She had only told Tommy about the baby, but now that Lou knew, Brad was sure to find out and fire her.

She felt like such a loser.

This was her first job since graduating high school last summer and leaving home. Her father told her the day she left, she was dead to them, and to never come back. She was glad to leave, though she would miss her mother, who when the time came, just stood behind her father mouthing the words she was sorry. Karol had walked out, never to return or talk to her parents again.

Now faced with the biggest decision in her life, she knew if she lost her job, she would have nowhere to go. She has been living at the YWCA until she could save enough to get her own apartment, but they were strict about it being a temporary living arrangement. But with a baby on the way, would they make her leave? Laying her head on her desk, she felt her stomach flutter, forcing her to make a mad dash back to the ladies' room, this time to throw up.

***

Over the next three weeks, Lou and Karol exchanged few words. Karol looked tired and had dark circles under her eyes. When Lou asked if she was eating, Karol said she was fine, so Lou let it go for now. She had other things on her mind and had been busy working on her story.

Jason would be in town tomorrow and they were going to discuss a wedding date. She still hadn't chosen a day but had finally decided she wanted a simple ceremony with Dad and Mary, and Fred and Joan and of course Julie, depending on the date they chose.

As for her story, she was running in to dead ends. Though she could use Jason's help, she wanted to prove she could do this on her own. Besides, she didn't want to waste their time together discussing work. Lost in thought, she jumped when her cell phone buzzed.

It was Jason.

"Well hello handsome," she swooned into the phone, then glanced at the clock. "Where are you? It's after five. Shouldn't you be here by now?" She felt her stomach do a flip.

Something was wrong.

"Hi, sweetheart. There's been a minor glitch but before you say anything, please hear me out."

His voice sounded strained to her.

"There was this story I had been working on before Annie died. It was important to me. Anyway, I have a chance to finish it. The bad part is, I'll be overseas for three months, but I will call, and we can Skype if the signal is good."

Silence filled the air.

"Are you still there?"

"Yes, Jason, I'm here. I'm just trying to understand what you are saying."

She knew he could hear the disappointment in her voice.

"I know this is crazy to spring on you right now, but the clearance finally came through and I have to take it if I want to go. I really want to finish this project. Do you understand?"

The room spun with a kaleidoscope of colors swirling around her head as a searing pain above her right eye seemed to pierce her brain.

Did she hear him correctly?

"You're telling me you are going overseas for three months and asking me if I'm okay with that?"

"I'm sorry Lou, but I have to do this, just the way you had to do your story. Please understand."

She knew she couldn't deny him his moment and choked back the lump in her throat, trying to pull herself together. By the time he got back she would have the wedding planned out, plus it would give her time to work on her own story. She was trying to convince herself, but it burned like fire in her heart.

"You're right Jason, you have to do the story. It's for only three months and when you get back, we will get married. I'll take care of everything and...." She could hear the sigh of relief in his voice.

"I love you Lou, more than you will ever know. And yes,

we'll marry the day I return. I don't care where. I just want you to be my wife. Thank you for understanding. I'm not sure when I can call, so don't get worried if you don't hear from me for a while. Just know I'm thinking of you and you are always in my heart. Please tell you dad and Mary how sorry I am about missing their wedding."

"Jason, I."

"They're calling my flight. I have to go. I love you—and I'll be home soon."

He clicked off and Lou dropped the phone on her desk in a rush to the bathroom, before throwing up her lunch until she had the dry heaves, then collapsing on the floor in racking sobs.

Karol had just exited the stall and was washing her hands when Lou rushed in. This time she grabbed the towels and slid down next to Lou.

Lou lifted her head for a moment and realized who was sitting next to her. How ironic, she thought. Closing her eyes, she buried her face in her hands and continued to sob.

Why was love so complicated?

***

Karol couldn't imagine what had sent Lou in here in such a frenzy, so she sat and tried to comfort Lou the way she had done for her.

Lou lifted her head, took the towels, and wiped her face.

Karol rose, offered Lou her hand, then helped her to her feet, guiding her to the sink and watched Lou's look of shock as she glanced into the mirror at the two of them. What a sight they were.

For the first time, Karol noticed the dark circles under her own eyes. Lou's eyes were red from crying, with black streaks of mascara running down her cheeks.

Lou began to laugh, and Karol joined in until the two

hung on to each other to keep from falling over. The laughter subsided and Lou gently pulled back from Karol.

***

Lou felt embarrassed by her outburst, but grateful for the comfort.

"Thank you. That was kind of you."

Karol dropped her hands to her sides and looked away.

"I was just trying to help."

Lou splashed her face with warm water, trying to remove the smeared mascara. Another reason she hated to wear make-up. Content she had succeeded in getting it off, she took a deep breath, lifted her shoulders, tucked her curly hair behind her ears, then straightened her blouse.

"You did and I'm grateful. Enough about me. How are you doing?"

Lou turned and looked Karol straight in the eyes. The girl looked worse in the harsh lights of the bathroom.

"I'm... I have to leave the Y at the end of the month." Karol seemed barely able to say the words. "They won't let me stay any longer."

Lou gasped. "Did you tell them about the baby?"

Karol shook her head.

"Why not? I'm sure they would let you stay under these circumstances."

"I just couldn't tell them. I don't know what to do. Tommy is still pressuring me to get rid of the baby. He said it's all my fault!" Karol started sobbing.

Fury pulsed through Lou to the point she wanted to find this Tommy kid and wring his neck. Why did men always blame the woman for babies? Karol was better off without him. But the housing situation worried Lou.

"What about your family? Could you go home until the baby is born?"

Karol shot her a look of horror. "I can't. I mean, I have

no family to go home to."

"But I thought you were from Lyle? Isn't your family still there?"

"No, they all moved away. I don't know where they are. Please Lou, don't ask me about them. I'll think of something." Her voice trailed off to a whisper.

Lou heaved a deep sigh and chewed on her lower lip. Jason said she always did that when she was troubled and smiled to herself. What was she going to do? She couldn't let Karol end up on the street, and Jason was going to be gone for three months.

Suddenly she had a crazy idea.

"Listen. I have an idea, but it's totally up to you. What if you came to stay with me until you figure out what is best for you and the baby?"

"You would do that for me?" Karol sniffed. "I thought you were getting married soon, from the gossip around the office."

Lou bit her lip again.

"Yes, I am, but it won't be for at least three months. Jason is on assignment overseas, so you could stay until he gets back. But remember, it's only temporary."

Karol grabbed Lou's hands. "Are you sure? I mean, thank you. I promise I won't be any trouble and I'll help any way I can."

Lou gave Karol a gentle squeeze, released her hands and rubbed her temples. What was she thinking?

"I said you can stay, but there will be rules. You are not to allow Tommy to come to the house. You will go see a doctor for a checkup, plus help with light chores. As for paying, just help with the groceries. I want you to start a savings account, so you can get your own place by the time Jason returns. Remember, this is only for three months. Is that agreeable?"

Karol's head was bobbing up and down, making Lou dizzy. "When did you say you had to leave?"

"Next Friday." She hung her head as if afraid Lou would see the look of fear in her eyes. "Are you sure about this Lou? Maybe I can find some other place to go."

"I wouldn't have offered if I didn't mean it. Have your things ready and I will pick you up at the YWCA after work. This will give me a chance to prepare your room."

Karol threw her arms around Lou and hugged her tight. Lou grinned. Karol was growing on her.

Chapter Three

George set his morning newspaper aside, glanced over at Mary and smiled. She was humming to herself while she finished setting out the fresh-baked pastries for the other residents of their boarding house. He still couldn't believe how lucky he had been the day he stopped to inquire about a room to rent.

Last year had been a roller coaster ride for all of them. It started with reconnecting with Lou, then falling in love with Mary. He had consigned himself to spend the rest of his life alone, but God had other plans. He was admiring his beautiful bride to be, as she set the cinnamon roll in front of him.

"You sure are joyful today, Mary," he said dipping his finger in the gooey icing and licking it off.

Mary kissed his forehead.

"Well George, it's only a month until we are husband and wife and I still have so many things to do."

George pulled her to his lap and held her tight.

"You have nothing to worry about. I have everything under control."

"Oh, you do say."

George smiled. "Yes, my love. All you must do is show up. And to make sure that happens, we're going to the chapel together."

Mary laughed and hugged his neck. "That's one thing you don't have to worry about George. I never dreamed I would love again until I met you. So, you're stuck with me like the sticky icing on that cinnamon roll."

George burst out laughing, then kissed her.

"George McClelland, now look what you have done!"

"What? I just wanted to taste it on your lips."

Mary shook her head, kissing him back and smearing the icing all over his face and hers. They were still laughing when Lou walked into the room.

"Whoa now! What in the world are you two doing? Should I come back at another time?" She put her hands over her eyes and peeked through her fingers.

Mary jumped up from George's lap and hurried to the sink for a wet cloth. She wiped her red face before throwing the washcloth at George.

"Hi Lou, we were just discussing the finer points of sticking together," Dad said.

Lou plopped down in the chair across from her father

"I can see that. So, what did you discover, Dad?"

She pointed to her chin indicating he still had icing on his.

George finished cleaning his face. "Is if all off?"

Lou nodded, laughing.

He loved to hear his daughter laugh. It had been a long time coming.

Mary returned to the table and took the seat next to him.

"What brings you over here today Lou? Shouldn't you be at work? Is something wrong?"

He felt an uneasiness rising in his chest. Something was troubling her, and it showed on her face. She was chewing on her lip.

"Can't I stop by to see my two favorite people and ask if you need any help with the wedding?" Lou avoided his eyes.

"Lou."

"Okay, okay. There is something, but it's not really a big deal."

George took her hand in his own. "From the look on your face, it appears to be a big deal to me."

Lou pulled her hand back and leaned against the chair.

"Jason isn't coming home this weekend, or the next, or the next." Her voice lowered. "And Karol from work will be staying with me for a while."

"I thought he was coming tonight. I have his room ready. And why would Karol be staying with you?" Mary asked, looking confused.

Lou gave a deep sigh. "Jason left on a special assignment for three months."

George sat straight in his chair and Lou put up her hand.

"Before you say anything, Dad, hear me out. Jason had been working on a special story about the troops, but never completed it after he lost his family. He said it's been eating at him and now he has a chance to finish what he started. He can't tell me much, but he will be gone three months and will contact me when he can. He asked me to believe in him the way he did with my story."

Mary reached out and touched Lou's hand.

"Are you okay with this?"

"Not really. But how do I deny him his chance? You both remember how I was with Kelly's story and how I'm still trying to find answers. I have to trust God to bring him home safe to me." A tear rolled over the edge of her eyelid and slid down her cheek.

George cleared his throat.

"Okay, I think I understand about Jason, but what is this about Karol staying with you? Isn't she the receptionist at the paper? I didn't know you were friends."

Lou swiped the tear away with the back of her finger.

"We aren't friends the way Julie and I are, but something has come up. I can't have her living on the streets. So, I offered her a place to stay. It's only temporary while Jason is gone. I'm just trying to be a better person. She needs my help."

George had nothing to say. Her generosity amazed him, but he worried about her too and would talk with her later in private, but for now he would support her decisions.

"I think that's commendable of you to help. Do you know much about this girl? Where's her family? Can't she go home to them?" George noticed the frown on Lou's face. "I'm just asking Lou, for your own sake."

"I know, Dad. Like I said, it's only for three months. Anyway, I just wanted you both to know, in case you came by the house and found her there, or why Jason didn't come home this weekend."

Lou dropped her head, focusing on the stain on her khaki slacks. "He wants you to know how sorry he is about not being here for your wedding."

George rose from his seat and put out his arms. Lou did the same. Father and daughter held each other tight.

"When you hear from him, tell him we understand and get home soon."

Lou buried her face in his chest. "Thanks Dad. And you too, Mary."

Mary rose and joined them.

George prayed silently it would all work out.

***

After a restless night, Lou approached Brad's office door and knocked.

"Come in," the voice on the other side bellowed.

Lou chewed her lip as she opened the door and entered.

"Hey Brad, you got a minute?"

Brad set his paper aside and motioned for her to shut the door and take a seat.

"What's up Lou? How's the new story going? Is Jason back yet?"

Lou took a moment to register his rapid-fire questions before answering.

"The story is coming along, though I'm running into dead ends, but don't worry, I'll find my way around them. Jason is still on assignment and should be back soon, but that's not why I wanted to talk to you."

Brad sat forward with a frown on his face.

"What's up, Lou? You're not quitting, are you? I mean, I just gave you this big promotion."

"No, I'm not quitting. Besides, where could I find a better boss than you?" She forced a smile.

Brad relaxed back in his chair. "Okay then spill it."

Lou glanced around the room for a moment, not sure how to start the conversation.

"Well, first this has to be in the strictest of confidence and cannot leave this room."

"Lou, get to the point." He sounded agitated.

"Do you agree first?"

"Yes. Now what's going on?"

"Karol is pregnant and will be living with me just until Jason gets back. She's been living at the YWCA but must leave. The baby's father is Tommy Parker. He works in the warehouse but wants nothing to do with the baby or her. She has no family and I just couldn't let her be homeless."

Brad remained silent.

"Well, say something."

"I don't know what to say. Are you sure about letting her live in your house?"

Lou shrugged her shoulders.

"It's only until she can find another place to live and decides what she wants to do about the baby. What I want to know is, can she keep her job, and does she have medical to cover this?"

Brad let out a slow whistle and leaned back in his chair.

"Wow. That was a mouthful I didn't see coming. Yes, she can keep her job if she does it. You know she's not the best receptionist. I realize she's young, but she must show up on time and do what I ask of her. Also, our medical will cover her and the baby. This is a big step for you, Lou, I'm impressed."

Lou frowned as she stood. "Yes, it is, but hold your judgement. We haven't gotten through the first day yet," she replied, then left his office.

The biggest decision she made was to give her room to Karol and she would move into her mother's room. It had been such an emotional battle she had waited to the last day and now stood at the door with trepidation.

She could do this.

Pushing the door open, she stepped through and waited. Nothing happened. Lightning didn't strike her, and a screaming ghost didn't push her out the door. It was just an empty room.

Releasing her breath, she set the boxes next to the bed and turned to the closet first. Sliding the doors aside, Lou ran her hands gently over all her mother's pretty dresses. She thought she might keep several for special occasions...if they fit. Carefully, one by one, she pulled them out and lay them on the bed. A couple dresses caught her eye, and she set them aside. The rest she packed in the first three boxes.

Next, she went through the shoes doing the same. Boxes filled quickly with sweaters, coats, scarfs, and hats, along with handbags, after she checked for hidden treasures but found none. With the closet empty except for the luggage, Lou turned to the dresser and gently pulled the top drawer open. Simple cotton panties and bras neatly lined the drawer. Lou was surprised at her mother's choice of undergarments, expecting silk and lace. Sliding the drawer closed, she decided she would do that one last. The next two had pants and blouses. Nothing that was her style, so she placed them in another box.

Finished with the other drawers, she returned to the top one. Though she felt uncomfortable touching her mother's underwear, Lou quickly lifted out the contents and dropped them into one of the smaller boxes and closed the top.

After sealing and labeling everything, she hustled them to the garage to take to the Goodwill later. Returning to the room, she wiped out the dresser, dusted everything, then went to get her own clothes. By the time she finished changing rooms, she was breaking a sweat and it was time to get Karol.

***

Karol stood at the front entrance to the YWCA with everything she owned packed into the tattered suitcase by her feet. The staff had been kind to her since she had arrived, and when she said she had found a place to stay, they were glad for her. She wished she were happy. Tommy was still harassing her about the baby, and she didn't know if this would work living with Lou. But it was the only choice if she didn't want to be sleeping on the street. She was sure the Y would let her come back, but it was time to move on. This was no place to have a baby.

***

Lou pulled up to the curb where Karol was standing and parked the car. The poor girl looked miserable, and Lou knew she had done the right thing.

Karol wasted no time stowing her suitcase in the back seat, then jumped in the passenger seat.

"Thanks for doing this Lou. I promise to help and not get in your way." Her voice trailed off to the sound of sobs.

Lou felt awkward but reached over and patted Karol's hand. "It will be okay. Let's go home and get you settled, then we can work out the rest."

Karol gave her a weak smile and turned her head towards the window, not saying a word during the ride.

Lou said a silent prayer, hoping that this would work out

as she pulled into her driveway and parked.

"Well, here we are."

Karol dabbed at her eyes and opened the door.

Lou did the same, then helped get the suitcase and led the way.

During the next few weeks as Lou and Karol try to adjust to their new lives as roommates, Karol's moods and crying reminded Lou of her mother, and she thinks she may have bitten off more than she can chew. Feeling at her wits' end, Lou realizes she needs a new perspective and calls her father. He suggested Karol talk with Pastor Bill for help to figure out what is the right path for her. Lou had completely forgotten about him. Thankfully, Karol agrees.

Lou sets up a meeting and Pastor Bill gives Karol the names of people who can help, but she is adamant about not giving up her baby. He asks Karol to keep in touch and Lou is feeling hopeful things will get better, until they arrive home and Karol rushes into her room slamming the door.

Shaking her head, Lou shuffles to the kitchen for a needed cup of coffee. All these distractions are putting her behind on her story. Reaching for her notebook, she searches for anything that will drive her in the right direction to find Kelly's family. She is still flipping through her notes when she hears Karol shuffle into the kitchen and looks up.

"Hey Karol."

"Hi Lou." Opening the cupboard, she finds a box of crackers, then pours herself a glass of milk before plopping down next to Lou. "What are you working on?"

Lou grabs a cracker and realizes she hasn't eaten all day. Checking the clock, it was 6:15. Where had the time gone?

"Have you had dinner yet?"

Karol shook her head. "I wasn't hungry."

Lou rose and opened the fridge door. It was empty. She forgot to get groceries today. How could Karol eat healthy for her and the baby if she didn't provide her with food?

"How about we go get a hamburger and fries tonight? I promise I will get groceries tomorrow."

Karol smiled. "Can I have a chocolate milkshake too?"

Lou laughed. "Go get your shoes on. I'm starved."

Karol got up and hugged Lou.

Startled, Lou accepted the young girl's gesture and hugged her back.

"Thanks." Karol whispered as she went to get her shoes and was opening the front door. "Come on, Lou," she called.

Lou grabbed her bag and coat and hurried to catch up.

Chapter Four

Lou woke with a bittersweet smile on her face. She had survived six weeks with Karol, and today Dad and Mary were getting married. She still hadn't heard from Jason but knew in her heart God was watching over him. She would not let missing him ruin this day. She also called Julie last night for an update. Though her friend couldn't travel, she was holding her own with the baby and just had to take it easy. Lou thought she might take time off after the wedding for a visit.

Jumping out of bed, she hurried to get ready. The wedding was in two hours and it was already ten. She could kick herself for sleeping so late. She wanted to arrive early in case Mary or Dad needed any last-minute help.

Slipping on one of her mother's dresses she had kept for the occasion, she did a little turn in the full-length mirror. It was a simple A-line design in a rose color and fit her nicely. It felt strange wearing the dress, but also comforting in a way.

The wedding would be bittersweet without Jason. They were to have been standing with Dad and Mary. Lou had to accept things change and not let her feelings upset this important day for all of them. Dad was getting a second chance at love and she was getting a chance to have a mother again.

Lou was ready to leave for the chapel, when she saw Karol come out of the bathroom crying and stopped.

"What's the matter? Is the baby all right?"

Karol wiped her nose in the tissues she was holding. "Oh, the baby is fine. I guess it's the hormones or something. Don't worry about me. Enjoy your dad's wedding. I think I'll go back to bed for a while." Slipping past, she stopped in the hallway. "And Lou, thanks again for letting me stay here. I really appreciate it."

"Your welcome." Lou patted Karol on the shoulder. "Remember, if you need anything to let me know."

"I will," she said, then disappeared into her room.

***

George looked in the mirror, frustrated with his bow tie. He had tried three times to tie it and it still looked crooked.

"Mary," he called out. "Can you help me?"

Mary entered the room wearing a lavender-colored satin and chiffon dress that ended at her ankles. She looked like an angel, leaving him speechless.

"What's the problem, George?"

"I ah... Mary, you're so beautiful. But am I supposed to see you before the wedding?"

"Oh George, don't be silly. We're riding together. Remember? Anyway, what do you need?"

George pointed at his tie.

"Come here." Gently, she tied the bow tie and adjusted his collar. "You look handsome George. I'm a lucky woman." Tears welled in her eyes. "Don't go making me cry on my wedding day."

George handed her a tissue. "I love you Mary. Cry if you want to." Then he took her hand. "Let's go get hitched."

***

Lou parked and hurried into the chapel, relieved she had arrived before the bride and groom. Friends were filling the seats, and she was straitening the guest book when Dad and Mary walked through the doors.

"Oh Mary. You look so lovely. Doesn't she, Dad? And you. My goodness, you clean up nice." Lou kissed them both on the cheeks. "Dad, go take your place at the alter and Mary and I will wait here until the music starts."

George gave both women a kiss and hurried to take his place.

Mary reached out and took hold of Lou's hand. "Thank you for being here today. I'm sorry about Jason. I know you miss him. We do too."

A lump formed in her throat, but she would not cry and upset Mary. "I'm so excited for you and Dad. You both deserve this." She heard music begin to play. "Well, that's our cue. See you at the other end."

Lou turned and walked up the aisle towards where her father stood. She was halfway up when a man stepped from the shadows and stood next to her father. He had a beard covering his face, but she knew those eyes. Jason! Lou felt lightheaded but pulled herself together and took her place.

The wedding march began, the guests stood, and Mary entered, making her way to her husband to be.

Jason winked at Lou. She chewed on her lip.

George and Mary said their vows, promising to love one another for the rest of their lives. When the minister pronounced them husband and wife, George took Mary in his arms for their first kiss. Everyone clapped as they walked down the aisle hand in hand.

Lou and Jason followed holding hands, and she squeezed his hand a little harder than necessary, but he didn't pull away. Once Dad and Mary went through the doors into the reception hall, Lou pushed Jason out the door to the back of the chapel but didn't have a chance to say a word, before he covered her mouth with his own. Lou closed her eyes, swooning in his kiss, then pulled back.

"What are you doing here? I thought you said...? Never mind kiss me again!"

Jason obliged until they both had to come up for air. "Hi Lou. Did I surprise you?"

Lou stepped back and stared at him. He looked tired, but he was here. "Yes, you did. So, what's with the fur on your face?" She reached up and stroked his beard. It was softer than she thought it would be and dotted with specks of gray.

"Yeah, what do you think? I always wanted to grow one."

"It's different for sure. Is this a permanent thing?" Lou wasn't sure if she wanted it to be.

"Only for a while, so don't worry. It helps me fit in better over there. Most of the men have them."

"Why didn't you call and let me know you were coming?" She had a feeling he wasn't home for good.

"I wasn't sure if I could get a flight and didn't want to upset you or George and Mary if I couldn't make it. I'm sorry Lou, I've missed you." Jason put his arm around her, pulling her to his chest.

Lou buried her face and drank in his scent as if trying to imbed it into her brain for safekeeping. She wanted to stay that way forever, but it was time to go back.

"Jason, we have to go inside. Dad will wonder what happened to us."

The reception was in full swing when they entered, and Dad was feeding a slice of cake to Mary as they approached the table. Mary picked up her piece and with a twinkle in her eyes, smashed it in Dad's face. Everyone was hooting and hollering at the happy couple.

Lou idled up to her father and wiped the frosting from his cheek.

"Good job, Mary. That might be a trick I use at our wedding." She turned towards Jason. "What do you think, future husband of mine?"

Jason grinned through the thick beard. "I think I'll make sure I shave before that day. Otherwise I'll end up looking like Santa Claus."

Dad and Mary laughed in unison, then moved out to the dance floor for their first dance as husband and wife. Lou and

Jason soon joined them, then the rest of the guests followed.

As the music played, Lou watched her father and her new stepmom basking in the glow of the lights. The love they shared with each other shone brighter than any light in the chapel. Lou couldn't be happier now that Jason was here to share this with her.

The reception ended, and Dad and Mary were getting ready to leave on their honeymoon, to the coast for the weekend.

Lou approached her dad and wrapped her arm around his. "It was a beautiful wedding. Do you want to plan mine? You might have found a new calling. And Mary, the cake. I can't believe you made your own wedding cake. What a team you two are."

Lou knew she was talking too much but couldn't help herself. She kissed them both and turned away. Now that Dad was married, he wouldn't need her anymore. She knew in her heart Jason was leaving again and she had a house guest she wasn't sure she wanted.

Jason saw the frown on her face and moved next to her.

"Congratulations George and Mary. I'm glad I could make it back in time."

George stretched out his hand. Jason shook it, and the two men exchanged a knowing glance.

"Thanks, Jason. It was a delight to see you walk in. At first, I wasn't sure who you were with the beard and all. I would like to talk to you, but my wife is signaling it's time to go." George paused. "I like the sound of that. That's something you need to take care of soon."

Jason nodded as George walked away.

Lou and Jason followed them out to the car decorated with shoe polish and tin cans dangling off the bumper. The guests lined the driveway, each throwing rice as Dad and Mary drove away. Lou dropped the rest of hers from her hands and turned to Jason.

"We have to talk. There's something I need to tell you."

Jason had a look of panic on his face. "I need to tell you something too."

Lou took his hand and pulled him towards her car. Once inside, she threw her arms around his neck and kissed him.

Jason pulled back and looked her in the eyes. "Just give it to me straight Lou."

"What are you talking about?"

"Are you calling off the wedding?" he asked.

"I'm not calling off the wedding. Are you?"

"Absolutely not. But what is it you need to tell me?"

"What do you need to tell me?" she asked.

Jason fidgeted in his seat. "I'm only here for one night. I have to return tomorrow."

Lou gasped.

"Listen honey, it's only for a few more months. The story is bigger than I thought, but I must finish it. People are depending on me."

"I guess I knew when I saw you, that you weren't staying."

"I'm sorry, Lou. I know you are depending on me too, and I worry about you."

"I'm doing all right, although I miss you terribly." Lou bit her lip and shove down the lump in her throat. "I don't want you to worry. You must stay focused, so you get back safe. I have my job and the new story I'm working on. And I have a new roommate."

"You have what?" He had a look of confusion on his face.

"A roommate. Karol from the office is staying with me until she can find a place of her own."

"Is she going to be there when we get married?"

Lou sighed. "No Jason. It's only until you come home for good and she gets a place of her own. She needed help, and I offered it."

Jason blew out a slow whistle. "Boy, I'm gone just a few weeks and things have changed."

"Oh, don't be silly. I'm just trying to be a better person."

"Don't get upset. I think what you're doing is wonderful. And it makes me feel better you're not alone while I'm gone. It just surprised me that's all."

Lou laughed. "Yes, it took me by surprise too. But I don't want to talk about that now if we only have until tomorrow."

Jason pulled her towards him and held her in his arms. "Let's get out of here and go someplace so we can talk without all these people watching us."

She could feel the pounding of his heart. "I agree, but we can't go to my house. Buckle your seatbelt, there's someplace I want to take you."

Ten minutes later they were parked by the river, watching the sun set over the horizon. The evening air flowed through the open window while they talked for hours until they fell asleep in each other's arms.

Lou was the first to wake as the light of morning peered over the hilltop, spilling rays of orange and yellow across the water. Jason was still sleeping, and she didn't want to wake him, but her back was cramping and she had to use the bathroom. Lifting his arm from around her neck, she slid out the door and rushed to the outhouse, grateful they hadn't closed them for winter yet. When she came out the door, Jason was bouncing up and down.

"Morning Lou. Please hurry."

Lou laughed as he rushed pass her and slammed the door. All she could hear was water splashing and the sound of awes coming from the other side. Finally, the door opened, and Jason exited with relief in his eyes and rubbing his hands with sanitizer.

"So, where was I. Good morning beautiful." Leaning down, he kissed her.

"Good morning to you too." Folding her arm around his waist, they walked back to the car. Lou noticed Jason was checking his watch. "What time do you have to leave?"

"As soon as you get me back to my car. It's parked at the chapel."

Lou frowned but kept quiet.

Jason stopped and turned her towards him. "Are you sure you'll be all right until I get back? Maybe I should just forget this whole thing and stay here with you."

Lou held up her hand. "Oh, no you're not. I won't be the reason you don't finish your story. If you quit now, someday you'll blame me, and I can't let that happen. I'll be here waiting, no matter how long it takes. Just promise you will come back to me." She bit her lip until it hurt to stop the urge to cry.

Jason lifted her chin. "I promise the minute I get back I'm taking you to the courthouse and we're getting married."

Lou sniffed and tried to smile. "Sounds good to me. I'm not the churchy type anyway."

Jason laughed as they got into the car. Fifteen minutes later, after more heart wrenching kisses, Lou watched him drive away. There was nothing more to do but go home... alone.

***

Karol had been up all night worried when Lou hadn't come home after the wedding. She was still pacing in the living room when she saw Lou's car pull into the driveway. Relieved, Karol hurried back to her room before Lou made it to the front door. By the look on Lou's face, whatever had kept her out all night didn't seem to make her happy. Maybe if she let her be, Lou might tell her about it, but right now she needed to sleep.

***

Lou slipped the key into the lock as quietly as she could. It was barely seven in the morning and she didn't want to wake Karol or explain where she had been. Though it was none of her business. What she wanted was a hot shower and to sleep.

Tiptoeing down the hall, she felt relieved Karol had her door closed. Closing her own door behind her, she stripped off her dress and was soon under the hot spray trying to work the knots out of her neck, until the water cooled.

Grabbing a towel, she dried off, then slipped on her fuzzy bathrobe, before climbing into bed, robe, and all. Exhausted, she was asleep as soon as her head touched the pillow.

Chapter Five

Lou seemed miserable all the time, but Karol didn't know how to cheer her up. She was rubbing her growing belly when she felt the baby kick and laughed.

"Oh, wow!"

Lou jerked her head. "Is something wrong? Do you want me to pull over?" They were going for burgers and shakes again.

"No, I'm fine. The baby just kicked me."

"Is that the first time you felt it do that?" Lou asked, concerned.

"Here, give me your hand." She reached for Lou's hand and placed it on the side of her belly. "There. Did you feel it?"

Lou nodded, unable to speak as she retracted her hand, then pulled into the diner and parked.

"Oh my God, Karol, that's amazing. Does it hurt?"

"Not really. Just a little uncomfortable. At first it felt like butterflies, but now it feels like a foot or a hand punching me gently and letting me know this little person is in there growing. The doctor said at the next appointment I could learn if it's a boy or girl if I wanted to."

"Are you going to find out?" Lou asked as they got out of the car and headed for the door.

Karol followed her to the counter. "Do you think I should?"

"I guess it would be fun to know. At least it would be easier to buy what you need instead of rushing to get things after the baby comes."

"What can I get you?" the girl at the counter asked.

Lou scanned the menu. "How about two burger baskets with fries and large chocolate milkshakes?" She turned to Karol. "Does that sound good to you?"

Karol nodded with a big smile on her face. "Sounds wonderful. But let me pay for dinner."

Lou pushed Karol's money away and payed the bill. "No. It's the least I can do since you let me feel the baby and I forgot the groceries, again," she laughed.

The two women found a booth and waited for their order to come. Lou noticed the glow on Karol's face. She had never been around anyone having a baby before. Julie moved away after she got married and Lou hasn't been to see her since she found out she was pregnant. She wondered if Julie had the same glow and was still pondering the thought when the server placed their order on the table.

"That sure smells good and look at those shakes," Lou said.

Karol was already sipping on hers with a look of pleasure on her face. "They put lots of chocolate in it." She continued sipping, then suddenly stopped, and slid the shake aside. "Oh, brain freeze."

Lou chuckled. "How about pacing yourself?" Picking up a fry, she popped it into her mouth. The hot salty potato tasted delicious, and she relaxed.

"So, have you talked to Pastor Bill again or called the helpline number he gave you?"

Karol set her burger down. "I was going to, but I don't know what to say."

Lou could tell something was on her mind by the look on her face and reached over and touched her hand. "Listen Karol, we have to figure this stuff out. Like where you will live, and who will help you after the baby is born. Remember, this was only temporary. Jason will be home soon."

Tears slid down Karol's face and she felt like a heal. "Please don't cry."

Karol grabbed a napkin and dabbed her eyes. "I'm sorry, Lou. You've been so kind to me. I don't know what I'd do without you. I can never repay you. Especially since Brad fired me."

Lou sat back against the cushions. "He didn't fire you. He gave you maternity leave. I was thinking maybe you could help me with research for my new story if you wanted to."

"Really? That would be cool. But only if you're sure."

Lou wanted to say no, but kept her mouth shut. Besides, Karol might find something that she had overlooked.

"Yes, I'm sure. How about we finish dinner and tomorrow we make a plan?"

Karol smiled from ear to ear before gulping down the rest of her burger and shake, shelving the discussion about the baby for now.

The next day they searched for any clues to what orphanage Kelly lived in, checking all records for The Dalles and surrounding towns, but Lou was still hitting dead ends. She was about to give up, when Karol found a small order of nuns in Madras, Oregon, who ran an orphanage during that time. This could be the break Lou's been waiting for. Checking the internet, she discovered the order still existed.

"I can't believe you found this. I've been over those papers for months."

Karol leaned against the chair. "I'm glad I could help. Do you think this is where Kelly lived? Who leaves their baby like that?"

Lou took a seat next to her. "Maybe her mother couldn't take care of her by herself or maybe she died giving birth. I won't know unless I go ask. Hopefully, this is the right place because there are no others that we can find."

Karol cradled her growing belly. "I still don't see how a mother can give away their baby. I know I can't, and I won't. I hope you aren't suggesting I do that."

Lou shook her head. This wasn't a conversation she

wanted right now. "I think I'll call and see if I can make an appointment for tomorrow. Will you be all right by yourself?"

Karol nodded.

"If you need anything, Dad and Mary's number is on the fridge."

Retrieving her notes, she left Karol sitting at the table and went to her room to call the orphanage. Lou wondered what might have led Kelly's mother to give her up and if she'll ever find the truth.

***

Karol sat quietly thinking about what Lou said. She knew she would have to leave when Jason got back and had been hoping that Tommy would change his mind. But the last time they talked; he had been so nasty to her. He didn't want her or the baby and knew she should call the number Pastor Bill gave her. A tiny place in her mind wished Lou would just let her stay. But why would she? Lou didn't owe her anything.

She wished she could call her mom, but that wasn't possible. Her father told her never to contact them again. What was so wrong with wanting to get away from a life of drudgery?

Life had been hard growing up, never having things the other kids had, and she suffered bullying at school for her homemade clothes. None of the girls wanted to be her friend, and the boys made fun of her. Life had been hell. Though hard, school had been her only salvation, and she swore as soon as she graduated, she was out of there. Though she only moved across the river, it seemed a world away. Sighing, she knew she had to do something. Tomorrow, she would take the bus and go talk to Pastor Bill.

***

Lou ended her call; excited tomorrow might be her lucky day. She wished Jason were here so she could share the news, but she hadn't heard from him in a month. The separation was grating on her nerves and she was having trouble sleeping again. What if he never came back? The thought shocked her. He will be back, and they'll get married. Life will settle down and they might think of having their own children.

Julie was still holding on and with Karol in the house, this was the first time she ever considered having children. Lou laughed at herself. How about she gets to the alter before she thinks of kids? In a reflex motion, Lou checked her phone for messages but was disappointed when she found none. Scrolling through her contacts, she tapped Dad's number. It had been a week since she last visited. She wanted to give them time to settle into their lives after returning from their honeymoon. Lou had to admit she envied them. When would it be her turn?

George had just returned from taking the garbage out when his cell phone buzzed. Pulling it out, he smiled. "Well, hello there Louie. What's up?"

"Hey Dad. Just thought I'd call and check in on you love birds. How's Mary?"

"She's great and misses you. When are you coming over for dinner?"

"I miss her too. I would, but I hate to leave Karol by herself."

"Then bring her with you. We always have room at the table." George paused. "Have you heard from Jason?" She didn't answer. "Lou?"

"No, I haven't. But he said it could be weeks. I'm sure it will be soon." Her voice cracked. "Anyway, I just wanted to hear your voice. Oh yeah, I found a new lead on Kelly and I'm going to Madras tomorrow. Wish me luck."

"That's great. Let us know what you find out and call me

when you get back. We'll plan dinner soon and bring Karol. I love you, Lou."

"I love you too Dad. Talk to you tomorrow."

Lou clicked off before she couldn't talk anymore. She needed to check on Julie; she needed to figure out Karol's living arrangements before the baby comes, and she was worried about Jason. But that would all have to wait. Tomorrow she might finally find the information she needs to finish Kelly's story.

The next morning, Lou felt anxious during the drive to Madras. Following her MapQuest directions, she found the Sisters of the Saints Orphanage without trouble. Parking her car, she grabbed her bag and made her way to the front door. The Orphanage would be considered minor compared to other's she had visited. Closing her eyes, she said a quick prayer then knocked. The door opened, and a kind face greeted her.

"May I help you?" the elderly nun asked.

Lou relaxed her body at the sound of the woman's voice.

"I... hello, my name is Lou McClelland, I called yesterday."

The nun opened the door wider. "We have been expecting you. Please come in."

Lou stepped past the woman and stood in awe. The inside was nothing compared to the plain brick exterior. Marble, in shades of creams and flecked with gold, lined the walls. Candle lanterns, converted to electricity, gave off a soft glow, and Lou felt a sense of peace.

"Thank you for seeing me on such brief notice."

"Mother Superior is waiting in her office." The nun turned and strolled down the corridor.

Lou followed. Were these the same halls Kelly walked, if she had been here? So many questions peppered her brain, and she hoped this wouldn't be a wild goose chase. She was still daydreaming when the nun stopped, and she almost ran into her. "I'm sorry. This is so beautiful."

"Thank you. Here is Mother superior's office. Just knock and enter. I hope you find what you are looking for. May God be with you," she said, then disappeared down the hall.

Lou bit her lip, knocked, and opened the door. A woman, much older than the last one, sat behind a large ornately carved mahogany desk, with her hands folded in front of her. The crisp white habit framed her ivory colored face and a slight smile crossed her lips. Lou shut the door and approached the desk.

"Hello, I'm Lou McClelland."

"Welcome Lou. Would you like to take a seat?" She gestured towards the chairs in front of the desk.

"Thank you for seeing me today."

"My pleasure. We don't get visitors these days and you piqued my interest from what you told me on the phone. What exactly are you searching for?"

Lou cleared her throat. "I'm looking for a child that was possibly brought here in 1910. A girl. I was hoping you might have records of that time."

"My, that is long ago. Well, before even my time."

Lou felt her shoulders slump. "I was hoping... this is my last lead."

"Why is this so important to you? Is this person family?"

"No, but she saved my life." Lou saw the quizzical look on her face. "Oh, I guess I need to tell you the story first, so you can understand."

Lou spent the next twenty minutes recapping her story, and all that had happened. When she finished, she noticed a hint of a tear in the woman's eyes.

"So, you see, I am trying to honor her and find her family."

Mother Superior wiped back the tear that had escaped with her hankie.

"That is commendable of you." Picking up a tattered book from the edge of her desk, she opened the cover. "After you

Return to Bakeoven Road

called, I had Sister Abigail search through the archives and the registers for that time. Luckily, we throw nothing away. This is the record book from 1895 to 1950. When did you say the child came here?"

Lou flipped open her notebook. "From what I can guess, it was around April 1910. Kelly mentions it's her 18th birthday when she is getting ready to leave the orphanage."

Mother Superior gently turned the yellowing pages while Lou watched for any signs of hope on her face as her eyes scanned the entries. The suspense was unbearable. After ten minutes she was about to give up hope, when Mother Superior stopped, and her eyes widened. Lou leaned closer to the desk.

"Did you find something?"

"I think I might have. Hold on for a moment." Picking up her phone, she waited. "Sister Abigail? Yes, would you mind going to the records room and pull file number 746? Thank you and yes, bring it to my office as soon as you can."

Lou felt her skin prickle. Could this be the break she prayed for? Seconds ticked by, but it seemed like it was taking forever, until the door opened, and a young nun entered carrying a brown envelope presenting it to Mother Superior. Lou bit her lip, almost drawing blood as she watched it open and what looked like a letter drawn from it, along with a photo.

She leaned forward again. "Is that?" Lou held her breath.

"What did you tell me her name was?"

"Kelly Turner." She said, exhaling.

Mother Superior handed the photo to Lou. "I think this is the person you have been looking for. This picture must be of Kelly when she graduated from nursing school."

Lou studied the photo. Something about the girl looked familiar, sending chills down her spine.

"Does the letter have any information about Kelly's mother or who brought her here?"

Mother Superior picked up the file again. "The notation says a young man handed over the baby. I think the letter is from the mother. She says she is seventeen and is forced to give up her baby. The father is dead. She asks us to save her baby and hopes God will forgive her. She signed it, Rosalie Scherrer."

Lou let out a mournful sigh. She knew women married young and started their families. But who would be so cruel to force her to give up her baby? Was life so barbaric back then? By their standards, Lou would be an old maid at her age.

"Do you think I could have a copy of the letter and the picture?"

Mother Superior slipped the photo and the letter back into the envelope, then slid it towards Lou.

"I think you should have these. If you can find her family, I trust you will pass them on. God seems to have chosen you for this task and our prayers will be with you on this journey."

"I don't know what to say." Lou wanted to jump up and hug the woman but remained seated.

Mother Superior stood, circled around the desk, and placed her hand on Lou's shoulder.

"You have a great heart, Lou. Life may not be easy, but God is always with you. I ask if you do find Kelly's family, please let us know. From what I understand, she held a special place in the hearts of all here at the orphanage."

"I promise," was all Lou could say.

Gathering her things and the precious envelope, she left the office and headed for her car. Now she had a name. Rosalie Scherrer. But where did she come from? Was there still family alive and if so, where did they live?

Lou couldn't wait to get back to her office and headed to The Dalles by Bakeoven Road. She wanted to make a quick stop near the rosebush to let Kelly know she had found the name of her mother, and she loved her. It sounded funny talking to the rose vines, but Lou felt a close bond with Kelly.

"I won't give up Kelly. I'll find your family and bring you home to them. Just know, for now you are safe. God and I are watching over you." Lou closed her eyes and was sure she felt Kelly's presence.

Once back at her office Lou searched for names in Madras but found nothing. Expanding her search to other surrounding counties, she still came up empty. With nothing to lose, she searched her own county. When the Scherrer name popped up on the screen, Lou thought she might faint. Kelly's family had lived right here in her own town. Glancing at her watch, it was after six and time to go home. Karol was entering her seventh month and Lou didn't like leaving her alone.

Opening the front door, she could hear Karol sobbing.

"What's going on?" Lou asked as she entered the kitchen.

Karol was sitting at the table, and her eyes were puffy, and red. Wadded tissues sat piled on the table in front of her. "Oh Lou. Everything is all wrong," she cried.

Lou sat down next to her. "What do you mean?"

Karol blew her nose and added the tissue to the pile. "I thought he would change his mind if he knew he was having a son, but he doesn't care. He said it wasn't even his kid. He called me terrible names and said if I didn't get rid of it, he would. I'm frightened, Lou."

Lou was at a loss for words. What kind of monster was this Tommy? Should she call the police and report him? Anger flooded over her for Karol's situation. "Did he actually threaten to harm you?"

Karol shrugged her shoulders. "Not in those exact words. But he was mad."

"Do you want to call the police and file a report? Maybe get a restraining order against him?"

"What does a restraining order do?"

"Well, if he bothers you again, they can arrest him."

"Oh, I couldn't do that," Karol gasped.

Lou was tiring of the drama surrounding Karol and Tommy, and she wanted her house back. She wanted Jason back. She wanted her life back.

"He hasn't been coming to the house to see you when I'm not here, has he?"

"Only once and I told him he can't come here again. I'm sorry, Lou, but I thought... no, I wasn't thinking." Karol hung her head. "If you want me to leave, I guess the Y might take me back."

Lou wanted to scream. "No, I will not make you leave... yet. But if you do it again, we will have a genuine problem. Do you understand? "

Karol didn't say a word.

"I mean it Karol. It's for your own safety. We don't know what Tommy will do. So, from now on, make sure you lock the doors when I leave the house. If you need to go somewhere, you call me. And we are going to see Pastor Bill again. Hopefully, he will have ideas about where you can live. You will also call the help lines and apply for aid. You only have eight weeks left, and this baby is coming whether you're ready or not. Do you understand me?"

Karol threw her arms around Lou's neck and hugged her tight. "I'll do whatever you say. Thank you, Lou. I love you."

Her words and unexpected display of emotions went straight to Lou's heart, and she hugged Karol back.

"It will be all right. We'll get through this together."

Releasing herself from Karol's grip, she stood and walked to the sink for a glass of water. She didn't want Karol to see she was on the verge of crying. This emotional stuff was exhausting. She needed to talk to Dad and get his perspective. Maybe put in an alarm system too. She thought of calling Julie but didn't want to upset her. She had made it to six months, and Lou didn't want to cause any problems.

"Lou?" Karol shuffled up behind her. "Lou?"

"What?" she snapped, then regretted how she sounded.

"I was wondering if you found anything at the orphanage today."

Lou could see Karol was trying to change the subject and welcomed the diversion. "Come sit down and I will tell you all about it."

An hour later they were still talking.

"That's so cool. And to think they might have lived right here in town. What are you going to do next?" Karol asked.

"I thought I would go to the courthouse tomorrow and you can use my computer to search the newspaper archives for any Scherrer's. Look through the obituaries, weddings, and such. I think we are getting closer to finding Kelly's family." Lou was silent for a moment. "I had another idea."

"What's that?"

"I think I want to search for my family too."

Karol looked confused. "But you have a family. Your dad and Mary."

Lou set her pen down. "True, I have Dad and Mary. But I know nothing about my mom's side of the family. I can't remember her ever talk about them when I was young. Tomorrow I will ask my dad what he knows, and we can add them to our list." Lou looked straight at Karol. "Do you want to find your family?"

"No! I mean no."

"Karol? Is there something you haven't told me? I don't want any more secrets between us."

Karol seemed to struggle for a moment, then like a dam breaking, she spilled everything about her parents and why she left. Lou was angry and disgusted. She wanted to find them, but Karol begged her not to. Finally, Lou relented and would let it go for now, but made Karol promise if something went wrong with the baby or with her, Lou would contact her parents. Karol reluctantly agreed.

The two women sat holding each other's hands with a newfound understanding between them, then went to bed.

Chapter Six

Excited about what was on her schedule for the day, Lou bounded out of bed. The search for Kelly's family had suddenly opened a door to her desire to know more about her own family. It never dawned on her she might have other relatives.

She knew that her father's parents had died, there were no other siblings and that he was an only child, so that side was a dead end. But Mom's side was a mystery, one Lou hoped to solve and headed for Dad's house.

Mary was in the kitchen doing her daily baking when Lou walked in. The aroma from her wonderful cinnamon rolls made Lou's stomach yearn for one.

"Good morning, Mary."

"Well, hello, Lou. It's so nice to see you. Hang on a minute while I put this batch in the oven, then we can sit and talk."

"No problem, I'll just pour myself a cup of coffee."

Mary slid the pan into the oven and set the timer before turning to face Lou. "Did you want to see your father? I think he's around here somewhere."

Lou noticed the twinkle in Mary's eyes when she mentioned him. "I bet he's hard to keep track of. What project is he working on this time?"

Mary scooped up a cinnamon roll, setting it on a plate for Lou. "He was working on the back steps fixing the railing last time I saw him. Thank goodness for his carpentry skills. I could never keep this place up without him. I'll go get him while you finish your roll."

Lou could only nod since her mouth was full. Looking around the kitchen, she felt at home and had been thinking of redoing hers but still hadn't found the time or the energy. Especially with Karol living there for the time being. She would let it wait until Jason got back and they could do it together. A cloud of loneliness covered her. She missed him more than she ever imagined and was finishing her roll when she heard the door open and Dad and Mary entered.

"Hey, Dad."

George hung his jacket on the hook by the door before he encircled Lou in his arms. "Hello yourself. Are you eating? You seem skinny." He kissed her cheek before releasing her.

"Yeah right Dad. I just ate a whole cinnamon roll." Lou licked the remaining frosting off her fork and was eying another one. She forced herself to set it aside.

Pouring himself a cup of coffee, he slid on to the stool next to her. Mary excused herself, saying she had a load of laundry to tend to. Lou knew she was giving them time alone and appreciated the gesture.

"So, little girl. What brings you over here today besides rolls? Is everything all right at home?"

Lou sat for a moment gathering her thoughts. Should she tell him about Karol or ask about Mom first? Karol could wait. "I think I found a lead on Kelly's family."

George set his coffee cup down. "That's great Lou. I'm so proud of you and all you are doing. Your job, dealing with Karol and Jason. Just don't over-due it. Be sure to take time for yourself." He paused. "Don't give me that look. You know what I mean."

Lou smiled and hugged him. "I'm pacing myself. So, don't worry. Anyway, back to my story. I went to Madras yesterday and discovered the place where they took Kelly in as a baby. Miraculously, they still had records and even a picture of her." Lou fished into her bag and pulled out the photo, setting it on the counter. "She looked so young. This is her graduation picture from nursing school."

Dad lifted the photo to examine it closer. "She looks

familiar."

Lou nodded. "I know. I thought the same thing. Isn't that weird? They also had a letter from her mother. Her name was Rosalie Scherrer, and she was only seventeen. From her brief note, she says she was being forced to give the baby up and the father was dead." Lou felt a familiar tightness in her throat.

"What are you going to do now?" Dad set the photo down.

Lou chewed her lip. "I want to find her family and I'm hoping someone's still living. I have Karol searching the paper's archives and I thought I would go to the courthouse and look through some old records."

"That's amazing. You're quite the investigative reporter."

"There's one more thing I would like to do."

"What's that?" he asked.

Lou hesitated. "I want to know about Mom's family. We never talk about her side. Did she have brothers or sisters? Where are her parents? Aunts or uncles? Do I have any cousins?"

Dad leaned back on the stool. "Gosh Lou, I'm afraid I don't know. Your mother never talked about her family. Since I didn't have any, it never crossed my mind to ask. I'm sorry."

A look of disappointment flowed across her face.

"Now don't look like that. Did you check her birth certificate? It should have something on it you can use. We had to have it when we got married. I think it's in the file cabinet in the hall closet."

Lou perked up. She hadn't thought of that. Were the answers right in front of her? She couldn't wait to get home and threw her arms around his neck.

"Thanks, Dad."

He took her hands and held them, giving her a serious look. "I don't want you to get your hopes up too high. Your mother was not one to share. Just remember she loved you."

Lou lifted his hands and kissed them. "I know Dad, but I

have to try. You understand, don't you?"

"If anyone can find what you need, it will be you. On another note, how is life with Karol? Any problems?"

Lou hoped she might get out of talking about that, instead she decided to just be honest.

"We had a slight problem the other day. Seems Tommy is threatening Karol about the baby. I told her if he does it again, she is getting a restraining order against him."

Dad had a concerned look on his face. "Are you sure you two are safe? This worries me, Lou."

"We're fine. I was thinking of getting an alarm system, but maybe that's overdoing it."

"What exactly did this Tommy say to Karol?" He stood and paced the kitchen.

"Tommy said if Karol didn't get rid of the baby, he would. I think he's just afraid of being a father and blowing hot air. I'm sure it's nothing." She hoped so.

"I think an alarm would be a good idea. I'll pick up one and install it today. They have these new ones that go straight to your phone. I saw it on television last night."

"Thanks Dad, you're the greatest. I will be in and out today, so I'll let Karol know you are coming by. I need to get going. I want to check the file cabinet tonight."

Mary returned just as Lou was leaving.

"Thanks for the cinnamon roll, Mary. You know you could sell those and make a fortune."

"That would take all the fun out of baking, but thanks for the suggestion." She wrapped Lou in a warm hug. "Come for dinner soon. We miss you."

Lou loved the calming effect Mary's lavender scent had over her and returned the hug.

"I will." Gently releasing her grip, she headed for the door. "Later Dad" she called as she bounded out of the house.

Excitement coursed through her. Could the cabinet hold answers to what she was looking for? Anything was possible, but first she had to retrieve notes from the office. She also needed to let Karol know her dad would be coming by to install an alarm system.

***

Karol thought Lou was being overdramatic, but when she hung up the phone, she heaved a sigh of relief. Tommy's erratic behavior concerned her to the point she had to block his calls. His constant badgering was wearing on her, and she knew it couldn't be good for the baby. Her last doctor visit had shown her blood pressure was up. How could it not be with Tommy harassing her all the time? Why did he have to be so mean to her? It just wasn't fair.

She knew she wasn't ready for a baby. And how was she supposed to take care of it and herself, pay for a sitter and work and find a place for them to live? Her talk with Pastor Bill had helped her see she had to take this seriously, and she promised she would. All this stuff was giving her a headache, so she went to lie down.

***

Lou felt better after letting Karol know about the alarm. It might not stop Tommy totally; it should at least detour him until she and Karol could figure out what to do. Lou wished she could talk to Jason, but she still hadn't heard from him and her heart ached.

Parking the car at work, she got out and shivered when a gust of wind hit her. For the first of November, the sky looked ominous with thick black and grey clouds. The latest weather report was calling for snow and freezing rain, and it worried her for Karol's sake. The thought of Karol's baby prompted her to want to call Julie and check on her. It looked like she would make it to term.

Hurrying to her office, she settled behind her desk and retrieved her phone. Hitting send on Julie's number, she chewed on the end of her pen as she waited.

The phone kept ringing.

Something was wrong. Julie always answered by at least three rings, but now it was going to her voicemail. She pushed end and called John's number, but it went to his voicemail too. Now she was standing and began to pace the office. Her heart was racing when she found Julie's mother's number, hesitating for a moment before pushing send. The phone rang four times when she heard a voice on the other end.

"Hello? Patricia?" Lou could hear someone crying. "This is Lou. I'm trying to get ahold of Julie."

"Lou... I... Julie," was all she could say before bursting into uncontrollable sobbing.

"Hello?" A man had retrieved the phone.

Lou recognized the voice. It was Don, Julie's father. Lou couldn't breathe but pushed on.

"It's Lou. Is something wrong with Julie and the baby?"

"I don't know how to say this any easier, but Julie lost the baby about an hour ago."

Lou gasped and collapsed into her chair. "Oh, God! No! What happened?"

"We're not sure, but it looks like the placenta ruptured. There wasn't anything they could do that would save the baby, and they had to do a hysterectomy to save Julie's life."

Lou thought she would be sick. This baby had meant the world to Julie, and now she wouldn't be able to have a child. "How is she? Can I come see her?" Lou could hear Don cough.

"I would give her a few days. John, her mother, and I are here. She doesn't know yet."

Lou wanted to rush to her friend's side, but understood what Don was saying. "Will you call me when she wakes up?"

"Yes, I will."

"And tell her I love her, and I'll come when you think it's time."

"Listen Lou, I have to get back to her room. The nurse is signaling us she's waking up. We'll keep in touch."

Before Lou could answer, he had hung up. Shock and disbelief reverberated through her body. Julie never hurt a soul in her life. She and John would have made the perfect parents.

How could God let this happen to someone so sweet and brave as her friend? Lou wanted to be with Julie but would wait. She wanted to work on her story, but she couldn't get control of her emotions and went home.

***

Karol woke from her nap to the sound of a drill buzzing outside. Sliding into her slippers, she waddled down the hall to check out the noise, then saw George's truck pulling out of the driveway. He must have finished installing the alarm, though neither she nor Lou knew how to work it yet. Heaving a sigh of relief, she continued to the kitchen for a cup of coffee.

It was after four and Lou should come home soon. Karol decided she would be nice and fix dinner tonight. She wasn't the best cook, but she could make a great grilled ham and cheese sandwich. She was in the middle of slicing cheese when Lou rushed through the back door, straight to her room, and slammed the door behind her. Setting the knife aside, she went to see what the problem might be.

***

Lou collapsed onto her bed, unable to move. Her head pounded, and her eyes burned from crying. She knew she would have to pull herself together for Julie's and Karol's sake, but she didn't know how she would do it.

Taking a deep breath and letting it out slowly, she sat up and wiped her eyes and face with both hands. She had to be strong. They both needed her. Lou was straightening her shirt and hair when she heard a tapping on her door. Karol must be worried after she ran through the house like that. Time to suck it up and take back control. Grabbing a tissue, she blew her nose and went to answer the door.

"Are you all right?" Karol asked, with a concerned look on her face. "Did something happen to Jason?"

Lou straightened her shoulders and squeezed the tissue in her hand. "No, Jason is fine. Let's go to the kitchen and we can talk."

Karol looked like she would cry, and Lou wasn't up for more blubbering. The women returned to the kitchen and Karol eased herself on to the chair. Lou paced around, not sure where to begin.

"Lou, what is going on? If it's not Jason, then who? Your Dad was just here, and he seemed fine, though I didn't get to talk to him... oh no... is it Julie? Did something happen to the baby?"

Lou didn't want to frighten Karol but unfortunately, this was the reality of life and she knew too well with the loss of her own baby brother.

"Yes, it was Julie. She lost the baby."

Karol gasped and placed her hand on her stomach. "What happened?"

Lou stopped pacing and sat in the chair across from her. "Something about the placenta rupturing. I don't know all the details, other than they had to give Julie a hysterectomy to save her life." Lou noticed tears slip down Karol's cheek. "Now don't get worried about your baby. I can see it on your face."

Karol dipped her head. "But..."

"Listen to me Karol, you and the baby are fine. Julie was having trouble from the beginning and it was a gamble if she could carry to full term. It's unfortunate, but it happened, and she will have to look to other ways of having a family. It will be hard on her. I know she would have been a great mom." The lump in her throat was nearly choking her. "How about we get some dinner started? I'm hungry."

Karol tried to smile. "I was making dinner when you came in."

Lou turned and glanced at the counter. "Yum. I love toasted cheese and ham. Let's do this together." Lou rose and held out her hand.

Karol accepted and followed her to the stove. "Oh, your dad installed the alarm, but he left right before you got home, and I don't know how to use it."

Lou pulled two plates from the cupboard, setting them on the counter. "I guess I better get some instructions otherwise the thing is useless," she laughed, trying to ease the tension. "Let's eat first then I'll call him. After that, I wanted to work on the story for a while if you are not too tired." Lou hoped it would help take their minds off today's events.

Karol placed the sandwiches on to the plates and sliced them into quarters. "Sure, I would like that."

Lou and Karol finished dinner, then worked for a couple hours following leads for Lou's story. Lou also called Dad and got the rundown on the alarm system. It was simple enough after she and Karol downloaded the app on their cell phones. It wasn't fancy, but it would alert them if someone came to the front and back door. Exhausted from the day, both women said goodnight and retreated to their bedrooms.

Lou closed the door and sat on her bed. Would she ever find Kelly's family? What about her mother's family? Suddenly she remembered the filing cabinet in the hall closet Dad had told her about. For a so-called investigative reporter, she was lousy at following up.

Not wanting to bother Karol, she quietly opened her door and tiptoed down the hall to the closet. Her hands shook as she opened the door and stood looking at the file drawers. Would there be anything here to help in her search or just emptiness?

Unable to wait any longer, Lou pulled the top drawer open. It held the shoe box of cards from her father. She wondered where Dad had put them and remembering how that had all gone down nearly brought tears to her eyes. She slid the drawer closed.

The second drawer held an array of colored file folders, each labeled in alphabetical order. The usual things, water, and garbage bills, electrical, the mortgage and so on.

Flipping through to the "m's" she was disappointed when she saw nothing labeled marriage certificate. What if Mom had thrown it away after Dad left? Would she have?

Lou knew anything was possible with her mother but refused to let it deter her. Starting at the front she opened each file, scanning the contents on the slight chance Mom had misfiled it. She was at the last file and about to give up hope when she noticed a file crammed behind the divider and pulled it out. It was older and weathered, not like the others, and labeled SVJ.

Holding the file gently, she hurried back to her room and crawled onto her bed. Setting the file on the comforter, she ran her hands over it and suddenly became exhausted. The strangest sensation enveloped her body and she could barely keep her eyes open. Lou didn't know what was happening, but when she lay against the pillows, a quiet so thorough, so deep, took control of her mind lulling her to sleep.

Chapter Seven

Lou woke in the early hours feeling rested for the first time in months. It was the strangest feeling. Sitting upright, she remembered the file and scanned the covers. Panicking, she jumped from the bed and to her relief found it on the floor.

Carefully picking up her treasure she placed it back on the bed scolding herself for being careless before climbing on top of her blanket.

Lou was biting her lip when she opened the file. In front of her was her mother's birth certificate, along with her parent's marriage license. Lou scanned the documents and was surprise when she read her mother's full name.

Susan Vivian Johnson.

Picking up the paper to look closer, she read the names of her mother's parents, Elizabeth Wilson, and Cliff Johnson, but it listed both as deceased.

A feeling of wonder and loss floated over her like a black cloud. Were there any living relatives or was this another dead end?

Setting the file aside, she remembered she was going to call David, Jason's boss, and see if he had any news on Jason. Reaching for her phone, her hands felt clammy as she waited for the phone to connect.

"David Joner here."

"Good morning David, or should I say afternoon. This is Lou."

"Hello Lou. I recognized your number, and its noon here. What can I do for you?"

"Well, I was wondering if you've heard from Jason? I'm getting worried." Lou noticed he was taking his time answering her question.

"I... well to tell you the truth, I haven't heard from him either, though that's common when my reporters are on assignment. It's for their own safety."

Lou wasn't buying his answer. "What do you mean you haven't heard from him? Where is he anyway?" Her voice was rising. "Listen David, I want to know where Jason is and when will you get him home!"

"Try to calm down Lou. I'm sure he's fine. I can't tell you were he is, but I'll make some calls and get back to you as soon as I know something."

"You better," was all she could squeak out before the line went dead.

Tossing the phone aside, she was livid with anger at David and angry at Jason for leaving her. She knew she was being unreasonable, but it worried her. After a couple of deep breaths, she regained control of her emotions and returned to what she was doing.

Checking the certificate for the hometown of Elizabeth and Cliff Johnson, she saw the address was in Yakima, Washington and would start there. Taking a picture of her mother's birth certificate with her phone, she slid the originals back into the file. She was eager to get to her office and start searching, but mostly she wanted to hear from David.

Before leaving, she checked her messages, but there was nothing. She had a bad feeling about Jason but pushed it from her mind. She was worried about Julie. For now, all she could do was try to get through the day without falling apart.

Lou exited her room and headed for the kitchen. Karol was making tea for a change when she walked in.

"Good morning Karol, you're up early today." Lou grabbed a cup, tossed in a tea bag, watching the steam rise.

Karol dunked her tea bag and set it on the saucer. "I couldn't sleep. Baby decided to play in the middle of the night instead of sleeping."

Lou smiled. She was grateful Karol was in a good mood today. She didn't know what she would have done if it had been the other way.

"How about you take the day off? I have a lot of work to do at the office."

"Are you sure? Isn't there something I can do to help you with your research?"

Lou could use the help, but she wasn't sure if she wanted to share what she had found yet.

"No, you rest today. Tomorrow we'll hit it hard. I have leads I need to follow, and I might be late tonight. Be sure to lock the doors when I leave. I have the app loaded on my phone, so I'll be checking in during the day. If you need anything, you call me. Okay?" Lou set her teacup in the sink.

Karol smiled. "I'll do what you say." Then she jumped up. "Sorry Lou, got to pee."

Lou watched her waddle down the hall and couldn't help but smile, though it quickly faded when she thought of Julie. Calling out 'goodbye' she went out the back door locking it behind her making sure the alarm had activated.

Sweeping into her office, Lou plopped down in her chair, hoping today would be a break-through day on all fronts. Firing up her computer, she started plugging in the names from her phone. It required a little hunting, but one by one, she found the information she needed to trace the family line through the birth and death records of Oregon and Washington.

Scratching her head, she made a graph on her notepad and started adding names.

Elizabeth married Cliff Johnson and they had a daughter, Susan Vivian, Lou's mother. Elizabeth's parents were Irene and Hobart Wilson. They also had a son Gene, who would be in his eighties and was living here in The Dalles. Cliff Johnson was deceased, but it was unknown if Elizabeth was still alive.

Searching further, she discovered Irene's parents were Rosalie Scherrer and Haven Carter. Rosalie had two brothers, Max, and Jake, who never married, so the family line ended there. She couldn't find any relatives for Haven Carter. Kelly wasn't listed anywhere.

Lou leaned back in her chair, dumbfounded by all the people she had uncovered. Were they really her family or was this just coincidence? She did one last search for Gene Wilson and to her amazement; he was living six blocks from her office.

Her hands shook as she wrote the address and phone number. Should she call first or just show up? If he were family, would she be welcome, or would he think she was a crazy nut?

Lou decided she had to take the chance. Hitting save on the computer, she grabbed her coat. By the time she pulled her car into the driveway of Gene's house and parked, her stomach was doing flip-flops.

Standing on the sidewalk and staring up at the big house, it looked familiar, but she didn't know why. Suddenly she remembered she had seen this house in the newspaper.

The Historical Society had done an article about historic homes. This one, and the one next to it, were the oldest farmhouses still standing in The Dalles and listed on the Historic Register. Built on the bluff, both houses overlooked the railroad yard, with an unobstructed view of the Columbia River.

Lou was in awe as she made her way to the front door and knocked. She realized this could be the beginning, or the end, of her lost family.

**

Gene Wilson was reading his morning paper when the doorbell rang. Easing himself from the kitchen chair, he shuffled towards the front door unprepared for the shock he received from the young woman standing on his doorstep. For a moment, Gene thought he was seeing a ghost.

She looked just like his great-grandmother Rosalie.

"Can I help you Miss?"

"Hello. Are you Gene Wilson?"

"Yes, I am. May I ask who you are?"

"I'm sorry to bother you, and I know this may sound strange, but I think we are related. My name is Lou McClelland. Do you think I could come in and talk to you for a few minutes?"

Gene knew he couldn't say no to those unbelievable cornflower blue eyes and pushed the screen door open.

"Please come in. I think we will have a lot to talk about."

***

Lou hurried through the door before he could change his mind. Standing in the entry, she felt she had stepped back in time, when she glanced into what must be the sitting room.

Red velvet curtains framed the windows, with a gleaming black grand piano at the center. Exquisite oil lamps sat upon gilded end tables next to a love seat, equally adorned in red velvet, with gold braided trim. She wondered about the sitting room but would leave those questions for later.

Gene motioned her to follow and as she continued down the hall, Lou noticed the stark contrast between the front room and the colorless hallway with lofty ceilings before they entered the kitchen. This room was also plain with few decorations. A wood-burning stove sat on a weathered brick hearth next to the back door. Lou noticed a kettle on the grate, with steam swirling into the air.

Gene gestured for her to take a seat at the wooden table by the window overlooking a stone-walled garden. The view was amazing, and she took a moment to compose herself.

"Thank you for agreeing to talk to me. I realize this might seem like an intrusion."

Gene took a seat across from her and seemed to study her face. "Not at all. I have been hoping for this day for an exceptionally long time."

"Why do you say that?"

Gene rose. "Please excuse me for a moment, I need to get something."

Before she could answer he was down the hall and out of sight. Lou looked around the kitchen and thought this wasn't such a clever idea. He could be a serial killer. She shook her head and laughed under her breath. She would have to stop watching all those crime shows and was about to get up when Gene returned. He was carrying a small hat box and placed it on the table in front of her.

"Sorry I took so long. I had to remember where I had put this." Gene grinned as he removed the lid, setting it aside, and pushed the box closer to her. "I think you will be interested in what's inside."

Lou felt a sudden pull to look. Reaching in, she found a smaller box and lifted it out. It was the color of faded ivory and held together with a pale blue satin ribbon. Embossed on the top of the lid were the initials RS. Lou's heart fluttered at the sight.

"Go ahead, open it," he said.

Lou stroked the satin ribbon. "Are you sure?"

"Oh yes. I think this has been waiting for you."

Confused but curious, she gently pulled the bow apart, releasing it from its constraints, and lifted the lid. The face on the photo staring up at her nearly made her faint.

It was Kelly!

"I don't understand. Where did you get this?"

Gene lifted the picture and set it on the table.

"This picture, along with others, have been handed down through the family for generations, in hopes someday the right person would come searching for them. I believe you are that person."

"I still don't understand. Why me? Who is that?"

Gene removed the rest of the photos and spread them across the table.

Lou could see the resemblance in all the women. Especially the last three pictures that were in color. She noticed right away the color of their eyes. Corn-flower blue.

"Are they all related?" She hoped she knew the answer.

"Yes. I believe this is your great-great-grandmother Rosalie. This one is her daughter Irene, your great-grandmother, and Irene's daughter Elizabeth, who would be your grandmother."

There were two left. Gene slid the larger one towards Lou causing her breath to catch in her throat. The hair was dark and curly like her own, but the face was her mother's. These were the women of Lou's past.

"I don't know what to say. My dad said my mother would never talk about her family, and he assumed they were all dead. Are you my family?" Her words caught in her throat.

Gene reached across the table and clasped Lou's hands in his own. "Yes, we are. I have been waiting for you ever since I read your article about the Angel on Bakeoven Road. Something told me you would keep looking. This small photo is of Rosalie's first daughter, Kelly. From what I understand, someone forced Rosalie to give Kelly up as an infant. I believe the photo is of the girl's graduation from nursing school. She left on her route but was never heard from again. It wasn't until I read your story, I realized you must be talking about Kelly."

Lou couldn't believe what he was saying. Had she found Kelly's family? But if Kelly was Rosalie's daughter that made Lou, Kelly's great-great-niece! This had to be a joke, but the pictures didn't lie.

Lifting the photo of her mother, she turned it over. On the back, written for all to see, was *Susan Vivian Johnson*. Lou held it to her heart and let the tears flow.

Gene handed Lou a tissue. "I didn't mean to make you cry. It's just that I have been waiting so long to hand this to its rightful owner."

"I don't know what to say." Lou sniffled and dried her eyes. "I never thought my story would lead me to this. It's a lot to take in at one time."

Gene smiled. "I would like you to take these pictures. I hope you will come back and see me again. I have one more thing to share with you, but I think this is enough for now."

Lou rose and stood in front of the man who was now her relative. "Thank you. This means the world to me and I will be back."

He held out his arms, and she melted in his embrace, then pulled back and reached into her pocket. "Here is my card with my numbers. Call me anytime."

Gene took the card and slid it into his shirt pocket as he ushered her towards the front door.

"Call me when you're ready, and we'll talk again."

Lou held the little box tight as she returned to her car. She wasn't sure what she should do first. She was still contemplating her next move when her phone pinged with a text message. Pulling it from her purse, she saw it was from Julie's mother. Lou's pulse quickened as she read the message.

"Julie is awake and understands what has happened. She is trying to be strong for John's sake, but I know she is hurting inside. I told her you called, and she asked if you would wait until she is home from the hospital to visit. She should be home in a couple of days. She said to tell you she is waiting to hear about your wedding plans, and you would frown. I will let you know for sure when she is up to visitors."

Lou frowned, but she also smiled. Only her best friend would think of her at a time like this. She checked her phone for any other messages, but nothing. She thought about calling Joan but decided against it. If something were wrong, Joan would have called her. For now, she just wanted to go home.

Pulling into the driveway, Lou noticed her front door open and had a bad feeling. Why didn't her phone ping her? Worried, she called Dad.

"Hey, Lou, what's up?"

"Dad, the front door's wide open, but the alarm didn't go off. I think something is wrong."

"Where are you?"

"I'm in the car. I just pulled in."

"Stay where you are. I'm calling 911 and I'm on my way."

"But what about Karol?" Lou panicked.

"Lou! Stay in the car until the police get there. Lou? Lou, can you hear me?"

Lou jumped from her car and headed through the front door. She heard loud voices coming from the kitchen. A man was yelling, then Karol screamed, and the backdoor slammed. Rushing into the kitchen, she found Karol on the floor in a pool of blood. Grabbing a towel from the counter, she pressed it across the gash on Karol's stomach, trying to stop the bleeding.

By the time the police and paramedics arrive, Lou was sitting on the floor in shock, cradling Karol's head in her lap, keeping pressure on the wound. When the paramedics took over, Lou stepped aside to give them room to lift Karol onto the gurney, then began to hyperventilate. The last thing she remembered was reaching for the counter before passing out.

***

George arrived as the ambulance was speeding out of the driveway, lights, and sirens blaring. Police cars were lined along the road and the house was crawling with uniformed men and women. He felt like his heart was in his throat when he approached an officer at the front door.

"My name is George McClelland, my daughter Lou, lives here along with another young woman. Was that Lou?" He could feel his chest constricting as the officer checked his notepad.

"No, the woman's name was Karol. Lou is in the living room."

George rushed past the officer and found Lou on the couch.

***

The ringing in her head slowly subsided as she woke. Disoriented, Lou looked around the room, then saw her dad next to her. Throwing her arms around his neck, she held him tight, until her pulse slowed, before releasing herself.

"What do we do now?" Lou tried to stand but wobbled, nearly toppling over.

George grabbed her arm to steady her. "The officer needs a statement from you if you are up to it."

Lou nodded. "Yes, I want to get this over with."

George signaled for an officer, and Lou told them what she knew. She suggested they look for Tommy. He was the baby's father and had been threatening Karol, wanting her to get rid of the baby. Lou was sure it was his voice she heard coming from the kitchen.

"I think it would be better if you stayed somewhere else for a few days Miss. This is a crime scene," the officer said.

"She will stay with me," George said.

Lou protested, then gave in. She knew she couldn't stay in the house after what happened.

"What about Karol? Is she? The baby?" Lou was afraid to say the words.

The officer must have seen the look of horror on Lou's face.

"I understand from the paramedics the wound wasn't too deep, but they were concerned about the baby with the amount of blood loss. I'm sure if you call the hospital, they can give you an update. I would wait an hour to give them time to get there and take care of your friend."

Lou nodded in agreement. A half smile crossed her face when he said, 'your friend.' Yes, Karol was her friend. Thanking him, she went to her room to pack a bag.

***

George found her sitting on the bed staring out the window. Shock was setting in and he knew he had to get her out of there. Gently he helped her stand, grabbed her bag, and guided her down the hall and out the door.

Police crime crews had arrived and after putting Lou in the car, George told them the place was theirs and lock up when done. Lou was sitting with her eyes closed as they drove away.

Returning to the boarding house, George helped Mary get Lou settled in the guest room, then called his doctor, who came and gave Lou a sedative to help her sleep through the night.

Once he made sure she was asleep, he called the hospital for an update on Karol, who had to have an emergency C-section to save the baby, a boy. Though small, he was breathing on his own and Karol could expect a full recovery.

George sighed with relief and would let Lou know when she woke up. He would also insist she stay with him and Mary until the Sherriff cleared the house as a crime scene, and he had time to repair the kitchen.

***

It had been over a week since that night and Lou was ready to get back home. Pulling into the driveway, she parked and stared at the house. Her emotions were raw, and she had to take a moment to compose herself before getting out.

Lou had been to the hospital every day to see Karol and the baby and realized that was another problem. She hadn't planned on having Karol and the baby living at the house. She figured they had enough time to get Karol a place of her own.

Besides the housing situation, her dad suggested she see a therapist, but Lou declined. She wanted to work things out on her own.

Climbing the steps to the front door, Lou didn't realize she was shaking until she tried to insert the key into the lock and failed. It took both hands to unlock the door, letting it swing open.

The smell of fresh paint greeted her when she entered, and she tried to relax. Setting her bag in the entry, she locked the door behind her, making sure the alarm was on, before advancing towards the kitchen. Her heart pounded the closer she got and realized she was holding her breath by the time she walked in. Letting out a sorrowful moan, she stood staring at the place Karol had fallen, but you wouldn't know what happened, unless you had been there.

The entire kitchen was new. Dad had replaced any sign a tragedy had taken place in here. Feeling her knees weaken, Lou reached for the kitchen chair and sat down. It took everything she could muster to keep from running out of the room. Staring at the floor, she jumped when the doorbell rang.

"Good morning Miss McClelland."

"Good morning, Sheriff. Something I can help you with?"

"I just wanted to let you know we arrested Tommy. He has pleaded guilty."

Lou felt as if a tremendous weight lifted from her shoulders. "Thank you so much for letting me know. I really appreciate it."

The Sheriff tipped his hat. "No problem. Have a good day."

Lou tried to smile, then closed the door, resetting the alarm. The house felt eerily quiet, leaving Lou rethinking if she should stay. Goosebumps ran up and down her arms each time she went near the kitchen and though she had gone through the house, turning on every light, she was afraid of the shadows.

Even knowing Tommy was in jail, Lou couldn't shake the feeling something bad would happen. Forcing herself back into the kitchen, she made tea, in hopes it would calm her, then retreated to her bedroom.

Sitting on her bed, she recalled her talk with Julie during the week. They cried on the phone together and Lou promised to come as soon as she could. Lou was grateful Julie hadn't asked her about wedding plans. She still hadn't heard from Jason.

Lou called David, who swore he knew nothing and told her not to worry, but even a call to Joan hadn't settle her nerves. She would have to let God handle this and get her mind back on her story.

Stretching out on her bed, she opened the box Gene had given her, taking out the pictures. With all that had happened recently, she hadn't told Dad about him or what she discovered about Mom. She didn't know why, but she wasn't ready to share her new family.

One by one, Lou studied the faces of the women she belonged to. It seemed surreal, but it had to be true. Pictures didn't lie. The other photos were of Max and Jake, and assorted family members. Lou picked up the one with Rosalie's name on it and studied the face, but her eyes drew heavy and she drifted off to sleep.

Chapter Eight

The alarm clock buzzed, jolting Lou awake, and she found herself in a pool of sweat. Hitting the off button, she sat on the edge of her bed shaking and held on to the nightstand as she stood. Feeling steadier, Lou gathered the pictures, stowed them safely back in the box, then set them on the dresser, before heading for the shower. She had a busy day ahead of her.

On her way out of the house Lou retrieved the box of pictures, wanting to take a closer look when she got to her office, but her first stop would be the hospital to check on Karol and the baby. Karol would get out soon, and there was still the question of where she would stay.

Lou knew it would be the right thing to bring her back to the house, but she didn't know if Karol could handle the memories of what happened, even with a new kitchen and paint. And where would the baby sleep?

Trying to clear her foggy brain, she hit the drive through at the local coffee shop for a quick cup and a pastry as she drove towards the hospital. Pushing the call button on her steering wheel, she instructed it to call Julie. She wanted to make a quick trip to Portland to check on her, but Patricia recommended she wait a little longer. Lou worried about her friend and wanted to see her, though she understood Julie's mom's concerns. She was licking her fingers when the phone rang.

"Hello Lou, I'm so glad you called." Julie's voice sounded strained.

"How's my best friend in the entire world doing?" Lou chirped, trying to keep it upbeat.

"I'm doing good, though the stitches were the worst. They itch so bad."

Lou smiled to herself. "I know. When I broke my arm, I thought I would end up tearing the cast off. But enough of the chitchat. How are you really doing? And don't lie because I will know." Lou could hear a sniffle.

"Okay, your right. It's terrible, Lou. I feel so empty and I know John is crushed. He says we can adopt when I am ready, but when will I ever be ready?" Sobs filled the line.

"Julie, listen to me. You're a strong, remarkable woman. Let yourself heal and worry about the other stuff later. God will let you know when the time is right."

She heard Julie laugh.

"That was deep. I miss you. Promise you'll come see me soon. I don't care what mother says. I need to see my best friend."

"I will and soon. I have a few things to wrap up here first, so I'm thinking in about two weeks. You should be cranky by then."

"Okay, I'm holding you to that. And Lou?"

"Yes, Julie."

"Thanks."

Lou finished her coffee and the last of her roll by the time she parked in the hospital lot. Before she made her way to Karol's room, she stopped by the NICU for a look at the baby. The nurse gave her a thumbs up, so she went to Karol's room and found her sitting in the chair by the bed.

"Hey Karol, it's good to see you up. How are you feeling today?" Lou set her bag on the tray table.

"Not too bad. I walked down to the NICU and could hold the baby this morning. He's so small. And all those tubes." Karol choked on her words. "I don't know how I will take care of him."

Lou crossed the room and gave her a hug. "We'll worry about that when the time comes. He's doing great and so are you. When can you leave this joint?"

Karol smiled. "The nurse said Friday. That's only three days, but the baby has to stay a little longer. Do you think I'm ready?"

Lou pulled a chair next to her and sat down. "Well, that's something we need to talk about." Lou saw the look of fear on Karol's face. "Now don't worry. I just want to know how you feel about coming back to my house after everything that happened. Tommy's in jail and will be there for a long time. My dad fixed the house and I've been staying there. I just need to know if you can."

Karol relaxed her shoulders. "I've been thinking about it. At first, I didn't want to, but your house has become my home. So, my answer is yes if it's all right with you." Karol lowered her head. "What about the baby?"

Lou exhaled a deep breath. "I think if we take out the queen bed and put in a full size, we should be able to fit a crib in your room and give you enough space for things you'll need to take care of him."

Karol lifted her head. "Really? Are you sure? You've done so much for me already. Without you, I'd have nowhere to go."

Lou felt ashamed for even thinking of not letting Karol come back to the house but knew things would have to change when Jason came back.

"Yes, I'm sure. We'll just take this one day at a time. And on that note, I want you to know I am going to drive to Portland and see Julie on Thursday, but I will be back Friday morning to pick you up." She had decided she would just show up and surprise her.

Karol picked at the belt on her robe. "How is she doing?"

Lou chewed on her lip. "Maybe someday they'll adopt."

Karol leaned back in her chair resting her head and Lou could see she was tired.

"Hey, enough of the sadness for now. You rest and I'll check on you both later." Lou pushed the chair back to the corner and grabbed her bag. "Call me if you need anything."

Karol nodded, and Lou could see she was on the verge of tears. Turning, she left the room. Her next stop was the office and a phone call to David.

***

Karol tried to understand what Julie must be feeling, especially since she had almost lost her baby too, but with God's help he was surviving. Only how was she going to take care of him? She could hardly care for herself.

Suddenly a thought formed in her mind. She tried to push it from her brain, but the seed was planted. Rising from the chair, Karol shuffled down the hall to see her son, then returned and placed a call to Pastor Bill.

***

Lou parked and retrieved the box. She wanted to look at the pictures again and promised Gene she would get back to him. But part of her wanted to forget the notion she could be related to Kelly and the other women. What good would it do to bring up the past since they were all dead? It just confirmed that she was alone.

Sure, there was Gene, and he was her relative, but she had been hoping... it was a silly idea and thrust it from her thoughts as she entered the building and hurried to her office. Setting the box on the end of her desk, she checked the time. It was still early, and David should be in his office.

Tapping her fingers on the desk, she placed the call using her office phone and waited for him to answer. While the phone rang, a lonely fly buzzed up the window of her office door, then slid down, only to start over. She had to curb the urge to get up and put it out of its misery.

The phone continued to ring until it went to voicemail. Lou figured he was avoiding her and hung up without leaving a message. He knew why she was calling and took it as a sign Jason was fine. She was sure David would have called if something had happened to him. Right? Jason told her to be patient so she would just have to trust he would be home soon.

Lou glanced over and noticed the buzzing had stopped. The fly was on its back on the floor, legs up, twitching with its last breath. She felt sad. So goes the life of a fly and refocused on the box sitting on the desk staring at her, beckoning her to open it, but her hands remained in her lap.

Finding Kelly's family, and discovering the connection to her own, had been the force driving her for months. So, what was she afraid of? She was reaching for the box when her desk phone rang and snatched the receiver.

"Hello? She prayed it was Jason.

"Is this Lou McClelland?" a woman asked.

"Yes. May I ask who's calling?"

"Oh, I'm sorry. This is the nurse's station and Karol asked that we call you."

Lou's shoulders tensed. "Is something wrong with Karol or the baby?"

"The baby is doing fine, but Karol has developed an infection in her incision and is running a fever. I know she was hoping to go home on Friday, but I think we will have to postpone that for another week or two. She wanted me to let you know."

Lou felt her shoulders relax but felt distressed for Karol, knowing she wanted to come home.

"Can't we take care of this at home with antibiotics?"

"I'm afraid not. It's best she's here in the hospital so we can monitor her."

"I understand. Will you tell Karol, I'll stop by later to see her and the baby?"

"Yes, I will let her know. Do you have questions?"

Lou couldn't think of any, but this would put a damper on her plans to surprise Julie. She couldn't leave Karol alone, even if just for the day.

"No, but thank you for the call."

The nurse hung up, leaving Lou holding the receiver in her hand until the beeping noise on the line reminded her to hang it up. Unable to keep her mind on track, she decided sitting here was a waste of time.

Calling the front desk, Lou let the temporary receptionist know that she would be working from home for the rest of the day, should anyone need to get ahold of her. Switching off her light, she picked up the box and hoped she could get at least two hours of work done before going to the hospital.

Karol was asleep when she got there and Lou didn't want to wake her, so she went by the NICU for an update on the baby. The nurse said he was getting stronger every day.

Lou thanked the nurse and God. This baby had a purpose, she just didn't know what it was yet, and left for home.

During the drive, she thought about Julie's baby and what he would have been like if he survived, and of her own baby brother again.

Had Mom's loss been so hard to accept that she hardened her heart to all those who loved her? She prayed this wouldn't happen to Julie. She knew it was selfish, but she wouldn't know what to do if she ever lost Julie's friendship.

Lou was still in a daze when she turned into her driveway and saw a strange car parked in front of her. She was about to call 911 when the door opened. To her surprise Julie got out. Lou shoved the car in park and shut it off before jumping out herself.

"Oh, my God! What are you doing here?" Lou threw her arms around her friend and hugged her tight, then worried, stepped back. "Did I hurt you?"

Julie grabbed Lou in a tight hug. "Don't be silly. I will not break. But I have to pee!"

Lou and Julie laughed as they walked arm in arm to the front door. Julie was doing a little jig by the time Lou got the door unlocked and turned off the alarm. She couldn't help laughing as her friend rushed down the hall towards the bathroom. Returning to the car, Lou grabbed her bag and her treasure. This was something she wanted to share with her best friend later.

Julie was just coming into the kitchen as Lou set the box and her bag on the counter.

"All better now?"

Julie nodded.

"So, what do I owe this unexpected surprise to?" Lou asked, pulling two cups from the cupboard.

Julie plopped her elbows on the counter and gazed up at Lou. "I was bored. And I missed you." Then she burst out laughing. "You should have seen the look on your face."

Lou smiled. "You're lucky I didn't call 911. Where's John? Did he come with you?"

Julie shook her head. "Nope. I drove myself."

Lou put tea bags in the cups and poured boiling water.

"What does your mother think of this little escapade? I'm sure you're on her naughty list." Lou motioned towards the chairs. "Sit. I can tell by the look on your face, that you're not feeling as well as you are trying to put on."

Julie gave a half smile and seated herself carefully in the chair. "I guess you're right. It still hurts a little. Mom was upset, but John understood I needed a little girl time with my bestie."

Lou set the cups on the table. "I hope you plan on staying and not driving back tonight."

Julie took a sip and sighed. "I was hoping you would insist I stay. I packed a bag on the chance." Her eyes twinkled with delight. "It will be like a slumber party; we can invite Karol to join us."

Lou coughed.

"Did I say something wrong?" Julie noticed the house was quiet. "Where is Karol? And when did you redecorate the kitchen?"

Lou figured she would have to tell Julie what happened since she planned to go back to the hospital to see Karol later. Taking a deep breath, she sprung into the horrid ordeal.

Julie sat listening intently, gasping, and holding back tears until Lou finished, then dabbed at her eyes.

"That's so awful. For Karol and you. You said they locked the father up?"

"Yes, and from what the Sherriff says, Tommy could get five to ten years for what he did. I got Karol a lawyer, and we would have had the book thrown at him, but Karol asked the judge to give Tommy the lower sentence, if he signed off all his rights to the baby. Tommy agreed and signed the papers without a word. He didn't want the baby anyway and doesn't want to be responsible for any medical problems the baby may have from being born early."

"How can anyone be so cruel?" Julie choked on her words.

"I don't know, but that baby is a real fighter. Hey, are you supposed to check in with John or your mother before they send the National Guard looking for you?"

Julie dug out her cell phone. "Thanks for reminding me. We definitely don't need that."

After a quick call informing both John and her mother that she was safe, she hung up. "So, that's done. What do you have to eat around here? I'm starved."

Lou snickered. "For your information, nothing. I haven't been to the store since Karol went to the hospital. I've been eating out. So, I guess we eat out."

Julie went to the cupboards and pulled each one open. Lou was right. Empty. Old Mother Hubbard had more food than Lou did. "Lou, Lou, Lou. What am I going to do with you?"

Lou held her hands up and shrugged as a wide smile spread across her face. "Okay, I'll get some groceries tomorrow. You can help me. Does that sound fair? How long are you staying? Not that I want you to leave soon."

Julie closed the cupboard door. "I was thinking a couple of days if that's all right with you?"

"Did you tell John that?" Lou frowned when she didn't answer. "Julie?"

"I'll call him later. He'll understand."

"How about we put your things in the spare room, then we can go see Karol and the baby, finishing the night off with burgers and milkshakes?"

Julie put her arm around Lou. "You sure know how to show a girl a good time."

Lou hugged her closer. "What are friends for?"

The two women chatted on the way to the hospital, and Lou could tell Julie was getting anxious the closer they got.

"You okay?" Lou asked.

"I'm fine. Just give me a minute."

Lou parked and waited until Julie signaled she was ready.

"Do you want to see the baby before we go see Karol?"

"Can we do that?"

"Sure, the nurses know me by sight. But we can only stay a few minutes."

Julie grabbed Lou's hand as they made their way to the NICU. Baby Edwards was close to the front window tonight and they could get an unobstructed view of him. Julie gasped. Lou worried she might faint.

"He's so tiny," Julie whispered, resting her hand on the window for a moment as if she were touching him.

"The nurse said he was gaining weight. He's a fighter for sure. Come on, let's go see Karol, then we can stop on our way out."

Julie followed Lou down the hall and stood back when Lou tapped gently on the door. "Hey, Karol. You up for some company?" Lou asked.

Karol was sitting up watching television, though she still had an IV hanging, giving her antibiotics for the infection.

Chapter Nine

Karol tossed and turned all day, running the thought she had planted in her mind over and over. She had prayed, asking God to guide her, and felt in her heart it would be the right thing to do. She had to believe God's will had brought her this far and everything would work out.

She was flipping channels when she heard a knock on her door and noticed Lou and another woman. Though she had never met her, Karol was sure this must be Julie and smiled.

"You bet. Come on in. Did you bring me a milkshake?"

Lou laughed, and Julie seemed to relax.

"No, but I will get you one tomorrow. Julie surprised me when I got home. She's going to stay for a couple of days."

Karol muted the sound on the television. "That's real nice. Um...Julie?"

Julie moved closer to the bed. "Yes Karol."

"I'm sorry to hear about your baby."

"Thank you. I appreciate your kindness. These things happen, and we have to believe God knows what he's doing." She took Karol's hand in her own. "I'm happy you and your baby are doing so well. We stopped by the NICU and I got to see him. He's beautiful."

Karol knew the moment she touched Julie's hand she had made the right decision. She just hoped Julie would see it that way.

"Would you and Lou sit down for a few minutes? There's something I want to talk about. I had planned on talking to Lou first, but since you're here, it will be easier to explain."

Lou pulled two chairs to the side of the bed, then closed the door. The women gave Karol a bewildered look before settling into the chairs.

Karol cleared her throat, twisting a tissue in her hands. "First, thank you Lou, for everything you have done. I know me, and the baby wouldn't be alive if not for you."

"Karol..."

"Please let me finish. You took me in when I had no place to go. You put up with my moods, tears, and tantrums. You are willing to bring me and the baby back to your home and all while trying to work on your story, worried about your friend here, and mostly Jason. You are my rock and you've shown me I can be strong. I hope someday I can repay you for your kindness. I have been praying a lot about this and I have talked to Pastor Bill."

Lou grinned.

"Don't look so surprised. I listen sometimes. Anyway, we've had long talks, and he's helped me come to this decision. I didn't plan this, but I think God did."

"I'm not sure what you are getting at," Julie said.

Karol put her hands to her head. "I know I'm not making much sense, and maybe it's not the right time for you, Julie, after losing your baby, but I was hoping you would take my son and raise him as your own."

Julie and Lou looked at each other dumbstruck. Julie was the first to speak. "You want me to have your baby?"

Karol nodded

"But why me?"

Karol grabbed another tissue. "I heard how much you wanted to be a mom and when you lost the baby, I realized how selfish I was being. If I keep him just to prove to others that I can do it, would only hurt him. He needs more love and care then I'll ever be able to give. I know it's a crazy thing to ask and if you don't want to do it, that's okay and I'll figure something out. I was just hoping...." Sobs took over and she couldn't go on.

***

Julie closed her eyes and asked God for his guidance. Could she accept this child as her own? Could John? Would she ever have the opportunity again? What about Karol? Was she sure she wanted this or was someone pressuring her?

She opened her eyes, and searched Lou's face for answers but knew she would have to find them in her own heart. Karol was saying something to her.

Julie shook her head, trying to focus. "I'm sorry, I didn't hear you. What did you say?"

"I was wondering if you would like to hold him?" Karol pointed behind them. The nurse had entered and was carrying a baby wrapped in a blue blanket, and a knitted hat covered his head. He looked like a little doll, but his eyes were open, and he let out a squeal that surprised everyone in the room. "I think he wants to say hello," Karol said.

Julie approached the nurse and held out her arms. She turned to face Karol and Lou.

"If you're sure this is what you want, Karol, it would honor me to be his mother."

Lou moved up next to the baby and smiled. "Karol, have you thought this through?"

Karol blew her nose. The look in Julie's eye said it all. "I'm sure. The only thing I ask is when he's older, you might tell him about me and let him know how much I loved him."

Julie nodded, lowering herself and the baby into the nearest chair. "I'll tell him about his brave mother and her love for him."

Lou saw the sudden panic on her face. "What's wrong Julie?"

"Karol can't just give me the baby. There are papers to file. And the courts. What will they say?"

Karol reached for the drawer in her nightstand and pulled out a packet of documents. "I have taken care of everything. Pastor Bill helped me. The baby's father already signed his rights away, and I have signed mine. The birth certificate will list you and your husband as his parents. I didn't think it would happen this soon, but I feel God brought you here today to help us both."

Julie felt the baby move in her arms and held him to her face. The moment she touched his cheeks with her lips, her heart melted and when his eyes locked on hers, she felt her soul restored. Drinking in his scent, she knew this was God's answer to her prayers. This could be her son.

"What will you do after you get out of the hospital?" Julie asked, nuzzling the baby.

Karol looked at Lou. "If Lou will have me, I would like to stay with her until I heal and can go back to work. Then get a place of my own. I was thinking about looking into the community college for fashion design."

Lou reached out her hand to Karol. "You can stay as long as it takes." She turned to Julie. "So, are you going to sign the papers?"

"What about John? He needs to be here."

Lou took the baby from her arms. "Then go call him. He can be here in over an hour."

Julie jumped up. "Your right! I'll be right back…" she stopped. "You're convinced this is what you want to do, Karol?"

"Yes Julie. Go call your husband."

Lou waited until Julie left the room and turned to Karol. "Are you sure about this, Karol?"

"I feel it's the right thing to do though it's tearing my heart apart. Pastor Bill helped me see this was the path I needed to take; I just didn't know how hard it would be to walk it."

***

Julie paced the corridor, trying to think of the right words to break the news to John. She wanted this baby more than life. But what if he said no? Would Karol let her have him if John weren't on board? Punching in his number, she prayed he would give her the right answer.

"Hello honey, what's up? Are you having a quiet evening with Lou?" He sounded upbeat.

"John, there's something I need to ask you."

"What's that? You want to buy something? You know you don't have to ask me."

"John, listen and don't say a word until I'm finished." With that, she quickly recapped what was happening and what it meant for them. When she finished, there was silence. "John? What do you think?" She heard him let out a low whistle.

"Where are you now?"

"I'm at the Columbia Ridge Hospital. Why?"

"Because I need to know where to come see my wife and our new son!" he whooped into the phone.

She was crying. "Are you sure?"

"Listen to me. God is giving us a second chance. I love you and I'll be there as soon as I can."

Julie returned to the room as Karol and Lou searched her face for an answer. She took the baby back from Lou and brought him close to Karol.

"John is on his way."

Karol reached her hand out to touch his face but pulled back. The nurse returned and said it was time for him to return to the NICU.

"Is it all right if I carry him back?" Julie asked, addressing Karol.

She nodded, then turned away.

Lou held Karol's hand as Julie, the baby, and the nurse left the room.

"I can't imagine how much this hurts you, but that was the greatest gift anyone could give another person. I want you to know how proud I am of you." Lou handed her the box of tissues.

Karol reached for Lou and sobbed until it exhausted her. Lou lay Karol against the pillow, waiting for her to drift off to sleep, then went to find Julie.

***

Julie watched as they hooked the baby back up to the monitors for the night. The nurse assured her it was just for precautions when she asked. He was still small, so they wanted to monitor him until he was ready to go home. Julie asked when that might be. The nurse figured in a week or two because his weight was still low.

Julie pulled the chair over and sat next to him, sliding her arm through the incubator portal where he lay. Touching his fingers, he wrapped his hand around hers, and though his eyes remained closed, she noticed a little smile drift across his face. She was still holding onto him when Lou walked up behind her.

"He sure is pretty. Or should I say handsome?" Lou whispered.

Julie lifted her head; she had been crying. "I think he's the most beautiful baby I've ever seen." She searched Lou's face. "She won't take him back, will she?"

Lou kneeled next to her best friend. "No. She's decided this is the right thing to do and as soon as John gets here, and you sign the papers, that little angel from God will be yours."

"How is Karol doing?"

"She cried herself to sleep, but I think she'll be fine. It will take a while, but I believe she knows this is her second chance too."

Julie nodded and continued her wait for John.

***

Lou excused herself, saying she needed to use the restroom and went down the hall to check her phone, hoping for a message from Jason or at least David, but there wasn't one. Loneliness engulfed her, and she felt like she couldn't breathe.

Rushing for the exit, she had to get outside for fresh air, only to find she was in the smoking section for the employees. Shaking her head, she returned inside to the stairwell and sat on the step where it was quiet and smoke free.

Glancing at her phone again, she scrolled through her pictures until she found one of Jason. His smile was so big that when she closed her eyes, she could feel his arms around her. When she opened them again, she realized she was hugging herself and tears were splashing onto the concrete floor.

Wiping her face with the backs of her hands, she stood and decided crying was a waste of time and energy. What good does it do? Life had been going on without her. Dad got married, Julie will have a new baby, and Karol will start a new life. It was time to stop feeling sorry for herself and take her life back.

Opening the stairwell door, Lou hurried to the restroom to clean up. She wouldn't ruin the happiest day of Julie and John's life with a haggard look on her face. Checking her reflection, she recalled Julie saying Lou was going to be her babies Godmother. She wasn't sure what that entailed, but she would be the best Godmother ever.

As for Karol, she would get her home, healed up and back to work so she could move out. She would help her get into college and on with her life. For herself, she had a box of pictures to the family she had been searching for. It was time to embrace what she had and stop wallowing in self-pity.

Lou saw John coming down the hall and stopped in front of him. "Hey there, John."

He paused, then recognized her. "Lou is this for real?" He looked like he might faint.

"I believe it is. Would you like to meet him?"

John didn't say a word but bobbed his head up and down. Lou took his arm and guided him towards the NICU where Julie and their soon to be son, waited. She stayed at the door for a moment, then went back to Karol's room to give them time together.

Karol was still asleep, so she sat in the chair and waited until John and Julie returned.

Ten minutes later Karol must have heard voices, opened her eyes, and sat up. After introductions, Lou was amazed how calm Karol appeared as she retrieved the papers from the drawer.

John and Julie signed the documents and Lou signed as a witness. The baby was officially theirs, short of filing the papers at the courthouse tomorrow.

"So, have you thought of a name?" Lou asked, setting the pen down.

Julie looked at John. "What do you think? We had chosen Daniel for...but if you want something else, I will understand."

John slipped his arm around Julie's shoulder. "I think Daniel is perfect." He turned to Karol. "Would that be all right with you?"

Lou saw Karol swallow hard and knew her emotions were riding on the surface.

"I think that's a strong name for your son." Karol's voice quivered. "I'd like to be alone for a while if you don't mind."

Lou slid the papers into the envelope and handed them to John. "Do you want me to stay with you, Karol?"

Karol shook her head. "Not right now." She turned her face into the pillow to hide the tears.

Lou, John, and Julie left the room and walked back to the NICU.

"I think I'll go get myself a cup of coffee. You guys want anything?" Both were staring at their new son, oblivious to what she was saying. Lou grinned and walked towards the vending machines, returning with three cups.

"Thanks for the coffee, Lou. I don't know about John, but I can really use this. It's been an unusual day."

John nodded in agreement, sipping his coffee.

"When do they say little Daniel can leave?" Lou sounded melancholy. She didn't want Julie to leave yet.

Julie looked at the baby for a moment, then back at Lou. "The doctor came by, and we told him we were the baby's new parents. He gave us an update and said Daniel should be able to leave in a week... so... I was wondering if I could stay with you until then. But, honestly Lou, if it's too much for you I can get a hotel room."

"For heaven's sake Julie, of course you can stay with me. Will you be staying, John?"

John was staring at his new son. "What? Oh, no, I have to get back to town and put the crib up."

His face beamed, and Lou knew in her heart Karol had made the right choice choosing them as her baby's parents.

"Okay, but not tonight. Tomorrow, after you file the papers, you can figure out a plan to get your son home."

She knew she sounded bossy, but someone had to be in control right now.

Lou gave them each a big hug. "I don't know about you, but I'm starving. I say you tell your son goodnight and we get something to eat."

John grinned. "You don't have to ask me twice." Julie was still staring at the baby. He was sleeping now. "Come on honey, he's in the best hands possible. After we eat, I can bring you back."

Julie gave her husband a big kiss. "John Parker, you're the best husband in the entire world. And Lou, you are the greatest friend I could ever have. Did you have any clue what would happen today?"

Lou shook her head. "Nope, not even one. As they say, God works in mysterious ways. Let's go eat."

With all the talking, it was after ten by the time they got back to Lou's place. Julie looked exhausted and was having pain, and John wanted her to lie down. They all agreed the baby was safe, and they needed rest themselves. Tomorrow would be another exciting day.

Chapter Ten

It was a long night for everyone. Lou could hear John and Julie talking late into the night, and she herself hadn't fallen asleep until after two in the morning.

Rising at seven, she was the first into the kitchen and made coffee, embarrassed she had little to nothing to feed her guests. Since Karol has been in the hospital, Lou had reverted to her old habits. She had to admit she missed the meals she and Karol shared like family.

Family. Lou said the words over again in her mind. She had a family. Her father and Mary, her newfound relative Gene, and a box waiting to show her the way.

Once she had Julie and John taken care of, she promised she would sit down and finish her research. Right now, she had a pair of emotional new parents and a heartbroken teenage girl to deal with.

Watching the coffee dripping into the pot, she got an idea. They could go to Dads. She figured with a little persuading she might get Mary to feed them until she could get groceries. Besides, she wanted Dad and Mary to know what Karol had decided and have them meet Julie and John.

***

Julie had been awake for hours watching John sleeping beside her. The events of last night played over and over in her mind, but she still was having a tough time understanding what had happened. She came to Lou to escape the pain of losing her baby, only to receive the gift of life from Karol. Part of her feared it had all been a dream and nothing was real.

She had to talk to Lou.

Slipping gently out of bed, as not to wake John, she could smell coffee brewing and knew Lou was up. Pulling on her robe, she tiptoed out the door to the kitchen. Lou had her back to her and seemed deep in thought when she entered.

"Good morning."

Lou jumped. "Oh... good morning. Did you sleep well?" Lou poured a cup and handed it to her. "Coffee?"

Julie accepted the cup. "Thanks." Blowing on the steaming dark liquid, Julie inhaled the inviting aroma, instantly calming her before she even took a sip. "This is so good. You always make a great cup of coffee. And to answer your other question. No, I did not sleep well. How could I?"

Julie set the cup on the counter and took Lou's hands in her own. "Okay Lou, tell me the truth. Did Karol give me her baby last night or was I just dreaming? But John is here, and I feel this wonderful love in my heart."

Lou smiled. "You were not dreaming. You and John are the proud parents of a little boy, or will be, as soon as you file the papers at the courthouse this morning. So, why don't you wake up that sleepy husband of yours and since I don't have any food here, we go surprise Dad and Mary. I'm sure they will feed us if I beg enough." Lou laughed at the look on Julie's face.

"Really, it's okay. I'll call and let them know there will be three more for breakfast. Dad likes me dropping in, and Mary loves company. Go get John up. We have a lot to do today."

Lou shooed her like a child, and Julie skipped down the hall acting like one. After a quick phone call and a brief explanation, Lou hurried and dressed. Ten minutes later, they were on their way to Dad and Mary's.

***

Mary was lifting cinnamon rolls from the oven when George entered, shaking his head.

"Well, that was an interesting phone call from Lou."

Mary looked up. "What do you mean by that? And good morning, dear husband."

George rounded the counter and gave her a kiss. "Good morning dear wife. Anyway, do you have room for three more? Lou has guests and, as usual, no food."

Mary grinned. "There's always room for Lou and her friends. Who are they if I may ask?"

"It's her friend Julie and her husband John, from Portland. She said she had some exciting news to share about Karol and would fill us in when they get here." George looked at his watch. "In about five minutes, she was saying. I better hurry and get the table set."

George got out the plates and silverware and promptly set the table. This had become his new job since he and Mary returned from their honeymoon. He loved working next to her and marveled at the wonderful meals she fixed for everyone who stayed at their boarding house.

They had four full-time residents and two rooms available for short-term renters. The house kept him busy making repairs, and he loved every sore muscle he had. He was finishing the table when he saw Lou and another car pull in and park.

"They're here," he called out and went to answer the door.

***

Lou hoped she would be lucky Mary was making cinnamon rolls this morning. She wasn't disappointed when Dad opened the door and the sweet smell drifted through the air, drawing her in.

"Julie, John, this is my dad, George, and my step-mom Mary, over there in the kitchen."

George barely had time to say hello before Lou bounded past him into the kitchen with her guests following.

"Hey Mary, those smell so delicious. Can I help put the icing on?" Lou gave her a kiss on the cheek. "Can I?"

Mary smiled. "You can, silly girl. Here, take the icing bag and do it the way I showed you. That's right, back, and forth, then repeat the other direction. See, I'll make a baker out of you yet." Mary gave her a hug and Lou held up her creations.

Julie looked astounded at Lou's new skill. "I didn't know you could bake Lou. Those look amazing."

Lou flashed a sheepish grin. "Well, Mary baked them, but I did the icing and that's the best part."

Everyone laughed then settled down at the table with rolls and coffee in hand.

"So, Lou, what's the news you have about Karol? Is she ready to leave the hospital with the baby?" Mary asked.

George noticed Julie and John give each other a sideways glance, and Lou was chewing on her lower lip. It was a sure sign something was up.

Lou licked her fork. "Well, the strangest thing happened last night. I don't know if you will believe it."

George set his coffee down. "We won't know unless you tell us."

***

Lou continued chewing on her lip for a moment then began her story.

"First, Julie arrived to surprise me, and then we went to the hospital, and Karol surprised Julie by wanting her and John to adopt her son. Julie called John and told him, and he hurried to get here. They signed the papers and once they file them at the courthouse, they will be new parents. Karol will come back home with me until she can go to work and get her own place and see about going to college."

George looked at Mary, Mary looked at him. Julie and John glanced at each other, then everyone looked at Lou. George smiled and shook his head. "That was a mouthful."

"Karol is sure this is what she wants to do?" Mary asked.

Lou cleared her throat. "Yes, she had this all worked out in her mind and on paper before Julie and I got there. She believes God spared her and the baby, so she could give him to Julie and John, to love and raise as their own son." Lou sniffed. "She's braver than I would be."

Julie reached for Lou's hand. "John and I feel blessed Karol has chosen us. I don't know if Lou has told you, but we lost our son to a miscarriage last month and I can't have children. She has given us the greatest gift we could ever hope for, and we will cherish him forever."

George stood and lifted his coffee cup. "Well. This calls for a toast. To Karol and the happy new parents."

Everyone cheered, then settled back to eating their cinnamon rolls until it was time to go to the courthouse. After promising they would come again, John and Julie left to file their papers.

Lou said she would catch up at the hospital and waved as they drove away. She had something else she wanted to discuss with Dad and Mary. Walking back to the kitchen, Lou poured herself another cup of coffee, trying to figure out the best way to approach the subject.

"What's going on with you today Lou? I can tell something is on your mind." Dad refreshed his own cup and Mary cleared the table. "You want another cup, Mary?" She shook her head.

"I have some information that may astound you. It has me," Lou said.

Dad and Mary sat down at the table. "Please, no more suspense," he said.

Lou slid into the chair next to Dad. "You know I have been working on my new story, trying to find Kelly's family, and Mom's, when I'm not being interrupted by all the drama lately. Anyway, I think I found her."

"Kelly's family?" Dad asked, taking a sip of his coffee.

Lou hesitated for a moment. "And Mom's family."

Mary leaned forward. "Really? How exciting for you. Are they from this area?"

Lou gave a quick recap on what she discovered and how she was still working it all out.

Dad let out a low whistle when she finished. "That's amazing if you can trace your heritage back to Kelly. I knew nothing about your mother's family. I asked often, especially after we lost your brother, but she never said a word. You say you have spoken to this Gene fellow?"

"Yes, I found his address and went to talk to him. He was friendly and said he hoped I would keep looking after he read the story about Kelly. He gave me a box with pictures. Mom's was in there, her hair was dark and curly, but she had our same corn-flower blue eyes. All the women in the family seem to have them. Anyway, I took it home to look at with the other pictures that first night but fell asleep. Before I had another chance, everything happened with Karol and the baby, then Julie arrived."

Lou leaned back in the chair.

Dad reached for her hand. "You have had a lot on your plate lately. Have you heard from Jason?"

"No. I called David, but he was no help." Her voice lowered. "I'm really worried Dad."

"I'm sure he's fine." Dad tried to sound convincing.

"What if he isn't? What if something happened to him and they aren't telling me?" Lou pulled her hand back and covered her face with her hands. The stress of not knowing was eating away at her.

Mary rose and put her arm around Lou. "It will be all right. God is watching over him."

Lou wasn't so sure. "Sorry I'm such a baby." Lou stood. "You two have a wonderful day and I'll call you later."

Before either of them could respond, she was out the door and driving away. Lou made it three blocks before she was hyperventilating so bad; she couldn't see the road and had to pull over and park.

A flood of emotions rushed over her like a raging river until anger replaced the sadness. Anger at Jason for leaving her, anger at herself for being angry at him. What did it matter if she had found a new family member? She was still alone. She knew she was being petty, but right now she didn't care.

The phone pinged, pulling her back to reality. It was Julie. Lou decided that no matter what was happening in her own life, she would not ruin this time for Julie or Karol. She would deal with her problems later.

"Hey, new mom. What's up?" She hoped she sounded convincing.

"Where are you? I got a strange call from your Dad. He said you rushed off."

"Oh that. Everything is fine." She hated lying.

"Are you sure?"

Lou laughed, trying to disguise the emptiness she felt. "Yes, I'm sure. So, did you get the papers filed? Is that little boy yours?" Lou could hear John in the background.

"John says to tell you he loves you and we can't thank you enough."

"Hey, I'm not the one to thank. This was Karol's decision. I just brought you together."

"You know what I mean. Anyway, we are going back to the hospital to check on Daniel and Karol. Will we see you there later?"

"I have to go to the office for a while. I'm not sure if the alarm is on, but if it is, the code is 5476. Just make yourselves at home until I get there." Lou hung up before Julie could respond.

Once she was back at the office, she placed a call to David, only to have it go to voicemail again. She sent a text but still got no answer. She was about to call Joan, then decided against it. Besides, if there was a problem with Jason, they would have let Joan know, and she would have called.

Booting up her computer, Lou opened Kelly's story file. Her readers were waiting. Brad was waiting. It was time to bring Kelly home to her family.

Lou's family.

For the next week Lou spent time working on her story, keeping up with Julie and visiting Karol. The courts pushed through the adoption papers since there were no objections and Julie and her family would leave in two days. Karol's infection had cleared up and she too would be coming home.

Life was falling in place for all those around her, but not for herself. She hadn't had time to go see Gene and felt ashamed, especially since she had pushed her way into his life, then dropped the ball. It was like a dark cloud hovered over her constantly and she had to fight the despair she felt.

Dad and Mary checked on her every day, and as much as she loved them, it was getting on her nerves. She had to snap out of this mood she was in, and soon.

The day had finally arrived for Julie to leave. John was taking the bus to town so he could drive his new family home and would arrive in an hour. Julie was trying to fit all of Daniel's new clothes into her suitcase without success when Lou walked into the bedroom.

"My goodness, do you think you have enough things for that tiny baby?" Lou laughed and gave her a hug.

"I might have overdone it a little."

"You think?"

Julie sat on the bed next to the suitcase. "If you think I'm bad, wait until you see what John bought."

Lou sat next to her. "Didn't you have things from—you know?"

Julie sighed. "After we lost him, my mother gathered all his clothes and toys and gave it all away. She thought it would be too hard on me and John to have to look at them when I came home from the hospital. The pain was so deep I said nothing. I know she was only trying to help but I hated her for making it look like he never existed. Thankfully, John insisted on keeping the crib and the rocking chair." She picked up a little shirt and held it to her chest. "I'll have John pick up another suitcase after he gets here."

Lou jumped up and went to the closet in her mother's old room. The suitcases were still sitting on the floor, tucked in the back. She had forgotten to take them to the garage with the rest of her mother's things. Grabbing the big one, she carried it back to Julie.

"Here's one of my mom's cases. You can use it to get Daniels things home and I can pick it up later. It will give me an excuse to come see you. Not that I need one." Lou laid the case on the bed and popped the locks. When she lifted the top, she gasped and slammed it shut.

Julie was standing next to her. "What's wrong, Lou? Here sit down."

Lou plopped on the bed, shaking.

Julie lifted the top and folded it back. "Oh, look. It's a little teddy bear." She held the bear up for Lou to see. "He's so cute. Is he yours?"

Lou nodded, unable to speak.

"But what's he doing inside your mother's suitcase?" Julie handed her the bear.

Lou stroked the soft fur and held him to her face. Tears rushed down her cheeks and she knew Julie didn't have a clue what was going on.

"My mom told me she threw him away when I was seven, during one of her crazy spells. I cried for a week." Lou held the bear out to get a better look. "I can't believe she had him all this time hiding in her suitcase."

Julie sat next to Lou. "Maybe she planned on giving it back later and forgot where she had put it."

Lou frowned at her.

"It could have happened. Didn't you tell me she would forget the things she would do or say?"

Julie was right. Maybe Mom was going to give it back and just forgot. Lou wanted to believe that was true but doubted it.

She handed the little bear to Julie.

"I want you to take this for Daniel. You can tell him later it's from his Godmother. I still get to be his Godmother, don't I?"

Julie gave Lou a big hug. "Of course, you do. But are you sure about the bear?"

"Yes, and I hope he will love it as much as I did."

Together they finished packing and were setting the bags by the door when a cab pulled up and John got out. It was time.

Lou followed in her car to the hospital. Tears flowed from everyone when the proud new parents drove away, and Lou returned to Karol's room.

"Do you have your things packed?" Lou checked the drawers, making sure they left nothing behind.

Karol fumbled with the buttons on her sweater. "It was the right thing to do, wasn't it, Lou?"

Lou walked over and put her arms around Karol. "Remember what Julie said, you can call her anytime."

Karol shook her head. "No, I think it's better to let him go. They're his parents now. It would hurt too much." Tears dripped down her cheeks, hitting the bed sheets like raindrops.

Lou held her tighter and let her cry it out. Picking up her bag, they walked out of the hospital and headed home.

***

Karol stared out the window on the ride back to the house. Her entire life had changed over the last few weeks, making her head spin. The incision was finally healing, but her heart felt like it had shattered. John and Julie wanted to help her, so they set up a fund to pay for her college. She tried to protest, but Julie insisted she deserved a fresh start.

Glancing over at Lou, she knew she could never repay her for her kindness. Karol had thought about it long and hard and decided she would move back to the YWCA until she figured out where she wanted to go to college. Julie told her she could go anywhere she wanted, and they would pay for housing along with the tuition. She just had to choose.

It was time to be independent and Karol didn't want to be a burden when Jason returned. She would still see Lou at work. Brad said she could come back if she wanted to and Karol was surprised how much she had grown up in a short amount of time.

***

Lou pulled into the driveway, parked, and let out a deep sigh. "Well, we're here. Are you sure you're ready for this?"

Karol didn't answer but opened the door and got out.

Lou could tell she was shaking. "Listen to me, if this is too much, I can take you over to Dad and Mary's place. You could stay there"

Karol turned and faced her. "I can do this, Lou. I will not let Tommy take anything else from me." Opening the back door, she retrieved her things and headed for the house.

Lou followed, amazed at the strength this young girl had, and swore to quit whining about her own life. They stood for a moment as Lou unlocked the door, then pushed it open.

Karol stepped through the threshold and paused. "Wow. It smells nice in here. And it's so much brighter."

Lou closed the door behind them and re-set the alarm. It was something she had been doing ever since that night.

"Yeah, Dad had the entire house painted. He thought it was time to brighten things up a little. I hope you like your room. I think Mary calls it buttercup yellow, but if you don't, I can have it changed." Lou knew she was rambling.

Karol gave her a smile. "I'm sure it's beautiful. I think I'll put my things away then meet you in the kitchen, if you would like to have a cup of tea."

"I think that would be nice. Wait until you see the kitchen. I mean, it's so bright and cheery too."

Karol touched Lou's arm. "I'm okay. Just give me a minute to get settled."

Lou nodded, then went to the kitchen to fix tea. She was setting the cups on the table when her cell phone buzzed, startling her. Picking it up, she noticed it was Dad calling.

"Hey Dad, how's it going?"

"I would ask the same of you. Are you both at the house? How is Karol doing being back? Is she okay with the whole situation with Julie?"

"Whoa, Dad. One question at a time. We just got home, and Karol is in her room, though I suggested she come to your place, but she said no. She's stronger than I am right now." She could hear Dad sigh and Mary talking in the background. "Really Dad, I'm okay. Give Mary a hug for me and I'll call you tomorrow."

Lou clicked off so he couldn't ask any more questions. She was pouring the boiling water into the cups when she heard Karol let out a little gasp.

"Are you sure you want to stay here, Karol?" Lou set the teapot down as she watched Karol scanning the room.

"Yes. It's so pretty in here. You would... I mean, I like the color. Did you help pick them out?" Looking like she might collapse any moment; Karol moved to the table and took a seat.

Lou sat across from her. "Nope, Mary and Dad did it all. Besides, I'm not much on decorating. You saw that from the way the place was before. Anyway, I think they did a fantastic job. I love the sky-blue cabinets; the white marble countertops and the oak floors. I think those two should start their own remodeling business along with everything else they do."

Lou took a sip of tea to stop herself from talking and noticed Karol scanning her surroundings as if she expected someone to burst in any moment. "You're safe here, Karol. He can't hurt you anymore."

Karol could only nod. "This is good. I've missed having tea with you."

Lou smiled. She had to admit she missed their time together. It had helped with Jason being gone, but now she questioned what the future held for all of them.

Karol rose and returned with the teakettle. "Would you like more hot water?"

Lou held out her cup. "Thanks. Does the quiet bother you? I could turn on the radio."

"No. This is nice. After listening to bells and voices over the intercom system for the last few weeks, this is heavenly, unless you want to."

"Your right, this is nice. So, have you thought about where you would like to go to college? I understand Portland State College has a great fashion design course and you would be close to... or you could stay here."

Karol sat her teacup down. "I thought I would go back to work for a while. You know, get my feet back on the ground, and I still want to help you do your research, if you want me to. I was also thinking about going back to the YWCA, if they have a room and get out of your hair."

"What? Absolutely not. I mean, yes go back to work, and yes help me on the research, but you don't have to leave. You are welcome as long as you want."

"What about Jason?"

Lou stretched her neck. "Yes, what about Jason? He's gone, and I don't know when he will be back, so I would like you to stay. And wait until I tell you what I discovered last week."

Lou told her about finding Gene and getting the box of pictures. Karol listened to the excitement in Lou's voice. It was good to think about someone else for a change. It looked like they both had something to look forward to.

Chapter Eleven

Karol returned to work and over the next month, Lou thought she was doing well under the circumstances. Julie called with weekly updates on the baby, excited he was gaining weight and meeting all his marks. Dad had called twice asking them to come to dinner, but both declined. Neither was up to company.

Christmas came and went, and the new year forced its way in, with no word from anyone about Jason. Lou didn't want to admit it, but she was giving up hope of a happy ending for herself.

Lou called Gene, apologizing for her bad manners, and asked when she could come for another visit. He told her she was welcome to come anytime, and they settled on the next day. She remembered he remarked there was something else to tell her, and she had totally forgotten about it.

How could she forget something so important?

This separation from Jason was fogging her brain, and she had to let it go. She decided she would take Karol with her. She had seemed a little down, and Lou figured she could use the outing.

"Hey Lou? What time are we leaving to see Gene? That's his name, right? Do you call him Uncle Gene or just Gene? Are you excited?" Karol set her bag on the counter. "This is so cool."

Karol's banter jolted Lou back to reality. "Well, I guess if he's really who he says he is, then it would be Uncle Gene. But let's hold our excitement until we have more facts. How's that sound to you?"

Karol's head bobbed up and down.

Lou headed for the door. "Are you coming or just stand there with a silly grin on your face?"

"Coming. I wouldn't miss this for sure. This is so exciting, just like detectives on a case."

Lou shook her head and tried to hide the smile as they got into the car. "Now listen, you let me do the talking, you're there to take notes."

"Right, right, like Sherlock Holmes and Watson." Karol laughed.

"Oh, for heaven's sake, will you be serious?" Lou glanced her way and couldn't help but join in the laughter.

When she pulled into the driveway and parked, Lou felt her heart flutter and realized she was chewing on her lip as they made their way to the door and knocked. "Now remember, I do the talking and you take notes."

"Right, Sherlock."

"Karol."

"Okay, okay. Just notes. But...," her voice stopped when the door opened, and a gray-haired gentleman stood before them.

"Good afternoon, Lou. I see you brought a friend. Please come in." Gene stepped back so they could enter. "Would you like to follow me to the kitchen? I have tea and cookies waiting for us."

Lou nodded her head towards Karol, who was gawking at the sitting room the same way she had. "Karol?"

Karol shrugged her shoulders. "Sure, lead the way. What a lovely room you have there. Do you play the piano? I've never seen such beautiful curtains and the loveseat...." Lou pinched her arm. "What? Oh yeah. Just take notes."

Gene smiled as he turned and led the way to the sunny kitchen. The aroma of fresh-baked cookies drifted through the air.

"Ladies, please take a seat. I have hot water and an assortment of teas, hopefully to your liking."

Lou and Karol grabbed the first bags they saw and set them in their cups. "This is very nice of you Gene; you didn't have to go to all this trouble."

Karol was already nibbling on a cookie.

"Indulge an old man. I rarely get visitors these days as lovely as you two." Gene leaned forward. "And what is your name, young lady?"

Karol swallowed hard. "Hi, I'm Karol, I work for, I mean I work with Lou. Doing research." She picked up her cookie. "These are great. Did you put cinnamon in them?"

"Karol, that's not polite to ask."

"Why not? Wait until you taste one?"

Gene leaned back in his chair. "If you would like, I can give you both a copy of the recipe. It was my sister's favorite."

Karol took a drink of her tea before answering. "Thank you, that would be very nice."

Lou wished she had left Karol at home. "I want to apologize again for leaving and not calling or coming back to see you. Just a lot of things have happened lately." Lou heard Karol whisper 'amen' under her breath. "So, what was it you wanted to talk to me about?

Karol dug out her notepad and waited.

Gene remained still for a moment, as if trying to gather his thoughts. "I have a confession to make Lou. It's been a long time since I saw you last."

Lou frowned. "I don't understand. It's only been a few months at most."

Gene cleared his throat. "Actually, before that. I would say it's been about twenty-years. I believe you were four at the time you came to visit."

Karol was scribbling as fast as she could.

"Why would I come here? I just found out you existed."

Gene continued. "Your mother, Susan, or Vivian as she was calling herself then, came to see her mother and me. She had you with her. I almost didn't recognize her. She had blond hair, but you never forget those corn-flower blue eyes. She wanted to talk to her mother, so I brought you into the kitchen for some milk and cookies."

Lou was shaking her head. "That can't be true. I don't remember this house or you."

Gene pulled a faded photo from his shirt pocket and handed it to her. "I took this that day not knowing we could never see you again."

Lou jerked the picture from his hand and stared at it. The black and white had faded, but she could make out the people in it. She was standing next to her mother and another woman who was holding a teddy bear, her teddy bear. "Who is this woman next to my mom?"

"That is your grandmother, Elizabeth, my sister, on the last day we saw either of you again."

Lou handed the photo back to Gene. "But why? What happened?"

"From what I overheard and from what Elizabeth told me later, your mother had just lost the baby. She was going through a rough patch and wanted to blame Elizabeth. The hurtful words that came out of your mother's mouth shocked me. I tried to keep you in the kitchen, but you went running when you heard her yelling. Her final words were that we would never see either of you again if she was alive. Elizabeth was heartbroken, and we never spoke about it again. When I heard your mother died, I hoped you might come looking for your family. I never realized a story in the newspaper would bring us back together."

Lou sat, trying to absorb what Gene was telling her. How could her mother have been so cruel? How could she deny her own daughter of a family? This was just too much to take in as tears forced their way to the rims of her eyes.

"I can't... I don't believe you... my mother... she."

Gene handed Lou his hanky. "I'm sorry Lou, but it's true. If you don't believe me, you can talk to your grandmother."

Lou's head snapped up as she dabbed at her eyes. "What did you say?"

Karol placed her hand on Lou's arm. "I think he said you can talk to your grandmother."

Lou was standing now. "But I thought she was dead? I didn't find any records of her being alive."

Gene pulled a card from his other shirt pocket and set it on the table. "That was a mistake on my part. This is where your grandmother lives now. If you want to, she would love to see you again. If not, she said to tell you she loves you and would understand."

Lou grabbed her bag and dashed out of the house, leaving Karol and Gene staring at each other.

Karol wasn't sure what to do but picked up the card. "Sorry, I have to go. It was nice meeting you and maybe I can get that recipe another day." She left him sitting with tears rolling down his cheeks.

Karol found Lou pacing around the car when she got outside. "Wow! That was intense. Do you think it's all true?"

Lou stopped and glared at her. "How am I supposed to know? My mom never told me anything about her family, and I never asked. I just learned to stay out of her way." Lou started pacing again, running her hands through her hair. "How could she do this to me? Making me believe we had no family? What kind of person does this to their own kid?"

"I guess you could ask your grandmother?"

Lou shot her a stern look.

"I'm just saying. Maybe she can tell you what you want to hear."

Lou leaned against the car. "What can she tell me I don't already know? My mother was a hateful, sad, vindictive woman. Let's get out of here. I wish I'd never come."

"But Lou."

Lou opened her car door. "Get in the car or I'll leave you here."

***

Karol jumped. Lou didn't have to tell her twice and was already starting the car by the time Karol got her seatbelt on. Silence filled the car on the ride back to the house and Karol wondered if once Lou calmed down if she would go see her grandmother.

At least her grandmother wanted to see her.

Karol's grandparents had died years ago, and she still hadn't talked to her parents, and it got her to thinking. Maybe if she and Lou could get past the hurt, they might have a second chance at happiness. One thing she had learned, life was too short to not try. Karol decided when she got home, she would start by writing a letter to her mother. If it came back unopened, she would move on with her life.

***

Lou's mind ran rampant with questions as she drove home. Thankfully, Karol was staying quiet for a change to let her think. This whole thing was crazy, but if she really thought about it, it was something her mother would do.

When had Mom changed?

Lou tried to remember back through her childhood. There were times she was so loving, and remembered sitting on her lap, holding the bear she gave to Julie for Daniel, as Mom read a bedtime story.

Then something happened.

That must have been when she lost the baby, her brother. Life was different after that. Dad was rarely home, and Mom cried all the time. Other days Mom would be like her old self, happy and laughing. Then a cloud would come over her and she would sink into such sadness.

Lou learned later it was depression.

Now she wondered if her life would have been different if she had known about her grandmother? Could she have gone to her when Mom was being irrational, instead of having to endure her outbursts? Did her grandmother know how unstable Mom was and if she did, why didn't she come and take Lou away?

Lou glanced over at Karol, grateful for her friendship. What if she hadn't heard Karol crying that day in the bathroom? What if she hadn't been so keen on finding a story to prove herself? And what if she had never met Jason?

Tears welled in her eyes for all the what ifs. Would she be better off having missed this part of her life? She knew the answers, but it did not relieve the pain she felt.

Chapter Twelve

Elizabeth Johnson sat staring out the picture window at the senior living center where she had been living for the last three years. Her husband Cliff had died five years before and with her arthritis advancing, she decided it was too much for her brother Gene to care for her. He was older than she was, but was in better shape, and continued to live in the old farmhouse on the cliff. How she missed looking out over the river.

The house belonged to their great-grandmother Rosalie and great-grandfather Haven. Her own mother and father had lived there, and she and Cliff had come back to live in the house after her parents died.

Gene had come to the house after Cliff died to help her. It was home, and she had hoped Susan, along with her family, would come to live there one day, but it was never to be. She never thought she would outlive her only child.

Reaching into her apron pocket, she pulled out the only picture she had of Susan and Louise. Where had the time gone and mostly, where had she gone wrong with Susan?

Gene had stopped by and filled her in on his visit with Louise and her friend Karol. Louise's reaction didn't surprise her, she only hoped with a little time she might see things differently. There was so much she wanted to tell her if she ever got the chance.

Elizabeth closed her eyes and asked God to help guide Louise home.

***

Karol had gone straight to her room when they got home, and Lou spent a restless night going over and over the conversation in her head. 'Should I call Dad and let him know that grandmother is alive? Do I tell him Mom kept this from both of us, and I could have had my grandmother in my life all these years?' Lou realized she was talking to herself. Isn't this what she had been dreaming of all her life, family? Now it was staring her right in the face and she was holding back.

Combing her hair, the reflection looking back disgusted her. Where had the confident person gone? It was time to pull herself together. Whether Jason ever came back, life would go on. She had a story to finish, and the possibility of a new family to get to know. Karol still needed her, Dad and Mary cared for her, and Julie and John had their new son. She would have to accept life was meant to be this way.

Karol was in the kitchen making toast when Lou entered.

"Morning Lou. Do you want some?" She motioned, holding up the plate.

Lou reached for a cup, slipped in a tea bag, and poured in hot water. "Sure, thanks. Hey, I want to apologize about yesterday. I shouldn't have sniped at you. I know you were only trying to help."

Karol set the toast on the table and opened the jam. "It's okay, Lou. Have you thought about going to see your grandmother?"

Lou sipped her tea. "Maybe but I don't have her address. I left the card on the table when I rushed out."

Karol dipped her hand into her bathrobe pocket and drew out the card. "Will this help?"

"When? How?" Her hand reached for the card.

"After you left, I picked it up. Also, if you visit again, your Uncle Gene said he would give us the cookie recipe."

Lou tried to give her a stern look.

"What? Those were the best cookies ever."

Lou couldn't help but laugh. Karol loved her sweets and so did she.

"If I go back, I promise I'll get it for us. Though you or Mary will have to bake them."

Karol nodded in agreement. "I'm surprised you haven't starved before I came here. Though after seeing all the take-out boxes in the garbage, I guess you're safe."

"Yes, thanks for takeout. I thought about it a lot last night and now with the address, I might go visit my grandmother today."

Karol clapped her hands. "Oh Lou, I was hoping you would say that. Do you want me to go with you? What am I saying? This is something you need to do on your own, but you have to promise to tell me everything when you get back."

Karol's enthusiasm was infectious, and Lou felt the familiar butterfly's in her stomach when she was excited about something. She enjoyed having that feeling once again.

"Yes, I'll tell you, but right now I have to get dressed. I will leave my phone off while I am there, so if my dad calls looking for me, tell him I left it on the charger, and I'll call him back."

"Sure, and Lou?"

"Yes, Karol?"

"Everything will work out. I can just feel it."

Lou turned towards her room. "I hope you're right."

Opening her closet, she picked through her clothes, not sure what to wear. She still hadn't enlarged her wardrobe. The same white blouses and khaki slacks hung on the rod in front of her. She did have the pastel lavender sweater she had kept of her mother's and could wear it over the blouse. At least she wouldn't look like a hospital worker.

Slipping it on, she felt a strange warmth surround her and smiled. Next, she tried to corral her curly hair, and added the minimal of make-up. She still didn't like all the drama about it and settled on mascara and lip gloss.

Strawberry. Jason's favorite.

A tear welled in her eye at the thought of him. Not knowing if he was dead or alive was the hardest part. It ate at her soul.

Brushing the tear away, she would try and put him out of her mind for the day, though she knew it would be impossible.

***

Elizabeth had finished lunch and returned to her room, when she received a message from the office, she had a visitor and was pleasantly surprised. She had been praying for this day, she just wished Susan were here to share it with her. Checking her hair in the mirror, she straightened her blouse and waited.

***

Lou found Elizabeth's room and stood outside, trying to gather her courage to knock. What if she was making a big mistake dragging up the past? Maybe Mom had a reason she didn't want to see her mother and she should leave it alone.

Chewing on her lip, Lou knew she couldn't stop now; she had been searching for answers her whole life. They might not be the ones she's hoping for, but she'd never know until she asked.

Raising her hand, she gently tapped on the door and was picking at her thumbnail when it opened.

A woman with beautiful white hair and the same cornflower blue eyes greeted her.

"You must be Louise. Please come in. It's been a long time."

Her voice was soothing as Lou stepped through the door. She seemed harmless enough, but as hard as Lou tried, she didn't remember her.

"Thank you for agreeing to see me. Most people call me Lou."

Elizabeth motioned towards the small table with the two chairs. "I have tea. Would you like a cup?"

Lou nodded. "That would be nice." For once in her life, Lou was at a loss for words. Was this really her grandmother standing in front of her?

Elizabeth poured the tea and sat, motioning Lou to do the same. "I'm sure you have a lot of questions, but first I would like to tell you a brief story if you don't mind."

Lou shrugged her shoulders and sat back.

Elizabeth told her about her mother, Irene, who made her life miserable and swore she had spawned the devil for her transgressions, when she became pregnant with Lou's mother. Irene was a rigid woman, and so was her father.

The only solace she found was from her grandmother Rosalie. She was Elisabeth's salvation and helped her through the challenging times in her life. When she died, Elizabeth felt she had lost a piece of herself.

As for her parents, they went to their graves never forgiving her. They also had never bonded with Susan as she grew up, and for that Elizabeth was sorry. She wondered if that was why Susan cut her and her father out of her life. She never knew for sure.

"I know this is a great deal to understand. Just know that Cliff and I loved your mother and you. It broke our hearts when she wouldn't let us see you again."

Lou shifted in her seat. "Did you know that she lost a baby? My brother?"

"Yes, I don't know if you remember, but you came to the big house to see me with your mother. She had just gotten home from the sanitorium after losing the baby. She was so different. I'm not sure how to explain it. There was just this vacant look in her eyes, and she looked so sad. Uncle Gene took you into the kitchen while we talked. I tried to understand, but what she was saying made little sense. She was blaming your father, the doctors and me for her loss, as if something we had done caused the baby's death. The more I tried to reason with her, the more she became agitated and soon was yelling. You must have heard her and came running in from the other room. You were clutching your teddy bear, the one I sent the Christmas before, and crying. She grabbed you by the arm and stormed out the door, spewing such hatred. Her final words, as she put you in the car, were to never contact her again. That we were dead to her. Susan didn't even come to her father's funeral when he died eight years ago."

Lou sat stunned. For over twenty years, she had believed she had no other family than her father. Now to learn her grandparents lived right here in town, along with her uncle, was more than she could understand. "Why didn't you contact me after Mom died?"

Elizabeth twisted the napkin in her hand. "I wanted to, but I didn't know what your mother might have told you about us."

"She never said a word. I didn't know you even existed and never would have, if not for Kelly's story, and deciding to trace my family." Lou shook her head. "I don't understand. How is Kelly related to all of us?"

"That remained a big secret for years. When I got pregnant, I went to Grandmother Rosalie for advice. My mother wanted me to give the baby away to save face in town, but I couldn't do it. When I told Grandmother, she told me of her first daughter and how someone forced her to give her up right after she gave birth. She was only seventeen at the time and never saw her again. She made me promise to keep my baby and she would help any way she could. Fortunately for me, Cliff, your grandfather, loved me very much, and we married before Susan was born, but we had to move away. My parents never forgave me, and we didn't come back until after they both had died. It wasn't until I read your story in the paper, I knew this had to have been Grandmother's daughter. I remember in your last article that you planned to keep searching for Kelly's family and I hoped someday you might knock on my door."

Lou felt the room was spinning around her and lowered her head. "Why didn't my mother love me?" she whispered.

Elizabeth took Lou's hands in her own, caressing them. "Oh, honey. Your mother loved you. She just couldn't love herself. Right before you had to put her in the home, she came to see me. She was lucid, and we had a long talk. Susan told me of the hard life she had put on you in hopes it would strengthen you. She blamed herself for the baby's death and for pushing your father away. I tried to explain that it wasn't her fault, but she couldn't get past her own guilt. She knew she was getting worse and hated the burden she had placed on you. She just didn't know how to tell you, so she pushed you further away."

"She should have told me. I thought she blamed me for the baby and hated me because Dad left us. I just wanted her to love me." Lou couldn't hold the tears back any longer.

Elizabeth rose and held her granddaughter in her arms. Lou smelled the familiar lavender scent and cried that much harder. Finally, she regained control of herself and pulled back.

Elizabeth pulled her chair closer to Lou and sat.

"Lou, believe me, she loved you with all her heart. You were the best thing that ever happened to her, even if she couldn't show you in the way you needed. She begged me to ask for your forgiveness should we ever meet. I told her I loved her, and we said goodbye. It was the last time I saw her. I read her obituary in the paper and have been praying to God to let me live long enough to do what your mother asked of me."

Lou jerked her head up. "You're not dying, are you?"

Elizabeth chuckled. "No, hopefully not anytime soon. Though old age is gaining on me."

Lou smiled for the first time. She liked this woman. A heavyweight lifted from her shoulders, knowing that her mother had loved her. Her grandmother said so, and she had no reason to lie. Her grandmother... she liked the sound of that.

"I can't believe we are sitting here after all these years, Grandmother."

Lou checked her watch. She had been there for over two hours and knew Dad would be chomping at the bit, along with Karol, wondering where she was and what was happening. She just didn't want to leave.

"I'm sorry but I have to get back to work and I have a lot to think about. I really need to talk to my dad. Can I come and see you again? Soon?"

"My darling Lou, you can come every day though it might get a little boring hanging out with an old woman," her smile lit the room.

Lou hugged her again, then made her way to the door. "Thank you, Grandmother. I'll call tomorrow and we can set up a time for you to meet my dad. He will never believe this."

"I would love that very much." Elizabeth pulled two recipe cards from her pocket. "Your Uncle Gene said to give these to you and your friend. Evidently he made quite an impression on her with his baking."

Lou chuckled. "Yes, he did. On both of us. I look forward to getting to know him too."

She gave Elizabeth a kiss on the cheek before she hurried out the door, leaving her with a smile on her face. She herself was still smiling when she got back to her car.

Turning her phone on she saw three missed calls from Karol, and two from Dad. Excited to share her discovery, she headed for Dad and Mary's. Karol would just have to wait.

Chapter Thirteen

George was getting worried Lou wasn't picking up when he called. Mary told him to just let her be. She was probably knee deep in research. He would have liked to believe that, except Karol told him Lou had gone out but left her phone at home. She never went anywhere without her phone. Reaching for his cell phone he punched in her number again and waited. This time she answered.

"Hey Dad. I see that you called twice. Sorry I missed you, but my phone was dead, and I left it on the charger."

"Karol told me that. I was getting worried. You never go without your phone."

"Well, you caught me this time. What did you need? Is Mary okay? You're not feeling sick, are you?"

"Hold on, Lou. I'm fine and Mary is fine. I called because I'm worried about you. You haven't been yourself with Jason being gone and then this whole Karol thing. I think you should talk to someone." He felt she needed help to get her through this period in her life, afraid she might end up like her mother.

"Look Dad, I know I've been a little on the wonky side lately, but really, I can manage it. I have something to talk to you about if you have a few minutes or hours."

"Sure, I think I can carve out a few minutes for my favorite daughter."

"Your only daughter," she laughed.

"The love of my life, next to Mary. She's standing across the room. So, when will we see you?"

"How about in two minutes? I'm parking the car now."

"The door is always open."

George hung up and turned to Mary. "Lou said she needs to talk to us."

"I heard that. She sounded a little serious. Do you have any idea what she wants to talk about? Should I give you two privacy?"

George put his arm around his wife. "Absolutely not. We're family. We stick together. Whatever she has to say, she can say to both of us." George heard the door open and close. "Okay act natural. Here she comes."

Mary smacked him on the arm and went to greet Lou.

"Hello. We have missed you lately. Can I get you something to drink? Tea, coffee, a soft drink?"

Lou gave her a hug. "You have any root beer? It just sounds good, but if you don't, water would be fine."

"You are your father's daughter. I just got him a case yesterday. Sit and I'll get everyone a glass. So, what have you been up to lately? How are Karol and Julie?"

George gave her an awkward glance. He was the one who was supposed to be asking all the questions. "Yes, how are Karol and Julie? And what have you been doing lately?"

Mary set the glasses on the table, as everyone took a seat.

Lou took a deep drink before answering. "Karol is doing well and is looking into colleges. Julie and John are settling into sleepless nights as new parents and I met my grandmother today."

George almost spit out his drink. "You did what? How is that possible? She's dead."

"George, give the girl a chance to answer."

***

Lou told them about her visit. "I know this is a lot, it was for me too, but talking to Grandmother has cleared up a lot of what I thought or believed about Mom. All these years I was sure she hated me for making you leave and for the baby dying. I understand now it wasn't my fault. It just happened. I wish I could tell her I love her once more."

Lou saw the look on her father's face and knew what he must be thinking. She reached out and touched his hand. He lifted his head with tears in his eyes.

"It's not your fault either, Dad. You can't blame yourself. All that matters, she loved us both. That's how I want to remember her from now on. It's time to let go of the hate and sorrow. I would like you both to meet Grandmother Elizabeth. You'll like her, Dad, and Uncle Gene. From what I noticed at his house; he likes to carve too."

Dad wiped his eyes. "I would like that. Thank you, Lou."

"For what?"

"For keeping an open heart and not closing it off when you have every right to."

Lou squeezed his hand. "I have to let go, to live. If that means forgiving Mom, then that's what I will do. I never knew this journey would lead me to finding Kelly's family, my family, our family." Lou smiled, really smiled for the first time in months. "Oh Mary, I almost forgot, I have something for you."

Lou searched her pockets until she found the recipe cards and held one out. "This is for you. Grandmother gave it to me, but since I can't bake, I figured you might like to teach me. It's an old family recipe for cookies. Uncle Gene made them when Karol and I visited. And she couldn't stop raving. You know, Karol. Anyway, I'd like you to have it."

Mary gently took the card and held it to her chest. "I will treasure it and I would love to teach you how to make them. Is that a deal?"

Lou nodded. "It's a deal. So, Dad, are you up to meeting your mother-in-law? That sounds weird doesn't it?"

"Yes, I would. It's been a long time coming."

Lou stood, "I thought I would give everyone a few days to get used to this new family dynamics. I plan on calling her tomorrow and I'll see what day is good for her and Uncle Gene, then let you know. Now I need to get home before Karol blows up my phone, wondering what's been happening. She's so nosy sometimes, but God, I love her." Lou paused at the door. "Don't you ever tell her that. It will go to her head and there'll be no living with her from then on."

Dad and Mary couldn't help but laugh, as Lou bounded out the door and down to her car.

***

Karol paced the floor, watching for any sign of Lou's car, wondering what in the world was keeping her so long, then figured she went to see her Dad. Glancing out the window once more, she saw Lou's car pull into the driveway and had the door open before Lou made it up the steps.

"Oh my God Lou, where have you been? I have been so worried. I thought she did something with you, but then that would be silly since she lives in a retirement home and they don't let them bake. Then I thought you might have gone off the deep end and all, but realized you're too smart for that, so I figured you must have gone to see your dad."

Karol was talking so fast she was making herself dizzy. "Right so, how did your dad take the news? How could he take the news? Hello, your mother-in-law is alive and lives down the street. I bet that was a brain burner." Exhausted, she plopped on the chair next to the door.

Lou walked right past her into the kitchen without saying a word. Karol jumped up, shut the door, and followed.

***

Lou set her bag on the counter, trying to catch her own breath and dizzy from all the questions. Boy, can that girl talk. It made her laugh. She needed to laugh. She needed to be happy.

"Sit down and I will tell you, if you keep your mouth shut."

"But... okay, not a word. Just tell me, tell me."

Lou took her time before she started and kept it short. Karol didn't need to know about her mother's problems, other than she suffered from depression and it had been difficult growing up not knowing what it was. Karol kept quiet while she talked, listening intently, and nodding occasionally. When Lou finished Karol gave her a quizzical look.

"What's that for?"

"Well, that's all fine and dandy, but why didn't she get ahold of you after your mother died."

"I told you if you were listening. Mom hoped I would find Grandmother on my own. Who knew it would happen because of a story about some crosses on that old road?"

Karol played with her teacup. "I guess you are right. Things happen as they should, when they should. I did something too."

"And what was that?"

"I wrote a letter to my mom."

"Did she write back?"

Karol nodded.

"Well, what did she say? Don't keep me in suspense."

"She wants to come and see me."

"Karol, that's wonderful. When?"

"I was thinking next Saturday. She gave me her number. We talked for a few minutes and I said I would have to clear it with you first and would call her back."

"For heaven's sake. This is your mother. You don't have to have my permission to see her. You call her right now and set it up."

Karol lowered her head. "Are you sure? I don't want to cause any more trouble than I have."

Lou swallowed hard. "You're not causing trouble. I asked you to stay to help you out, but really you have helped me. I value your friendship more than you will ever know. You are a strong young woman. If you can fix your relationship with your mother, then do it. Don't live the rest of your life with regrets for what could have been. I wish I had the chance you've been given."

Karol smiled. "I love you, Lou. More than you will ever know. Would you be here when she comes? I really would like you to meet her."

"If that's what you want. Now call your mom." Karol retrieved her cell phone and placed the call. Lou could see Karol was holding back the tears when she said 'I love you' to her mother, then hung up. Lou prayed this would be a joyous reunion. "There, now that's done. Is your father coming too?"

"No. Momma said she up and left him six months ago and went to live with her sister. Just walked out the door. He never said a word to stop her."

"Oh, I'm sorry."

Karol stiffened in her chair. "I'm not. He was a mean man. Momma deserved better than him, and I think he knew it. He never liked me for sure."

"Karol, how can you say that?"

"It's the truth. From my first memory of him, he was always telling me I was the devil's child. I didn't understand what he was talking about, so I, too, learned to stay out of his way. Momma tried to run interference, but as I got older, the meaner he became to both of us. I told no one, but he used to beat us, though Momma took the blows to protect me. I tried to talk her into leaving, but she said this was her bed, and she had to lie in it. Whatever that meant. When I graduated, she put me on the first bus out of town and I came to the YWCA here in The Dalles. That's as far as the little money Momma had saved would get me. She told me never to look back. The sadness in her eyes cut be to the bone that day. I've missed her so much."

Lou understood the feeling.

**

Karol spent all week cleaning the house from top to bottom, trying to burn off nervous energy. Lou spent her days at the office working on her story. Both seem jumpy at dinner that night.

"Momma will be here at noon tomorrow. I thought I would fix a light lunch. If that's okay with you?"

"Of course. Is there anything you need me to pick up? Dessert? I could ask Mary to make those cookies Uncle Gene gave us the recipe for, unless you want to make them?"

Karol fidgeted with her food. "I think I would like to make them. Momma loves cookies. She taught me how to bake when I was eight or nine. We spent hours in the kitchen making all kinds of things. I think it would make her happy."

"Perfect. Then cookies it shall be. I put the recipe card in the drawer next to the oven. Check the cupboards to make sure you have everything you need. Otherwise I'll pick it up for you."

Karol did a quick scan and assured Lou she had everything she needed. "Lou?"

"What? Is there something I missed?"

"I was wondering if you would like to help?"

Lou scraped the plates and set them in the sink. "Really?"

"I'll guide you."

Lou reached over and put her arm around Karol. "If you're sure."

"I'm sure."

For the next hour, Lou sat mesmerized watching Karol measure the ingredients, then mixing everything together until they had a delicious gooey batter. There were so many steps to this baking thing, but she was enjoying it. Karol showed her how to scoop the batter into balls, roll it into the cinnamon and sugar before setting on the baking sheet, far enough apart so as they baked, they wouldn't stick together.

Once everything was in the oven they sat and enjoyed a cup of tea waiting for their cookies to bake.

"My goodness, those smell heavenly. Do you think we made enough?"

Karol checked the timer. "I think so. Why?"

Lou licked her lips. "Because we must taste them, you know, to make sure they are good. I wouldn't want to serve terrible cookies to your mom."

Karol laughed. "That's true. I made an extra dozen for just that reason."

"Smart girl."

They were hovering over the oven when the timer went off. Karol pulled the trays out and slid them on the cooling racks. The aroma of cinnamon and vanilla filled the kitchen as they waited anxiously for the cookies to cool enough to eat.

"Are they ready yet?" Lou asked, licking her lips.

Karol tapped the top of the cookies with her fingers, then put them on a plate. "Here, set these on the table and I'll get more hot water."

Lou snatched the plate from her hand and stuffed a cookie in her mouth when Karol turned her back.

"I saw that Lou."

Lou had a silly grin on her face. "What?" She tried to say without spewing crumbs down the front of her blouse.

"You're worse than a kid in a candy store."

Lou put her hands up and shrugged her shoulders. "Couldn't help myself. You better try one. You know, just to make sure." She took a bite of another one.

"I guess I better, before you eat them all." Karol bit into the warm cookie and swooned. "Your right, these are delicious."

Lou reached for a third cookie and Karol smacked her hand. "Really Lou, you will make yourself sick."

Lou pretended to frown. "Okay, let's get the dishes done while these cool. Then I think we should try to get a good night's sleep. Tomorrow will be a wonderful day."

A look of worry crossed Karol's face. "Do you really think so?"

Lou dried the mixing bowl and set it on the counter. "I do. Now let's get this mess cleaned up." She splashed Karol with water.

Karol gasped and splashed her back, until they were soaked, and their sides hurt from laughing. It was just what they needed.

After cleaning up the wet floor and wrapping the cookies, they said goodnight. What ever happened tomorrow, Lou hoped it would be what Karol needed to finally heal.

Closing her door, she settled into her bed and hugged her pillow, burying her face so Karol couldn't hear her cry. She didn't want to sound like a broken record, but when would it be her time for happiness?

***

Karol rose early and walked to the market, returning with fresh flowers for the table. She wanted everything to be perfect. It had been two years since she had seen her mother and the anticipation was killing her. She was still fussing with the flowers when Lou came in.

"Those are lovely Karol. Your mother will be proud of you." Lou snatched a cookie off the plate before Karol could stop her. "Just one. I promise."

"I assume you won't be needing breakfast since we are having an early lunch, and you are eating cookies."

Lou licked the sugar from her fingers. "Nope, I'm good." She opened the fridge and spied the lunch trays Karol had fixed. "Those look good too. Maybe I should try them out?"

Karol shut the door and stood in front of it.

"Absolutely not. Don't you need to dress or something? It's already past ten."

Lou gave her a little smirk and waved as she left the kitchen. "I'll be back."

Karol sank into the chair. Lou was right, today would be a wonderful day.

***

Lou showered and washed her hair. By the time she had it dried and dressed, it was eleven-thirty. She had to admit she was excited about meeting Karol's mother when the doorbell rang. Karol had heard it too and followed behind.

Lou opened the door and greeted a woman in her late forties. Though taller than Karol, they shared a striking resemblance between them, except for the sadness in her eyes. Lou stepped back as Karol and her mother came face to face.

Neither said a word, then Miriam pulled Karol into her arms.

Lou felt she was intruding and retreated to the kitchen to give them privacy. How she wished she could hold her mother again.

***

Miriam hugged her daughter close to her body. She had been dreaming of this since the day she put Karol on the bus out of town. Even though she had never been that far away, the divide felt bigger than the river that separated them. Stepping back, she surveyed Karol, brushing the hair out of her eyes.

There was an air of maturity about her. She was no longer her little girl. She was a young woman of twenty.

"You're looking real nice Karol." She felt awkward standing next to her.

"You look good too, Momma. Though you could stand to gain a few pounds. You said on the phone you were living with Aunt Judy. Isn't she feeding you?"

Miriam smoothed out her dress. "Oh, you know your Aunt Judy's cooking can be a bit greasy for my liking. You don't go worrying about me. I'm so happy to hear from you. Good thing I sent my mail to her house or I would have missed your letter. I have so many questions and I'm sure you do too."

Trying not to cry, Karol took her mother by the arm, guiding her towards the kitchen. "I made lunch. I hope you're hungry. Lou and I, she's the lady I live with, we even made cookies last night, if she hasn't eaten all of them."

Karol laughed when they entered the kitchen to find Lou wiping the sugar from her lips.

"I can't leave you alone for five minutes. I would like you to meet my mom, Miriam. Mom, this is Lou."

Lou held out her hand, then moved in for a hug. Miriam hugged her back.

"It's nice to meet you Miriam. Please sit. Would you like tea? Karol has fixed quite a spread and I don't know about you, but I eat when I'm nervous."

"Thank you and tea would be nice. Do you have any honey?" She took a seat and waited. She liked this woman who had taken in her daughter and hoped to get to know her better.

Lou turned to the cupboard, grabbed the honey jar, and smiled at Karol. "See, everything will be fine."

Karol sighed and retrieved the lunch trays.

The silence was palatable until they relaxed, and the conversation began. It was light at first as Karol and Miriam got the simple questions out of the way, then the heavy stuff flowed out.

Miriam sat quietly, listening, as her daughter described what she had gone through. She dabbed her wet eyes with her napkin.

"I'm so sorry Karol. I should have been here for you. I was such a fool to let you go, but I knew it was the only way to save you. But I didn't. Can you ever forgive me?"

Karol took her mother's hands in her own. "Listen Mom, you did the best you could. I got myself into trouble. Thankfully, Lou took me in and helped me get through it all. Yes, it was traumatic and yes, it hurts to know I will never see my son again, but I know it was the right thing to do. You would love Julie and John and they love Daniel. That's what they named him. We were both given a second chance. I want to go to college to be a fashion designer and they will help me when I'm ready. As for you and me, I want us to be close again like we were. I've missed you so much. I'm happy you are no longer with Dad. I don't know why he hated me, but it doesn't matter anymore. It's time to get on with our lives."

Miriam looked around the kitchen, trying to gather her courage. It was time to stop the lies. "I never wanted to tell you, but you deserve to know the truth."

Karol looked confused, and Lou looked uncomfortable.

"What truth? What are you talking about Momma?"

"Daryl is not your real father. Your father's name was David, Daryl's twin brother." Karol started to protest, but Mariam stopped her. "No, please let me explain. David and I planned to get married, but before we could, David died in a logging accident. Right after the funeral, I found out I was pregnant. Daryl told me he loved me too, and he would marry me and claim the baby as his own. Lost in grief, I agreed against my better judgement. It was the worst mistake of my life. I wanted to love Daryl but longed for David when I looked at him and it nearly drove me mad. After you were born, Daryl came to hate us both, saying he was stuck with his brother's leftovers and not his own family. I tried to give him his own child, but it never happened. Daryl became more abusive towards you, always finding fault in anything you did. I had to protect you, so I took the beatings if he would leave you alone. It became a way of life for us. I know it's no excuse, but I didn't know what else to do. When I put you on that bus, I prayed he would change, but his behavior only escalated. Last year he hit me so hard he broke my hip—"

Karol and Lou gasped.

"I spent three weeks in the hospital and another two in rehab. When I came home, he swore he would never do it again. I wanted to believe him, but six months ago he snapped. He had me on the floor, choking me when Judy came by to check on me. She was screaming at him to stop and was on the phone with 911. She thought he would kill me, and so did I. The last thing I remembered was hearing a loud bang. When the police and paramedics arrived, they thought I was dead too. I learned later Judy tried to get him off me, but he shoved her against the table. His rifle was next to it and she picked it up, warning him she would shoot. Judy said he just laughed at her and started hitting me harder. She said she closed her eyes and pulled the trigger. The bullet hit him in the back and when he fell, he knocked the wind out of me. I couldn't breathe until they lifted him off.

I survived with just a broken jaw and the police cleared Judy of the shooting. After I got out of the hospital and sold the house, I moved in with her. I had him cremated then dumped his ashes in the garbage. I know that sounds cruel, but I didn't want to waste another day of my life on that man. I thought about moving away. Then I got your letter. When you said you wanted to see me, I felt reborn again."

Karol rubbed the sides of her temples with her fingers. Lou sipped her now lukewarm tea.

"You should have told me, Mom. I could have done something."

Miriam shook her head. "I couldn't, don't you see? He would have hurt you too. I will understand if you never want to see me again. I just thought if we start over, there couldn't be any lies between us." She rose, and Karol grabbed her arm.

"No Momma, please don't leave me. I need you now more than ever." Sobs racked her body.

Miriam pulled her close and stroked her head. "I'll never leave you again. I promise."

***

Lou rose from the table and excused herself to use the bathroom and to give them time alone. Splashing her face with cool water, she returned to the kitchen to hear laughter. She liked the sound. There had been too much crying in this house.

"What did I miss?" Lou aimlessly reached for a cookie.

"I was telling Mom how I thought your new grandmother might have thrown you in the oven and baked you like Hansel and Gretel, when you were late coming home."

Lou chuckled. "Your daughter has quite the imagination. Maye she should start writing stories too."

Karol gave her an odd look. "Really? Nah, you're just joking with me."

"I think you can do and be anything you want, if you put your mind to it. Isn't that right, Miriam?"

Miriam touched Lou's hand. "You are wise beyond your years Lou. Thank you for taking care of my little girl, I mean my daughter. I am forever grateful."

Lou gave her hand a little squeeze. "I can't say it's been easy, Right Karol?"

Karol smiled. "Right Lou."

"So, what are your plans from now on Miriam if you don't mind my asking? Are you going to stay in The Dalles or return to your sister's?"

"Well, I was thinking about getting an apartment here in town. I know this is sudden Karol. But maybe you would come and live with me until you decide where you want to go to college."

Lou felt the arrow go straight to her heart. Somehow, she knew this was coming. How could it not? Mother and daughter needed to be together so they could heal. As much as she wanted Karol to stay, she knew she couldn't be selfish.

"I think that's a wonderful idea. Don't you Karol."

"What about you? You'll be all alone." Karol was fighting back tears.

"We agreed from the start that this was temporary. Remember? Anyway, it's time for you to start the next chapter in your life and who better with than your mother. Besides, I have my story to finish and my new family to get to know. This is a new beginning for all of us. Now don't look so sad. We'll still see each other. I haven't invested all this time in you, to not make sure you get where you are going. We're friends and always will be." Lou stood. "Anyone want a cookie?"

The three women burst into laughter.

Miriam left two hours later with Karol in tow to visit her Aunt Judy. They would be back on Monday to look for an apartment. Lou was happy for them.

Walking through the empty house, room by room, it was so quiet; she thought she could hear the walls talking. *'It's time to leave Lou. Time to find your own place.'*

Grabbing her coat and bag, she decided there was only one place she wanted to be.

Chapter Fourteen

Lou stood at the open door holding the cookies she had brought with her.

"Mind if I come in Grandmother?"

Elizabeth was working on a jigsaw puzzle and looked up.

"Of course, you can. What do I deserve this wonderful surprise from you today?" She spied the baggie in Lou's hand. "Are those my favorite cookies?"

Lou crossed the room and pulled up a chair. "They sure are, and I even helped bake them."

"Are you going to share or just tease an old woman?" Her face was broad with a smile.

Lou handed her the bag, sitting next to her. "All yours."

She set the bag gently on the table next to her. "Don't you want any?"

"I would, except I think I've already eaten a dozen by myself." She leaned back and rubbed her tummy.

"Well then, I will take my time and savor each one." Grandmother set the bag aside. "How have you been since we last visited? Have you talked to your father? I'm sure the news came as a surprise to him."

Lou played with a puzzle piece in her hand, studying the board. "Yes, it was quite the shock. He thought you were dead too. Mom never let on once that you were alive. He would like to meet you and Uncle Gene. Did you know that Dad carves? I noticed Uncle Gene had tools and carvings on the windowsill when I visited. I think they would like each other. I know he would like you. And Mary, that's Dad's new wife, you would like her too." Lou placed the piece in the perfect spot and looked up. "Only if you want to."

"Dear child. I want to meet all your family. We could have a get together at the house. I know Gene would love to have everyone there. I'll talk to him and let you know the date."

Lou was studying another puzzle piece. She hadn't done a puzzle in years. It had been the one thing she and her mother had done together, and it made her smile.

"Lou?"

"What? Oh yes, that would be wonderful." She picked up another piece. "Do you mind if I stay a while and help you? Mom and I... we used to do puzzles."

"I would love it if you did. Your mother and I also shared a fascination for the wayward puzzle piece."

Lou relaxed and for the next two hours, they worked diligently sculpting the floral design, piece by piece. Lou shared more about her life with her mother and the situation with Jason. It was the first time she expressed her fears that something might have happened to him.

Grandmother asked if she could say a prayer for his safe return, and Lou prayed silently with her. By the time they slipped the last piece in place, both had forged a deeper bond between them.

Lou left with a renewed hope in her heart and a bounce in her step as the February sun was slipping over the hillside by the time she headed for home.

Winter had skipped The Dalles this year, though it gave a false sense of spring. This morning when she went to get the paper, she noticed the Crocuses and Daffodils trying to poke through the hardened soil near the walkway, eager to sprout.

Life was moving too fast for her and she hoped she could hold on.

***

Dad and Mary were standing on the porch when Lou's car turn the corner and pulled into the driveway.

"Hey Dad. Hi Mary. What are you guys doing over here?" Lou called out as she retrieved her things and headed for the steps. "I didn't know you were coming by. I went to visit Grandmother, and we got involved in a jigsaw puzzle and...?"

The look on his face stopped her in her tracks.

"What's wrong?"

"Can we go inside Lou? We need to talk. Is Karol here?"

Lou's hands shook as she opened the door and turned the alarm off.

"No, she went to visit family. What's going on, Dad? You're really freaking me out."

"Let's go into the kitchen where we can sit."

Mary looked like she had been crying as Lou led the way.

"Okay, we're sitting, and Mary's been crying. What did you do? You two aren't splitting up, are you?"

"Oh, heavens no, Lou. Mary and I are fine."

"Then why is she crying?" Lou's voice rose. "Why are you here?"

"I got a phone call this morning from Joan."

Lou sucked in her breath.

"Jason is missing in action and presumed dead."

The words hit her like a sludge hammer to the chest. How could he be missing in action? He wasn't in the military. Then she remembered he said he was working on a story about the troops. Surely, they had taken precautions to keep him safe.

This had to be a mistake.

Her mind could hear them talking, but nothing registered.

Jumping up from her chair, she rushed to the bathroom and slammed the door. Ten minutes later Lou returned to her seat.

"What did Joan tell you? And don't skip a word."

"Jason was with a scouting unit by the border. They bedded down for the night when the camp came under heavy fire. Casualties were heavy and by morning those who were still alive were airlifted out. Joan said they found his duffle bag about fifty feet from the place where he had been sleeping. The whole compound had been destroyed."

Lou didn't know how to respond as she twisted the engagement ring on her finger. She remembered the night he had proposed to her and they had been so happy. Now her worst fears had come true.

Dad cleared his throat, trying to get her attention. "Lou? What can we do for you?"

Lou looked up from her hand. "I think I would like to be alone, if you don't mind."

Mary gently touched her arm. "You could come stay at the house, at least until Karol gets back. We don't like you here by yourself."

Lou brushed the tears from her eyes. "I'll be okay, really I will. I have to get used to being alone again, anyway."

Dad looked confused. "Why would you say that? You said Karol went to visit relatives. Isn't she coming back?"

"I haven't filled you and Mary in on the newest development with Karol, since it only happened today."

"I don't understand. What happened today?" Dad asked.

"Karol's mother came to see her this afternoon. It's a long story, too long for tonight, but the condensed version is, they will find an apartment and move in together. At least until Karol decides where she wants to go to college. I think it will be best for everyone." The lump in her throat was nearly choking her. "As much as I would like the world to stop spinning, it halts for no one. Life goes on and so will I. I love you both. So, if you wouldn't mind leaving, I'm tired and I would like to go to bed."

Dad and Mary heeded her signal and stood.

"Promise you will call if you need anything. I don't care what time it is." Dad held her in his arms, and Lou forced herself not to cry.

"I promise." She knew she wouldn't, as she walked them to the door. "You drive safe and I'll talk to you tomorrow."

Closing the door behind them, she sank to the floor and didn't move until she heard the Sunday morning paper land on the porch next to the door.

Lou pulled her cramped body from the floor, shuffled to her room, and climbed into bed. She wanted to talk to Joan but didn't know if she could make the call. Dad told her everything Joan said, but she felt she owed it to her. Joan's pain was greater than Lou's. She had lost her brother.

Reaching for her phone, she made the call. Ten minutes later they hung up with a promise to stay in touch. Lou set the phone on the bed and lay against the pillows, trying to get her mind to slow down. It wasn't working, and she sat up.

The silence was eating at her. She knew she had to get out of the house and once again went to the only person who could help her.

***

Elizabeth finished her breakfast and was leaving the dining room when she saw Lou enter the lobby. The poor girl looked exhausted as she approached. Dark circles rimmed the bottom of her eyes and she looked like she had been crying. Elizabeth couldn't imagine what had brought this on unless...

Without saying a word, she guided Lou to her room and placed her in a chair by the table. The birds chirping outside the window was the only sound that disturbed the silence between them. Lou continued to stare into space, twisting something on her finger. Elizabeth realized it was her engagement ring.

"Lou? Do you want to talk about what is bothering you? Does it have to do with Jason?"

Lou lowered her head. "I don't know how to go on without him."

Her voice was so low Elizabeth had to lean forward.

"What did you say? I couldn't hear you."

"Oh Grandmother, he's never coming back," she cried out and buried her face in her hands.

"Can you tell me what happened?" She hated to ask, but wanted to keep Lou talking, for fear if she stopped, she may fall into a deep depression as her mother had. She couldn't risk losing Lou the way she had Susan.

Lou grabbed a tissue and wiped her nose before taking a deep breath and releasing it slowly.

"Dad and Mary were waiting for me when I got home last night. I thought it was strange, since they usually call first, but I was happy to see them, until I saw the look on Dad's face. Something in my heart told me this wasn't a social call. By the time we got to the kitchen, I think I knew what he would say. His words came so fast I had a tough time understanding until it finally sank in. Jason is missing and presumed dead."

Elizabeth gasped. "Are you sure that is what he said?"

Lou nodded, forcing herself to stay in control.

"Jason was doing a story with the troops; his unit took heavy fire. There were casualties, and the only thing they found was his duffle bag. They notified his sister Joan, and she called Dad. When I woke up this morning, I thought it had to be a bad dream, so I called her. When she answered the phone, the sound of her voice confirmed Dad was telling me the truth. Why is God doing this to me?"

Elizabeth reached across the table for Lou's hand.

"This is a terrible thing Lou, but it's not God's doing. As we talked before, life happens, and sometimes it catches us between the good and the bad. Time will lessen the pain, though right now I'm sure you don't believe me. I pray that you will not shut your heart away and let the despair swallow you like your mother did."

Lou exhaled again.

Elizabeth rose and walked to her dresser. Opening the top drawer, she pulled out a weathered journal. Returning to her seat, she gently placed it on the table in front of Lou.

"After my mother turned me away, your great-great-grandmother Rosalie gave me her journal to read, hoping it would help me understand what her life had been like and give me the strength to go on. Would you like to read it?"

Lou didn't know how a story would fix her broken heart, but she would read it if Grandmother thought it might help.

Picking up the book, she ran her hand over the cover. It was the same feeling she had when she had read Kelly's journal.

A feeling of connection.

Settling back against the chair, she flipped to the first page, transporting her back in time.

Chapter Fifteen

March 1909 Antelope, Oregon

"Rosalie. You gotta git up. It's almost dawn." Sixteen-year-old Rosalie Scherrer thought she heard her name called in the distance.

"Rosalie get up." The voice said once again before a hand nuzzled her shoulder. Rosalie shifted her arm hoping to ward off whoever was trying to disturb her dream. It was a beautiful day, and she was in the meadow laying on her back, watching the clouds drift by. The only sounds were of the birds and the wind in the trees, and she was happy here.

Her brother Max shoved her harder. Blinking her eyes to focus, Rosalie could see the hint of dawn cresting the horizon, spilling the morning sun through her bedroom window. She let out a mournful sigh, trying to clear her mind. What should have been a school day would now be another workday on the ranch. Touching her bruised lip, everything came rushing back from the night before.

Pa had made it clear. No more schooling. Rosalie begged him to let her keep going, but he wouldn't relent. She had turned to Ma, who told her to do what Pa said. Rosalie hated the way her mother cowered down to him.

Her brothers, Max, eighteen and Jake, who just turned twenty, stood back and stayed out of the way. Rosalie knew if they interfered, they would both feel the pain of Pa's belt. It wasn't fair making her quit school, but she continued to beg until he rose from his chair and came towards her.

"Enough Rosalie! I don't want to hear no more about this schooling nonsense. Girls don't need no book learning. They just need to know how to cook and clean. All that learning puts crazy ideas in your head, making you think you're better than the rest of us."

"That's not true. Max and Jake got to go to the eighth grade. Why can't I?" Rosalie whirled around to face her mother. "Ma? Please let me go. I only have one more year." Ma turned towards the wall. Rosalie twisted back around facing her father, her fists clenched.

"I hate you."

The words no sooner left her lips when the back of his hand hit her across the face, knocking her backward. Stumbling off balance, she had hit the chair and crashed to the floor. Ma screamed, and Jake jumped forward, but Max held him back. Rosalie tasted blood on her lip and Pa stomped from the house towards the barn.

Rosalie didn't move. Her mind tried to process what happened. He hit her. Pa had hit her. She was still on the floor when Jake broke away from Max's grip and kneeled by her side. Rosalie looked into his eyes and the tears came quickly until she was limp from crying.

Jake picked her off the floor and carried her to her bed, easing her down against the feather pillow and covered her with a blanket before leaving the room.

**

Walking through the kitchen, Jake gave his mother a disgusted look before he headed out the door to find his father.

Pushing his way through the barn door, Jake let his eyes become accustomed to the dim light coming out of the single bulb suspended from the rafter. He could see Pa pacing back and forth, muttering to himself. The barn door slammed shut, stopping Pa in his tracks.

"What do you want?" he growled.

Jake hoped Pa's first question would have been about Rosalie as disappointment turned to rage for all the beatings he and Max had endured through the years. He wouldn't stand for Pa hitting Rosalie.

"You did wrong Pa."

Pa glared at his son. "What right you got telling me I did wrong?"

Jake stood his ground. "You been beating on me and Max long enough. I won't let you do it anymore. And if you ever touch Rosalie again..."

"You'll do what? Get out of my sight." Pa hissed at him and turn his back.

Anger grabbed hold of Jake like a rattlesnake on a field mouse. Rushing forward, he rammed Pa square in the back. Pa let out a growl when he hit the hay-covered dirt, knocking the wind out of him. Trying to catch his breath, Pa turned to face his son. Before he could get up, Jake started kicking him. Startled, Pa tried to block the blows with his arms.

Jake kept striking as hard as he could, trying to give back the pain and hurt, until he was empty of the rage that had consumed him. Breathing heavily, with sweat dripping from his brow, Jake turned and walked out of the barn, leaving the door swinging in the night air.

***

Pa had laid on the scratchy hay for hours after Jake stormed out of the barn. That girl mouthed off just like her momma, and he wasn't going to have it.

Pushing himself to a sitting position, he flinched from the pain in his ribs. He had to admit, Jake did a number on him.

"Never thought the boy had it in him," he chortled to himself, then flinched again. He was sure he had some cracked ribs and there would be bruising from the toe of Jake's boot.

With a deep groan he worked himself until he was standing, though a little wobbly.

"That boy may think he's getting away with this, but one day I'll return the favor, and he won't see it coming." A look of evil crossed his face.

***

Rosalie heard the fighting coming from the barn and covered her head with her pillow. She prayed Pa hadn't hurt Jake. Then she prayed Jake hadn't killed Pa. It relieved her when she heard Jakes voice in the kitchen and Max asking about Pa. Jake said he was alive when he left him in the barn.

The last thing she recalled before falling asleep was the sound of Ma crying. Now it was morning, and she was wide awake.

Max stood silently next to her bed, gazing out the window.

"I'm sorry Pa hurt you Rosalie." His voice was just a whisper.

Rosalie swung her feet off the bed and felt a sharp pain on her thigh. Lifting her nightgown, she noticed a bruise forming. Standing, she put her arms around Max's waist and rested her head against the shirt on his back, hugging him. He slumped against her and she could feel him breathing.

Max was the sensitive one of her brothers, where Jake was the take charge type. She loved them without hesitation.

"It's not your fault, Max. I was sassing Pa."

Max turned and wrapped his arms around his little sister.

"I should have stopped Pa. I could feel he would do something mean, but..." he stopped and leaned his chin on the top of her head.

Stepping back, Rosalie lifted her head, meeting his eyes. They looked so sad. "I told you. It's my fault, so let it be."

Releasing herself, she walked to her dresser and grabbed an old pair of Max's jeans that he had outgrown. If it was a workday she better dress for the part.

"You best be going so I can get dressed and get to work. Like you said, it's almost dawn."

Max gave her a half smile, turned, and left as the brave front she had put up was crumbling. She licked her swollen lip and tears spilled down her cheeks.

Dashing them off with the back of her hand, she finished dressing and headed for the kitchen. She hoped this wouldn't be the beginning of the worst day of her young life.

***

Jake woke with a feeling of satisfaction. He just wished it had been sooner, for Max and for himself. Even Ma must know what an animal Pa had become. Jake shook his head. He feared she was too far gone to even understand. What had happened to her? Had Pa done something he didn't know about? He felt bad for thinking she was worthless. He had no right to judge her. Whatever Pa had done, she had kept it to herself. He promised he would try to be nicer to her.

Shucking on his jeans and boots, Jake grabbed a flannel shirt, slipping it over his tanned arms, then jammed it into his waistband and tightened the worn leather belt. He was trying to be quiet as not to wake Max, then realized his bed was empty. Queasiness gripped his stomach. Rosalie!

Entering the kitchen, Max was setting the table. "Is she all right?" he asked softly, searching his brother's face.

Max nodded.

Jake felt relieved and patted his brothers' arm, then grabbed a frying pan, skimming it with a slab of lard.

He had been cooking for the three of them for the last few years. Ma stayed in bed until mid-morning and Pa usually left before any of them got up. Jake hoped today would be no exception.

He was just setting the skillet full of eggs and potatoes on the table when Rosalie shuffled in, plopping down in the chair across from him. Her lip was swollen, and tears lined the edges of her eyes. He wished he could take her sadness away. The best he could do was keep Pa away from her until she was old enough to leave this hellhole of a ranch, they all lived on. He and Max had been talking about leaving and taking Rosalie with them, but they didn't know where they would go.

Shaniko was the next town, but only eight miles away. It was a bustling rail town where they were sure to get jobs, but he felt it was still too close to their father. He and Max knew they had to go further and after discussing it, figured they could go on to The Dalles. It was at least eighty miles away and accessible by train. Only problem was Rosalie. They could drop their bed rolls anywhere, but they couldn't expect their sister to sleep in a barn. Jake figured they would have to wait until they found jobs and lodging for all of them.

Max was the first to fill his plate, then motioned for Rosalie to hand him hers. Jake followed. The three siblings ate in silence. Rosalie picked at the eggs, barely eating. Jake placed his hand on hers and the look she gave him crushed his heart. He knew how much she loved school, but once Pa said no, he would never change his mind. Jake also knew after last night; he would have to be on guard. Pa wasn't going to let what happened slide by without striking back.

Jake decided tomorrow after his chores were done, he would ride to Shaniko and check the newspaper about jobs and lodging in The Dalles. He could send a telegram inquiring and figured with their ranch skills they should be able to find a job at any of the businesses. If he got lucky, he could get Max and Rosalie out of there sooner than later.

Finishing up the last of the eggs and potatoes, Jake scraped the crusty parts into the slop bucket for the pig. Max scraped his own plate then Rosalie's. Without saying a word, the three of them headed out to the barn to check on the animals.

***

Ma stood silently in the shadow of her bedroom door, watching the children. Burning tears streaked down her face. Pa didn't come back to the house last night after Jake returned from the barn and she figured he drank himself into a stupor and fell asleep in the bunk room. Ma hadn't slept, fearing he would return and take his anger out on her. She knew Jake and Max thought she was a terrible mother, even Rosalie, but to protect them, she endured the worst of what their father was capable of.

Exhausted, she shut the door and crawled back into bed. She knew she should have stood up to him about Rosalie finishing school, but the will to fight was gone. Laying her head against the feather pillow, she wished she would go to sleep and never wake up.

Watching Jake stand up to his Pa the way he did made her feel proud, if only for a moment. Why couldn't she do that? As she lay there in the silence, a plan formed in her mind and a sly smile crossed her lips.

***

Rosalie kicked the dust off her boots as she stood in the barn's doorway looking out over the wheat fields. Grabbing her handkerchief, she dabbed at the sweat dripping down her cheeks before it reached her lips and mix with the dirt she was already tasting. She was surprised how warm it was for March.

Max and Jake must have finished planting for the day and were walking towards her from the field. For teenage boys, they looked like old men from years of doing Pa's bidding. Pa always disappeared while she and the boys worked, only returning in time for supper. Though she often helped after school, she hadn't realized the work Max and Jake had to do on their own.

Rosalie thought about Ma, worried about her. She was thin as a rail and hardly ate. The only time she seemed to relax was while Pa was gone, but as soon as he returned, Rosalie noticed she would become silent and cower when he came into the room. She and Rosalie had been so close, but now Ma seemed to shy away. She was still pondering the whole thing when Jake startled her.

"What are you dreaming about now, Rosalie?" Jake brushed the top of her hair as he walked past into the barn. "You get all your work done?" he called from the milk cow's stall.

Rosalie smiled. She and Max followed to where Jake was now sitting.

"Yes, I got all my chores done. And I wasn't dreaming about nothing. Just stopping a moment to wipe the sweat off."

Standing behind her brother, she threw her arms around his neck, almost knocking him off the milk stool. Jake grabbed her hands and flipped her over his shoulder into the hay, then fell beside her laughing. Max stood watching with a wide grin on his face.

The cow jumped to the side and bellowed as if annoyed by the entire scene. Max dropped to his knees, then he and Jake tickled Rosalie until she was gasping for air.

Rosalie wiggled free and crawled towards the cow.

"You two better stop it before Bessie gets mad and kicks one of you," she huffed, trying to sound mad as she stood. Turning, she ran face first into her Pa's chest and screamed.

Pa grabbed her by the shoulders. "Whoa little girl. What are you and your brothers doing in here?"

The look in his eyes gave Rosalie the shivers.

Jake and Max hustled to their feet.

"Nothing, Pa. Jake was going to milk Bessie, and I knocked him off the stool. We were just kidding around." Rosalie stepped back; afraid he might hit her again.

Jake and Max were now standing behind her.

"That's right Pa. Max, and I were just funning. All the work's done for the day. So, if you don't mind, I'll milk the cow for supper." Jake stared Pa in the face, waiting for his reaction.

Pa stood silent, his face turning red with rage, then he snorted at them before leaving the barn heading for the house.

"That was close, Jake. I thought for sure he was going to hit you." Max said, shaking his head. "I think I'll go to the house just to make sure he doesn't do nothing to Ma. Rosalie, you better come with me. I'm worried about Ma. I think he's been beating on her when we aren't around and she's too afraid to say anything."

Rosalie gasped. "You think so, Max? She hardly talks to any of us anymore. What are we going to do? Jake? We can't let him do that. She's our mother."

Jake put his arm around her. "You try to talk to her. See if she'll tell you. Max and I will think of something."

Rosalie wiped her face with the sleeve of her shirt and followed Max to the house, leaving Jake to milk the cow.

***

Ma was standing at the stove frying chicken when Pa burst through the door spewing hateful words and approached her. She knew in her heart this was going to be ugly.

"What are you doing? Finally, get up and take care of your family?" He spat at her.

Ma kept her back to him. "Supper will be ready soon."

Pa came closer. "I wouldn't eat your slop if I was dying of hunger. You're a worthless wife and mother. I don't know why I ever married you." He continued to hiss at her.

Ma smelled the foul odor of whisky on his breath and something inside of her snapped. Before she could stop herself, she turned and flung the sizzling skillet full of lard and chicken into his face.

Pa dropped to his knees, screaming as she clubbed him in the head with the pan until Max rushed through the door.

"Ma! Stop!" He yelled, trying to break the trance she was in.

Ma slumped into Max's arms, dropping the skillet to the floor. Max gently set her in the chair furthest away from where Pa lay flopping in pain, more foul words sputtering from his mouth.

Rosalie had been standing at the door and watched in horror. Rushing to Ma's side, Rosalie put her arms around her and held her close. Ma just sat and stared at her husband on the floor.

Jake had heard the screaming and came running.

Max was soaking a rag in water and trying to put it on Pa's face, but he kept pushing it away.

"I'll kill her! Augh! My face!" Pa kept yelling until the pain overtook him and he passed out.

Jake stood next to him, glancing at Max. "Is he dead?"

Max shook his head. "No, but thankfully he quit yelling. Let's get him onto his bed. Grab an arm."

The boys dragged him into their parent's bedroom and lay him on the bed. The skin on Pa's face and chest had melted away from the lard, leaving a putrid burnt smell.

It looked bad.

Max got another wet towel, covering Pa's face and chest with it.

Jake had retreated to check on Ma, who was still rocking back and forth in Rosalie's' arms. He knelt next to the chair. "Ma? Can you hear me?"

Rosalie glanced at him with a worried look.

Jake took Ma's hands in his own, bringing them to his lips.

"It's okay Ma, he can't hurt you, but it's really bad. Do you understand me, Ma? I think we have to go for the doctor."

Ma snapped her head up. "No! I'll take care of him." She stood and faced her children. "Jake, have Max help you get him undressed. Rosalie, go get the bag balm we use for Bessie's udders." Not a single tear rolled down her cheek. "I love you and I hope someday you'll forgive me."

No one uttered another word as Max and Jake stripped Pa from his clothes and covered him with a blanket. Rosalie returned with the bag balm, handing it to her mother. Before they left the room, Ma gave them a weak smile, then closed the door.

Turning, Ma looked at her husband laying helpless on the bed, then slathered the thick ointment across his face and chest. Bits of his skin were coming off in her hand, but she didn't flinch. Instead, she rubbed harder. He jerked but didn't wake. She knew if he survived, he would kill her and the children too. Tonight, she would have to put her plan in motion sooner than she thought.

***

Jake, Max, and Rosalie stood in shock staring at each other. Had it been an accident, or had Ma tried to kill Pa? None of them wanted to say, but the way she was hitting him, left them all thinking the latter.

"Do you think he's going to make it?" Rosalie stooped to pick up the skillet. "He didn't look too good."

Max shrugged as he wiped the lard and their chicken dinner off the floor, tossing it in the slop pail.

Jake noticed the worried look on Max's face and fixed bacon and eggs for dinner. At least it would give them strength. He was sure they would need it in the coming days. They had to finish planting the fields. Jake gave a deep sigh. He didn't know what would happen if Pa died. He couldn't run this place even with Max and Rosalie helping. So much was weighing on his shoulders. And what about Ma? What would happen to her?

***

Ma sat beside Pa, studying what remained of his face. The lard had melted his nose and lips, and his head was swollen from the skillet beating. She suddenly felt free. She just didn't think it would be this soon.

Pa moaned, snapping Ma back to the present. Rising, she moved quickly around their bedroom until she had everything ready. Glancing in the cracked mirror on her dresser, Ma didn't recognize the broken woman staring back at her. Tucking her hair back into her bun, she smoothed her dress before opening the bedroom door. Her ultimate act would be to get the children out of the house. Rosalie, Jake, and Max were sitting around the table discussing what had happened when the bedroom door opened, and Ma entered the room.

"Is he?" Rosalie was afraid to say the words.

Ma shook her head. "No, he's still sleeping. I was wondering if you children would go to the barn for a little while. I need to tend to the burned skin, and he might yell if he wakes up. I don't want it to upset you." Ma noticed the look of concern on Max's face. "Don't you worry Max, I'll secure his hands, so he won't be able to flail around. It's for his own good."

"Are you sure you don't need help?" Jake asked.

"Thank you, Jake, but I created this mess, so I need to do this myself. I love you all and I'm so proud of you. I hope you can forgive me for not protecting you."

A look of sadness covered Ma's face, as if she were trying to tell them something.

Rising, Rosalie crossed the room and hugged Ma. Jake and Max joined her. The four held onto each other as if this would be the last time, they would all be together. Ma gave each of her children a kiss on the cheek, then shooed them out the door.

Rosalie turned just in time to see Ma mouth "I love you" before she closed the door.

"Jake, you think Ma will be all right?" Rosalie asked, pausing at the top of the porch step.

Max and Jake continued walking towards the barn.

"Come on, Rosalie," Max hollered back at her. "You heard what Ma said. She'll be fine. Besides, Pa's in no shape to do anything to her."

Rosalie hurried down the steps to catch up with her brothers and followed them into the barn.

Ma returned to the bedroom to check on Pa, who was sleeping from the Ludlum she had given him. She didn't care about his pain; she just didn't want him to wake up and hurt her. She needed a little more time to get everything ready now that the children had gone to the barn.

Hurrying into the kitchen, she got the can of kerosene sitting next to the sink and splashed it all over the table, chairs, and the walls. Stepping into the bedroom, she set the can down. She wanted to make sure the straps of cloth around Pa's wrists were tight to the metal frame of the bed he had abused her in. Confident the straps would hold, she bent over him.

"Well, looks like you won't be hurting me or those children no more," she whispered.

Pa's eyes snapped open, startling her. Pulling at his hands, he made a gurgling sound as he thrashed against the restraints.

Ma continued to smile at him as she picked up the can of kerosene, dousing the bed and floor until it was empty. Content with her handy work, she reached for the lamp as she headed for the door.

"Burn in Hell," she spat at him before dropping the lamp on the floor, igniting it.

The flames snaked along the wooden floorboards, heading for the bed and the man who had caused her so much pain. She watched for a moment, then closed the door. She knew as soon as the children smell smoke, they would come running to save her and Pa. She couldn't let that happen.

Grabbing the tin can that held the gunpowder; she sat down and tore off a piece of her petticoat. Twisting the fabric, she dipped it in the lamp oil, then stuffed it into the can before setting it by the door. The smoke from the bedroom filled the house, and Ma knew it was time. Taking the kerosene lamp from the table, she returned to her rocker. With her final breath, she asked God to forgive her, then threw the lamp at the twisted fabric.

***

Rosalie was the first to smell the smoke and ran for the barn door. "Jake! Max! Hurry! I think the house is on fire!"

As they ran for the house, it exploded tossing them to the ground and within minutes it burned out of control. Rosalie buried her face in her hands and wept unconsolably. She knew her parents were still in there.

Max got up, but Jake tackled him before he could reach the burning porch. Lying in the dirt, they huddled together watching the roof collapse, then the walls. Soon there was nothing left but a smoldering pile of what used to be their home.

Rosalie crawled to where her brothers sat in the dirt with shocked looks on their faces, huddling next to them, until the sound of horses neighing and people yelling broke the silence.

The neighbors to the south had seen the smoke and rushed to help, but there was nothing to do by the time Mr. Warner pulled his team to a stop next to the corral and jumped down.

"My God! What happened? Are you youngens hurt? Where are your folks?"

The questions were coming so fast none of them could answer. Mrs. Warner had worked her way down from the wagon and knelt next to Rosalie and the boys.

"Walter! Stop with the questions. Can't you see they're in shock?" Mrs. Warner turned back to face them. "Are any of you hurt?"

Rosalie, Jake, and Max shook their heads.

"Can you tell me where your folks are?"

Max sat stone faced, Rosalie burst into tears, and Jake pointed at the rubble. "In there," was all he could manage to say.

Mrs. Warner gasped. Mr. Warner tilted his hat back on his head and wiped his brow. There was nothing left standing but the chimney.

Max and Jake stood, then helped Mrs. Warner and Rosalie to their feet. No one said a word. What would happen to the three of them now? They had no parents. They had no home.

Chapter Sixteen

July 1909, Shaniko, Oregon

Staring out the window from the second floor of the hotel, the full moon lit the night sky like a beacon so bright Rosalie could see for miles across the desert plains.

Everything had changed since she left the farm. Her two older brothers, Max, and Jake sold off the ranch and went to The Dalles to start over. They begged her to come with them, but she had secured a job at the hotel in Shaniko and liked what she was doing.

Cleaning rooms all day was hard on a sixteen-year-old, but she got good pay, hot food, and a place to sleep. Maids were in high demand. The work either burned them out after a year or two, or they married a fancy man who came through on the train.

As part of her wages, she shared a room with two other maids. Patty was nineteen and Linda was eighteen. Both were looking for husbands and afraid they would be old maids if they couldn't find someone soon. They didn't want to clean rooms for the rest of their lives.

Rosalie wasn't interested in a boyfriend, she just wanted to not worry about her next meal or a warm bed. She thought she was in heaven with her own cot, feather pillow and real blankets. It differed from the hell she had lived in on the farm, but she didn't want to think about it anymore.

The railroad company built the town of Shaniko and it was considered the end of the line into Central Oregon. Ranchers came from everywhere, bringing their grain to sell, and cattle to market. The sheep herders drove their sheep to

Return to Bakeoven Road

town to shear at the giant barn built right next to the tracks, then sell the wool. People came from all over the country bringing business and people to Shaniko looking for a new life, and Shaniko had it all. Hotels, saloons, dance halls, dress shops, even a school. It had amazed Rosalie the first time she saw running water and flushing toilets. On the ranch, all they had was a hand pump for water and the outhouse for your business.

She had been working at the hotel for three months, when Mrs. Bates, the head housekeeper, instructed her to prepare the owner's room for their arrival.

Joseph and Mildred Powell owned the Hotel Shaniko and kept a large room on the third floor, for when they came to town. He was the president of the Columbia Southern Banking Company and well respected by the town. As for Mildred, she considered herself the town's first lady, always trying to impress everyone with their wealth, though it only made people think less of her and her snobbish friends.

Rosalie had never been to the third floor. It was off limits to the staff. Patty usually prepared the room since she had seniority over her and Linda, but today said she wasn't feeling well, and Linda said she was swamped with the wash, so Rosalie had to make sure the room was ready for the Powell's arrival later today.

Grabbing her cleaning supplies, she made her way up the staircase towards the third floor, when a chill ran down her spine. She didn't know why, but something was spooking her. Standing at the top of the stairs, Rosalie marveled at how elegant it was from the other two floors, and the way the kerosene lamps cast eerie shadows down the walls covered in red velvet wallpaper.

Near the railing sat an emerald green velvet couch, and crystal lamps rested on ornate side tables with leather-bound books stacked neatly next to the lamps. Did Mr. Powell or his wife ever sit and read them? Her curious mind wanted to see what they were, but something told her not to dally.

Hurrying down the hall, she found the door to the suite and knocked gently. Looking around, she waited, then knocked a little harder. Still no one answered. Taking the key Patty had given her, she unlocked the door and pushed it open. The room was empty, as it should be, but she had learned to always knock first. Once she walked in on a cowboy in a compromising position with one of the ladies from the saloon. She had gotten an eyeful and an education. That was something she didn't want to see again.

Entering the room, Rosalie stopped to catch her breath. It was even more elegant than the hallway. Gold velvet curtains, trimmed in red fringe, hung from the windows. A black velvet floral couch, covered with cream and pink rose fabric, sat in front of the fireplace. Ornate side tables flanked both sides, holding more crystal lamps. Across from the couch was the largest four poster bed she had ever seen. An entire family could sleep in it.

Rosalie had never seen such luxury in her life. Shaking her head, she knew she had to quit wasting time. Pulling back the downy comforter, she quickly changed the linens on the bed, smoothed out any wrinkles before fluffing the pillows properly. Grabbing her cleaning rag, she wiped down all the furniture, filled the pitcher with fresh water and placed clean towels on the washstand.

Next, she set the fireplace with kindling and logs, ready for a fire if the occupants so desired one. Finally, she placed the fresh flowers she had brought with her, in the vases next to the bed and on the fireplace mantle. She was hurrying as fast as she could when she felt the hair on the back of her neck prickle.

***

Return to Bakeoven Road

Joseph Powell had endured hours of Mildred's shrill tongue to last a lifetime and was looking forward to three days away from her. He had banking business to attend while in town but just wanted somewhere he couldn't hear her constant nagging. The woman was driving him mad and he didn't know how much more he could manage.

Divorce was not an option; he had worked too hard for what he had and refused to give any of it to her. By the time he reached the third floor, his anger towards her was building inside and he thought he would explode. Marching down the hall, he noticed his door was open.

"Who in God's name has left this door open?" he mumbled under his breath as he entered the room, then halted, casting his eyes upon a young girl standing at the fireplace with her back to him. Joseph remained silent as he watched her arranging the flowers on the mantle. Her long chestnut hair braided and tied with a violet ribbon ended at her waist. Even in her maid's uniform he could tell she was small and delicate, not like his large wife. 'Why couldn't he have found a woman like her?' he mused to himself. Yes, why not her?

The girl must have heard him enter and turned. A pink hue raced across her face and she quickly smoothed out her apron.

"Oh, I'm sorry, sir. I wasn't expecting you for another hour. I'm just finishing and will be gone in a minute." Picking up her rags, she stuffed them into her cleaning bags along with the dirty linens and towels, heading towards the door.

Joseph stepped into the room, trying to find his voice. "No problem, Miss. I guess I am a little early." His anger dissipated as he stared at her.

Rosalie paused for a moment. "Sorry sir, please don't report me, I really need this job. I didn't mean to not have it ready for you. I'll do better next time." Holding her breath, she waited for him to answer.

A sinister smile spread across Joseph's face as he looked her over. Not bad, not bad at all. She will do well with a little grooming. His mind was turning rapidly at the prospects if he played his cards right.

"What is your name?" he demanded, trying to sound gruff.

"Rosalie, sir." She said, exhaling as quietly as possible.

"Rosalie... that is a nice name. How long have you been working here, Rosalie?" He liked the name, the way it rolled off his tongue.

"Three months, sir."

Joseph moved across the room to distance himself from her. The urge to pull her into his arms and kiss her overwhelmed him and knew he had to stop himself before he went too far... yet.

"Well, I guess I can let it pass this time..." he replied, toying with her.

"Oh, thank you sir, I really appreciate it. And I'll be faster next time if I'm sent here. Patty was sick today and Linda was busy..." Rosalie grabbed the bags and hurried out the door. "Good day, sir," she called as she ran down the hall towards the stairs. Stopping for a moment, she looked back and saw him watching as she descended out of sight.

Joseph walked back into his room and shut the door, laughing to himself. Patty was sick today? Not like her to disappoint him. Reaching into his coat pocket, he pulled out a cigar. Clipping off the end, he tossed it into the fireplace and retrieved a match from the mantle. Lighting the other end, he drew in a deep breath of tobacco, exhaling rings of smoke into the air.

Three days... he thought to himself. I have three days. Joseph snuffed out his cigar and lay down on the bed. His mind was still fantasizing about the chestnut-haired maid named Rosalie.

Yes, Patty had disappointed him, but he was growing tired of her and now set his eyes on Rosalie. She was young, like Patty had been when he first met her, but now she was getting too old for his taste.

Over the years he had grown accustomed to the young farm girls who came to work at the hotel hoping for a better life than farm living. They were so naïve. Using his charm or authority, it was easy to get what he wanted. He had it all. A prestigious job at the bank, the owner of his own hotel and respect. The only downfall was a wife who liked all the finery he could supply but lacked the passion he wanted.

When they first married, Mildred was beautiful, but after ten years and no children, Joseph had grown tired of her whining and complaining. He eventually turned to other forms of satisfaction. The girls meant nothing to him; they were just a means to an end. Now he had his sights set on Rosalie without a thought to his wife.

***

Rosalie hurried down the stairs to the laundry room to drop off the linens and towels before stopping for lunch. How was she supposed to know he would show up early? This just wasn't fair. If Patty hadn't gotten sick, none of this would be happening. She still couldn't shake the creepy feeling Mr. Powell gave her. He seemed all right, so maybe she would keep her job.

Linda and Patty were sitting in the back room where the help could sit, giggling about something, only to stop when she walked in. Grabbing a sandwich and glass of milk, she went to sit down with them.

"I thought you were sick, Patty?" she asked, taking a bite of her butter sandwich. "And you Linda, what about all the laundry? I just dropped linens off, and the room was clear of wash. So, what's going on here?"

Patty and Linda looked at each other and burst out laughing.

"Sorry Rosalie, but neither one of us wanted to clean the Powell's room today. We can't stand him or his wife," Patty said.

Linda grabbed for a piece of Rosalie's bread crust, but Rosalie slapped her hand away.

"Hey, we're sorry but you're the low girl on the totem pole. Did she hassle you?"

Rosalie finished the bite she was chewing before answering.

"No, she wasn't there. Only Mr. Powell and he showed up early. Scared me to death at first, but he was nice about it. Do you think I'll get fired?" She was afraid they would say yes.

Patty and Linda looked at each other and let out a deep groan.

Rosalie saw the look on their faces. "What's that all about?"

"Should we tell her?" Linda asked, looking at Patty.

Rosalie felt that creepy feeling again. "Tell me what?"

Linda was about to speak, when they all noticed the hotel manager, Mrs. Bates, standing in the doorway glaring at them.

"I think your break time is over, don't you?" She snapped at them.

Patty and Linda grabbed their glass and hurried to the kitchen. Rosalie stuffed the rest of her sandwich in her mouth, then washed it down with the last of her milk, quickly rinsing her glass. She didn't want Mrs. Bates mad at her too.

***

Haven Carter sat on the bench outback of the hotel just like Mr. Powell told him to do. He liked Mr. Powell; he was nice to him. Not like his wife, she was mean. Called him names, terrible names. No, Haven didn't like her one bit.

Even though people told him he was slow, he knew how to do stuff. Haven had been working for the Powell's for the last two years. Mr. Powell hired him to take care of things for him. Not terrible things, just things he didn't want Mrs. Powell to know about. Haven liked having secrets, and Mr. Powell paid him to keep his.

Today was a secret day. Mr. Powell told Mrs. Powell he was going to The Dalles for business, but he was really staying at the hotel in Shaniko for three days. He told Haven he needed a rest from her, and it would be their secret. Haven understood, he needed a rest from her too. She was always yelling.

Yes, three days in town sounded good to him. He didn't get to stay at the hotel, but he got a room at the boarding house. Mr. Powell gave him an extra twenty-five cents to have a bath and get his hair cut. He sure liked Mr. Powell.

Tipping his hat back, Haven sat at his post watching the street in case Mrs. Powell came to town uninvited and Haven was to warn him.

***

Mildred Powell fussed over the wallpaper samples in front of her, unimpressed by any of them but realized she must choose something, if she wanted the room finished in time for the lady's tea, she was planning. Presentation was important to her.

The current paper on the walls seemed boring, even though she had replaced it two years earlier. Heaving a deep sigh, she settled on a striped pattern with tiny rosebuds. Handing the sample to her much-relieved housekeeper, Mildred rose and poured herself a cup of tea from the sideboard.

It wasn't the paper that was bothering her; it was the fight she and Joseph had before he left for The Dalles. He never seemed happy when they were together, and she worried he might leave her. Adjusting her dress, she knew she had gained weight over the years, but so had he. After ten years of marriage, people change.

Mildred came from Moro, a small town along the rail line, twenty-eight miles from Shaniko, and was working at her father's Mercantile. Joseph had been traveling from The Dalles to Shaniko to check on a new job opportunity and stopped in town. He was to be the new bank manager for the Columbia Southern Bank in Shaniko.

Both were smitten at first sight, and it wasn't long before Joseph asked her to be his wife. Mildred jumped at the chance to leave town and start a new life. When they arrived in Shaniko, he and Mildred stayed in the manager's suite on the third floor, until Joseph bought the largest sheep ranch in the area.

Mildred had it all, except she couldn't give them children. The one time she was expecting had ended in a miscarriage, and she was sure Joseph blamed her. The pain and heartache had devastated Mildred. Even though the doctor assured them it was God's will and to try again, her mind could not get over the trauma and intimacy was not something she looked forward to, leaving Joseph angry and confused until he no longer approached her. Mildred was sure he was finding comfort elsewhere, choosing to ignore his infidelity if he was discrete. She had her status to uphold amongst the ladies of the town.

***

There had been a full turnover at the hotel which made for a long day, and Rosalie didn't take another break until it was five o'clock and quitting time. She was too tired to get her supper but knew she needed her strength if she would keep up with the older girls, who she hadn't seen all day.

Grabbing a plate of stew and a hard biscuit, Rosalie found a comfortable chair to sit in and eat her dinner. She had finished her meal and was dozing off when she heard her name called, jolting her awake.

"Rosalie!" Mrs. Bates called out.

Rosalie jumped, sending the plate crashing to the floor. Scrambling to her feet, she quickly picked up the pieces, using her apron to hold the broken plate.

"I'm so sorry, Mrs. Bates, you startled me."

Mrs. Bates stood with her arms folded over her large belly, glaring at her. "Well, you shouldn't be sitting in the chair eating or sleeping. That's what the kitchen and your room are for."

Rosalie hung her head. "Yes ma'am, I won't do it again."

"No, you won't, and that plate will be deducted out of your wages."

Rosalie winced at the thought of losing any money for the chipped plate. It wasn't fair.

"Now I want you to get cleaned up and take Mr. Powell his tray."

"But isn't that Patty or Linda's job?" She wondered where the two of them were now.

Mrs. Bates tapped her foot. "Normally it is, but they asked for the evening off to go to the dance and since you are the only one left, you'll be taking care of Mr. Powell this evening."

Rosalie didn't know why she felt uneasy around him, but knew if she refused, Mrs. Bates would surely fire her. Nodding her head again, she hurried to the kitchen to dump the broken plate in the trash bin and put on a clean apron. Adjusting her collar and pushing back a stray hair, she picked up the heavy silver tray from the kitchen and made her way to the third floor.

Reaching the landing, the setting sun caught her eye, casting long shadows through the windows, reflecting off the crystal chandeliers. It was even more beautiful in the evening, almost magical the way the light danced across the walls and ceiling. She wondered what it must be like to be rich and have all this belong to you.

Stopping in front of his door, Rosalie adjusted the tray in one arm and knocked gently and waited. She wanted to leave the tray by the door and run downstairs. She was about to do that when the door swung open and she quickly straightened up.

"Well, hello, Rosalie. Nice to see you again."

"Good evening, Mr. Powel. Here's your tray."

Joseph stepped back, motioning for her to enter.

"Please come in."

Rosalie quickly moved past him and placed the tray on the table. She didn't see him close the door, turning the lock, but could feel him watching her. She didn't know what she was afraid of, but something was telling her to get out as fast as she could. She set his table, put the lid back on the tray, then turned towards the door.

"Your dinner is ready, Mr. Powell, so I'll be going."

Joseph stood in front of her, blocking the way to the door.

"What's the hurry, Rosalie? Can't you stay and visit for a few minutes?"

Rosalie stepped forward, but he did not move.

"I'm sorry, Mr. Powell, but they do not allow us to stay in the rooms, and I have a lot of work to do before I am done for the evening."

Joseph moved closer to her. "Now Rosalie, that's no way to treat your employer. I make the rules and I want you to stay."

He was so close; she could smell the cigar he had been smoking, and it turned her stomach.

"I really have to go..." she said, trying to get past him.

Joseph grabbed her arm, spinning her around. The tray slipped out of her hand, crashing to the carpet, startling both for a moment. Then a sick smile crept over his face.

"Please, Mr. Powell... let me go," she whimpered.

Joseph took her by the arms and pushed her toward the enormous bed. When she tried to scream, he covered her mouth with his hand.

"If you scream or fight me, it will be worse for you. Do you understand?"

Panic rushed through her and she wrench her hand free, striking him in the face, stunning him for a moment, before he shoved her down upon the bed, crushing her with his own body. Rosalie couldn't breathe from the weight upon her and tried to wiggle from beneath him.

"Now sweet Rosalie. Didn't I tell you not to fight this?"

Terror filled her eyes as he stuffed his handkerchief into her mouth, then grabbed the cords from the curtain, quickly binding her hands together above her head to the corner post of the bed.

Thrashing under him, she tried to spit the cloth from her mouth, but it wouldn't move. Before she knew what was happening a searing pain tore through her body and she screamed against the cloth until a deep darkness overtook her.

Rosalie slowly woke. Confused, her eyes search the room, until her mind clears. NO! She tried to scream, but no sound came from her mouth. Turning her head, she saw him lying next to her, his eyes closed, and his trousers undone. Looking down at her bloomers, she noticed a red stain and started thrashing her arms at the cords holding them.

Joseph rose, and they came face to face. The look he gave her made her stop moving.

"That's a good girl. I will clean up, then I will let you go. If you scream, I will hurt you. Do you understand?"

Rosalie nodded and closed her eyes. Every part of her body hurt as she listened to him moving around the room until he was standing next to the bed again. She wished she would just stop breathing and die.

"When I remove the gag from your mouth, you will be quiet. Understand?"

Rosalie nodded, coughing as he pulled it from her mouth.

"Good. I will untie your hands, then I want you to clean up this mess. You will tell no one what happened, or I will have you arrested as a prostitute and run out of town." Tossing the rag at her, he turned and walked to the window, looking out at the street below as if she didn't exist.

Rosalie dragged her arms down to her sides, rubbing her wrists. Her mind was numb, unable to form a simple word to respond. His tone scared her more than her body hurt as she rose from the bed.

Forcing the tears back, she reached for a washcloth from the laundry bag, pulled off her bloomers and cleaned herself, wiping the sticky blood from her legs, before tossing the soiled items back in the bag. Straightening her dress and hair, she picked up the tray, along with the bag, and silently left his room.

Standing alone in the hall, she burst into deep sobs. Her life would be worse than it is now if she told anyone, and who would believe her, anyway? She was just a maid.

Wiping her eyes with the sleeve of her dress, Rosalie used the back staircase to get to the boiler room without notice and stood in front of the furnace. Taking the soiled items from the bag, she opened the door and tossed them inside. As she watched the flames devour the fabric, she was tempted to throw herself in along with them, and might have, if a rat hadn't run past her foot, startling her.

Rosalie heard the clock in the hall strike eleven as she dumped the rest of the linens into the washtub and closed her eyes. The attack replayed so vividly in her mind, nausea rushed over her and she barely made it to the wash sink, retching until her sides ached. Rinsing the foul taste from her mouth, she grabbed the lye soap and a rag, pulled up her dress and scrubbed herself until she was raw, trying to wash away what had happened. She knew no amount of soap would ever make her clean again.

Drying her body, she straightened her dress, then hurried off to her room, hoping Patty and Linda were still at the dance.

All was quiet when she opened the door. Relieved, Rosalie changed from her uniform into clean bloomers and a nightgown, before crawling onto her cot. She hoped to be asleep before they came back, fearing if she saw them, she would blurt out what had happened.

It was after two in the morning when Patty and Linda snuck into the room and crawled into their beds. They never noticed the muffled cries coming from Rosalie as she lay in her cot tossing and turning, reliving the nightmare.

***

Joseph continued looking out the window over the main street until he was sure the girl had left. Stupid! Stupid! Stupid! He muttered to himself. Once again, he had let his desire overcome his moral sense and now would have to worry about her talking.

He hoped he scared her enough to keep quiet, but tomorrow he would make sure she understood the ramifications if she told anyone. Joseph let out a sinister laugh. Who would she tell? No one in this town would have the nerve to say anything to him. He owned this hotel; he held their money in his bank, and he owned their lives.

With a smug look on his face, he straightened his tie, slipped on his overcoat, and grabbed his top hat before making his way over to the Gold Nugget Saloon for a little libation. He wanted to make sure he had an alibi, should anyone bring up the subject. The time was nearing midnight when he strolled through the doors.

Cowboys, ranchers, and sheepherders, in town to sell their goods, crowded the place. Whisky flowed freely as the piano player banged out a ragtime tune. Everyone seemed to enjoy themselves as Joseph worked his way to the bar.

"Evening Mr. Powell. What can I get you?" The bartender asked, wiping the counter in front of him.

"Evening Cal. How about a shot of your best whisky?" Joseph turned and looked over the crowd. "Place looks busy tonight."

Cal nodded and grabbed the bottle he kept under the bar for Mr. Powell. Slapping the shot glass on the counter, he filled it to the brim and slid it towards him.

"Here you go, Mr. Powell, enjoy."

Joseph picked up the glass and slugged it back in one gulp. The sweet whisky burned his throat as it went down, bursting with heat when it hit his stomach, giving him a warm feeling throughout his body. He wanted to have another, but knew he had to keep his wits. People expected that of him.

"Thanks, Cal. That hit the spot."

"You want another?"

"No. Just one for tonight." Joseph tossed a five-dollar gold piece on the counter. "Keep the change."

Cal smiled, pocketed the money quickly, before he slid the bottle under the counter and went back to his business of serving the other patrons.

Joseph looked around the room and felt uncomfortable. He didn't fit in with these people. They weren't of his class and the place smelled. Putting his silk hanky to his nose, he decided this was a bad idea and turned to leave. He was about to the door when Gus Wheeler stopped him.

"Well, if it isn't the fancy Mr. Powell," he slurred, swaying a little. "You slumming it tonight or you down here taking someone else's land from them?"

Joseph edged closer to the door. "Now Gus, I don't know what you mean," he responded, trying to defuse the situation.

Earlier in the day he had foreclosed on Gus's property for not paying his loan. Gus begged him to reconsider, but Joseph told him it was out of his hands. Gus had stormed out of his office and headed straight to the bar where he must have been all night drinking up the last of his money.

Gus slammed his hand against the door frame, narrowly missing Joseph's face. "You know what I mean. You're a money-grubbing slime bag."

Joseph jumped back. He didn't like the look on Gus's face or the stench coming from his breath.

"How about you go sleep it off and we can talk tomorrow?"

"What's there to talk about? You're a thief." Gus teetered, nearly falling over.

Joseph feared the man may vomit on his silk suit and hurried out the door into the night, followed by Gus and two cowboys who must have wanted to see what the ruckus was all about.

"You wait up!" Gus yelled, stumbling across the street. "I'm talking to you!"

Joseph hurried to the hotel boardwalk, stopping to catch his breath. Suddenly a burning sensation rippled through his back and out his stomach. Looking down, a crimson spot formed on his starched white shirt spreading across his belly. Turning his head in shock, he looked at Gus standing in the street with a smoking pistol in his hand before he collapsed on the boardwalk.

Gus looked down at the gun in his hand, dropping it in the dirt before sinking to his knees.

"Oh god!" he wailed before passing out in the street.

The Sherriff heard the gun shot and came rushing out of his office to where Joseph lay bleeding on the steps of his hotel. By the time the doctor arrived it was too late, and he was dead. With the late hour, the Sheriff decided it could wait until tomorrow to inform Mrs. Powell. He summoned the undertaker, then dragged Gus to jail to sleep it off until morning, when he would be charged with murder.

Chapter Seventeen

Rosalie was up, dressed and working before Patty and Linda woke. Her body ached, and bruises were forming on her wrists, which she tried to hide by pulling her sweater over her hands. For a moment she thought of telling Mrs. Bates but worried she wouldn't believe her and fire her instead. Not willing to take the chance, Rosalie kept quiet. She would find a way to never go to the third floor again.

Picking up her cleaning supplies, she hurried to the kitchen to get her breakfast before starting the laundry. She was grateful it was her day to work in the washroom where she would be away from everyone.

***

Patty woke with a start, glancing at the clock next to her. It was half-past six and time to get up. Stretching, she smiled, remembering the fun she and Linda had last night. Turning her head, she could see Linda still asleep under her quilt. She wanted to stay in bed but knew there would be hell to pay if they were late to work.

Checking the other side of the room, she noticed Rosalie's bed was empty. Throwing back the quilt, she rose and pushed on Linda's shoulder to wake her. "Hey Linda."

"What do you want?" Linda murmured against her pillow. "Go away and let me sleep."

"Fine, but you will get fired if you don't get up." Patty said as she changed out of her dressing gown into her uniform.

***

Linda's eyes flew open as she sat up. "Why'd you let me sleep so long?"

"Me? I just woke up myself. Anyway, we better hurry. I see Rosalie's gone."

Brushing her hair up into a bun on her head, Patty fastened it with hair combs to keep it out of the way. Mrs. Bates frowned on the girls having their hair down.

Linda nodded and jumped from her bed, hurrying as fast as she could to dress and fix her hair. She already had two marks against her for being late and knew one more would get her sacked for sure. She hated her job but needed it until she found a husband to take care of her. Last night the rancher she had been with seemed promising. Linda figured by the end of the month if she played her cards right, she would be out of the hotel into her own home.

Grabbing her apron, she followed Patty to the kitchen to get breakfast before starting another day of drudgery. They had just entered when they heard the news about Mr. Powell.

***

Rosalie was on her second load of wash when Patty and Linda came busting through the door laughing.

"Oh, there you are, Rosalie. We didn't hear you get up this morning. It must have been early."

Patty dropped her bag of linens on the floor next to Rosalie, followed by Linda.

Rosalie ignored them as she continued with the wash. Patty must have noticed she seemed off and looked over at Linda and shrugged her shoulders.

"Hey... are you okay?" Linda asked. "Usually you are peppering us with questions."

Rosalie knew she had to pull herself together. Taking a deep breath and letting it out slowly, she turned to face her friends.

"Oh... I'm sorry, I guess I'm just not feeling well today. I think it's time for my monthly or something."

Both girls nodded, understanding what she meant. Patty walked over and put her arm around Rosalie's shoulder. "I understand. Tonight, put a warm water bottle on your tummy. It always helps me."

Rosalie gave her a weak smile. "Thanks Patty, I will." Trying to sound more cheerful. "How was your evening? Did you enjoy the dance?"

"It was wonderful!" Linda chirped up first. "So many good-looking cowboys. You should really go next time, Rosalie. You need to get out and enjoy yourself, instead of working all the time."

Patty nodded in agreement. "Yes, you work too much. But that's not the big news. You will never believe what we heard this morning."

Rosalie turned her head as if to ask. Linda moved over to stand next to Patty. "You know that Mr. Powell, who owns the place?"

Rosalie's eyes widened. Did they know?

"Well, he was killed last night. A rancher shot him for taking his land. Died right on the front porch of the hotel. Sherriff's got the guy over in the jail."

Rosalie felt the blood drain from her face and a vail of darkness wash over her before she collapsed onto the floor. She heard her name but couldn't answer. Finally, the spinning stopped, and she opened her eyes. Patty and Linda were standing over her, their faces white as a ghost.

"What happened?" She asked, pushing herself until she was sitting.

Linda and Patty grabbed her by the arms, helping her to stand.

"I don't know," Linda said. "We were telling you about Mr. Powell and you turned all white and fell on the floor."

Patty guided her to a chair, lowering her down. "Gosh Rosalie, you scared us to death. We thought you had died right in front of us. Maybe I should go get Mrs. Bates."

Rosalie's gut tightened. "No. I mean no thank you. I just need to rest for a few minutes, then I'll get back to work."

"If you're sure," Patty said.

Rosalie stood and smoothed back the loose curls dislodged when she collapsed. "See, I'm better already. You two hurry on before Mrs. Bates finds us, and we all get into trouble."

Patty smiled, picked up her cleaning supplies and headed for the door, pulling Linda with her.

"Take it easy today Rosalie. If you feel worse go tell Mrs. Bates, she'll understand. She's not as hard nose as she puts on."

"Thanks Patty, I will, but don't worry." Turning, she went back to the washing with a new vigor. She would never see him again, and it made her giddy with relief.

***

Linda followed Patty up the stairs to the first floor. They had twelve rooms to clean and they would have to hurry if they were to get them done before the new guests arrived.

"That was strange the way she keeled over in the washroom; don't you think?" Linda asked, as she stripped off the linens and dumped them in her basket.

"I mean, there we are telling her about Mr. Powell, and the next minute she's on the floor in a heap."

"Yes, seemed odd to me too, but who knows the real reason. It could be a touch of the flu. It's been going around." Patty finished wiping down the washstand, replacing the water and laying down clean towels. "But did you see the marks on her wrists?"

Linda stopped for a moment. She had seen them too. "Do you think?" she asked, not really wanting to know the answer.

Patty sat on the nearest chair. "If they are what I think they are, then it explains her reaction. But how... when? Oh, my God! Mrs. Bates would have sent her up with his tray."

Patty felt her stomach turn at the thought. Rosalie was so young to have that monster hurt her. She had felt the burn of the cords last year when he caught her off guard while she was cleaning his room. Linda too, had felt the cords. He had not been their first, but his brutality and the quick dismissal had shocked them. Though he paid both girls to keep quiet, he also made it clear they were to be available whenever he came to town. Now they were all free of him.

***

Mildred Powell sat in the drawing room of her fancy house, in her fancy clothes, trying to digest the news.

Sherriff Smith had been out to see her first thing this morning to let her know what had happened in town. She thanked him for his promptness and condolences, assuring him she would make the arrangements. Always acting the lady and being in control, Mildred bid him farewell, before retreating into the room she had recently redone with velvet wallpaper, trying to stifle the despair she felt.

Glancing around the room, she remembered how Joseph complained. He said it cost a month's wages to regular people, but finally gave in to her badgering.

Now it seemed so senseless.

Mildred rose and paced the room. Her breath caught in her throat when she thought of how the townspeople would pity her as the Widow Powell. Her husband killed by a drunk. A stray tear trickled down her cheek. Dabbing it away with her handkerchief, she scolded herself as this was no time to get emotional. She had things to do.

The funeral was a private affair. Joseph and Mildred didn't have many friends, so better to exclude everyone then have no-one show up. The man who shot her husband confessed his guilt to which they promptly hung him.

With those two issues managed, Mildred took over the third-floor room at the hotel, accustoming herself with its workings, and to monitor the bank. She would not let anyone swindle her.

Over the next few months Mildred took to sneaking up on the maids, watching as they made the beds, then complain, before she ripped it apart and made them do it over. Other times, she was in the bank watching over the manager's shoulder commenting on things she knew nothing about until finally; they escorted her from the bank. Mildred protested they couldn't do that as she was the owner, to which the current manager informed her the stockholders ran the bank. Joseph had only been the manager when he died. He never owned the bank. This was a major setback to Mildred. How was she supposed to live?

***

Rosalie was sick in the mornings and tired at night, and Mrs. Bates was thinking of letting her go, but Linda and Patty begged her to reconsider, promising to help until she was feeling better. Luckily, Mrs. Bates wasn't as hard-hearted as the girls thought and agreed, but she said if Mrs. Powell ever found out, she would have to fire them all.

Linda and Patty worked double shifts for the next three months until Rosalie felt better. Patty had her suspicions' and told Linda she thought Rosalie was carrying a baby. If it were true, what would happen when Mrs. Bates found out? The bigger question, what would happen when Mrs. Powell found out?

Patty and Linda were sure it had to be Mr. Powell's baby and confronted Rosalie late one night.

"I'm glad you're feeling better, Rosalie. Me and Linda were getting worried about you."

Rosalie chewed on her lower lip.

"Thank you both for helping. I don't know what was wrong with me, but I do feel better." She tugged at her uniform. "I can't understand why these dresses shrink so much in the wash."

Linda and Patty exchanged glances.

"I know this is personal Rosalie, but have you been having your monthlies?"

"Why would you ask such a thing?"

"Have you?" Linda asked, reaching out her hand to Rosalie.

"Well... I... but... no, that can't be," she cried.

Rosalie's face went white, and she hit the chair with a thud, placing her hand on her stomach.

"Honey, we think you're pregnant. We didn't want to think it could be true, but it makes sense now. The night we were at the dance and you went to Mr. Powell's room to take him his dinner. He did something to you, didn't he?"

Rosalie buried her face in her hands. Everything she had held inside came rushing out as she told them what he had done. Shocked, Linda and Patty wanted to kill him if he wasn't already dead.

Linda put her arms around Rosalie. "I'm so sorry he hurt you, but now you must think of the baby. What are you going to do? Do you have any family?"

Rosalie sniffed. "I have two brothers. They live in The Dalles. Maybe...." She shook her head. "I can't. It would be such a disgrace to them."

"Surely they would understand." Patty and Linda chimed in.

Rosalie continued to shake her head. "I'll think of something. Promise you won't tell anyone. I can't lose my job!" Rosalie was sobbing.

Linda handed Rosalie a strip of cloth to wipe her nose. "We promise, though it's going to be hard to hide your condition for too long. We'll help as much as we can. Mrs. Bates will figure it out, eventually."

"I know, but until then, I promise I'll work harder. I just don't want either of you to get into trouble on account of me."

As the three women hugged, Patty had a feeling this would not end well.

***

Six months later, Rosalie's world turned upside down. Mildred was prowling the halls when she overheard Patty and Linda talking on the back stairs and discovered Rosalie's secret. Shock, then anger washed over her. If word got out Joseph had assaulted the girl and this child was the result, Rosalie might lay claim to part of his estate.

Even if the courts didn't believe her, Mildred would become the laughingstock of the town, once his dirty laundry aired for all to see. It was something she had worried about when he was alive, and now it was coming back to haunt her.

Mildred decided that would never happen, if she had anything to say about it, and hatched a plan.

It was perfect.

She would wait until Rosalie gave birth, then claim the child as her own, sending Rosalie out of town with the threat of exposing her for seducing her husband for his money. The town would think Mildred had been in mourning and hiding her pregnancy under the circumstances. Yes, it was the perfect plan. The girl would have no choice if she wanted to save her reputation. Now she just had to inform Rosalie of her decision.

***

Rosalie had kept up her work with Linda and Patty's help. Mrs. Bates even praised her for a job well done, though she suggested Rosalie watch what she was eating as she was putting on weight. Rosalie commented that it must be Mrs. Bates great cooking and had to stifle a laugh when the baby kicked her.

Returning to the room she shared with Linda and Patty, Rosalie lay upon her cot. Her back had been hurting all day, and she just needed a brief rest. Suddenly she felt a crushing pain across her stomach and water rushed between her legs.

***

Patty was worried that Rosalie had been working herself too hard all day. When Rosalie asked if she could take a short rest, Patty said she would finish the laundry and sent her to their room. An hour later Patty went to check on her. She was walking down the hall towards their room when she heard Rosalie scream and went running.

Mildred was coming around the corner and saw Patty hurry through the door and followed. For a moment both women stood in shock, as Rosalie lay in a sweat, writhing in pain, before they realized she was in labor.

Patty knelt by her side. "I'm here, Rosalie. You can do this. Just breathe." Before she left home, Patty had helped her mother when she gave birth to her brother two years earlier.

Mildred was standing by the door, dumbfounded, watching.

Patty turned and gasped. She thought it was Linda who had followed her into the room.

"Mrs. Powell, what are you doing here?"

Mildred snapped out of her trance and stepped forward.

"I am here to claim the child on behalf of my dead husband."

Rosalie cried out. "You can't have it, it's mine!" Another contraction coursed across her body.

"Mrs. Powell, you can't be serious." Patty wiped the sweat from Rosalie's forehead.

"I am and I will have that baby."

"But he raped her!"

"Silence! Or I will have you run out of town for prostitution along with this harlot." She pointed at Rosalie. "I know all about you and my husband."

Patty didn't have time to argue. Rosalie's body pushed hard, and the baby's head crowned. Another push or two and it would be out.

"Push Rosalie, push. That's it, the baby's almost here."

Rosalie looked as if her life was draining from her body. The pain subsided, and the room was silent. Finally, a tiny cry filled the room and Rosalie wept. Patty had caught the baby as it came out, face down.

***

Mildred was standing over her anxiously waiting to see this illegitimate child of her husbands, only to look repulsed, when Patty turned it over.

It was a girl, but the left side of her face had a raspberry-colored birthmark from her chin to her forehead. Mildred raised her hand to her mouth. She had been ready to take the child and raise it as her own. Looking at it now she could never accept this creature. She couldn't let Rosalie keep it either.

Pacing back and forth, Mildred tried to think. Who else knew about this pregnancy besides Linda and Patty? It was obvious Mrs. Bates was in the dark or she would have told her. So that only left Linda and Patty.

With her grand plan out the door, Mildred knew she had to work fast. She would have Patty move Rosalie to Mildred's room upstairs, then have Linda and Patty removed from the hotel and forced to leave town. After she was sure they were gone, she would have Haven, that simpleton who had worked for her husband, dispose of it, before finally running Rosalie out of town. It was the only way if she hoped to save face.

Patty finished cleaning the baby, wrapped it tight in a towel, then handed her to Rosalie. Rosalie pushed again and cleared the placenta, which Patty wrapped in another towel and placed in the trash.

She had just finished cleaning Rosalie, when Mildred grabbed Patty by the arm and pulled her outside the room.

"I want you to move Rosalie upstairs to my room."

Patty looked startled. "But she just had the baby."

"I don't care. Get her up and take her to my room. Make sure you put extra linens on the bed. I don't want a mess. When you're done, return here promptly," she hissed.

Patty moved to Rosalie's side and whispered in her ear. Rosalie nodded and slowly pushed her body to the edge of the cot. Patty helped her stand with her daughter in her arms. Together they shuffled out the door and up the back staircase to Mildred's room. Rosalie nearly fainted by the time they reached the third floor. Patty helped her into the enormous bed where this nightmare all began. Holding her daughter close, she drifted off to sleep.

Mildred had stripped Rosalie's cot by the time Patty entered the room, handing her the linens.

"Burn these and the rest of this garbage, then pack your bags. Linda's too. I want you both out of this hotel and this town by sunset. If Linda asks where Rosalie is, you are to tell her she left to go be with her family. If you don't do this, I will tell the Sherriff you robbed me and that you and Linda are trying to get away and you will go to jail."

***

Patty stood in front of Mildred, with her mouth hanging open. The look in Mildred's eyes told her she wasn't bluffing and hurried to the furnace with the linens. When she returned to pack her bag along with Linda's, she noticed Mildred had removed all of Rosalie's things. Patty hurried and had both suitcases packed and was sitting on the bed when Linda bustled through the door.

"Hey Patty, what are you doing with our suitcases? Where's Rosalie? She needs to get back here before Mrs. Powell catches sight of her." She saw Patty point to something behind her and turned.

Mildred was glaring at her.

"Mrs. Powell, I didn't see you standing there."

Mildred stepped closer. "I am aware of that. I was just having a conversation with Patty, informing her that Rosalie has left to be with her family." She looked directly at Patty. "Isn't that correct?"

Patty opened her mouth, then closed it, swallowing hard before she spoke. "Ah... yes. It surprised me when I came back to the room to find Rosalie was gone. Mrs. Powell informed me of her leaving." She hated herself for saying this, but she didn't want either of them to go to jail.

"But what about?" Linda stopped in mid-sentence.

"About what?" Mildred asked.

Linda walked over and stood next to Patty.

"Nothing. I was just wondering who was going to be helping us."

Mildred paced the room, making Patty uneasy, as if she were conjuring up a spell. Mildred finally stopped in front of them.

"I've decided to let you both go. I don't feel your work is up to my standards and you are to leave now. Patty has already packed your bag. I will inform Mrs. Bates of your departure." Linda's face went ashen and Patty had to hold her up.

"But what about our wages?" They both asked.

Mildred pulled out a stack of bills from the pocket in her dress, peeling off fifty dollars for each of them. She was sure that neither girl had seen that amount of money at one time.

"I think this should cover your wages and help you settle somewhere else. Be on the stage or the train out of town today. There is no place for either of you in Shaniko."

Patty and Linda stared at the money, then grabbed the bills, picked up their suitcases and hustled out the door, leaving Mildred standing alone in the room.

They tried the stagecoach office but the last stage just left, so they went to the train depot and were able to secure tickets to Biggs Junction, leaving in ten minutes. Scrambling up the steps, they settled into coach seats and tried to catch their breaths.

"What was that all about Patty? Where is Rosalie?" Linda looked out the window towards town.

"I can't tell you right now. Trust me until we are out of this hell-hole." Patty gave her a pleading look.

Linda patted her hand. "Okay, I trust you."

The conductor was yelling "All Aboard" and they felt the train car lurch. This wasn't the way Patty had envisioned leaving town. Her only regret was leaving Rosalie behind.

Chapter Eighteen

The sound of crying woke Rosalie and she wondered where it was coming from, then realized it was her baby. Pushing herself up in the enormous bed, she remembered where she was and panicked, afraid he wasn't dead and had come back for her. She wanted to rise and leave the room but felt so tired.

Pressure was building in her breasts and fluid was leaking and realized it must be milk and her baby needed to eat. Unwrapping the tight bound that Patty had made around the baby, Rosalie nestled the baby's lips against her nipple. It took two tries, but finally she could feel the tug of the baby's mouth. Resting her head against the pillows, she could have stayed that way, except she kept hearing a tapping on the floor next to the bed.

Opening her eyes slowly, Rosalie made out the image of a woman standing in front of her. This time her eyes snapped open, and she clutched the bundle next to her.

"I see you are finally awake. It's about time." Mildred moved to the side of the bed where the baby lay next to Rosalie.

Rosalie felt a chill snake down her spine and the hair raise on the back of her neck. Something was not right. Why was she in Mildred's room? In her bed? What did she want? Then she remembered! Mildred wanted her baby. Rosalie pulled the child closer.

"You can't have her. She's my child."

Mildred laughed. "I don't want her, she's a freak. Have you taken a good look at her yet? Oh, I see from your expression you haven't."

Rosalie didn't know what Mildred was talking about as she looked down at her beautiful sleeping baby. Curious, she slowly unwrapped the blanket and lifted the child closer. That's when she saw it. The left side of the baby's face was red as molten lava. The mark ran from her chin up to her forehead and made the shape of a wing. Rosalie felt God's lips had kissed her baby.

"She's beautiful."

"You can't be serious," Mildred spat at her. "That child is a freak and always will be."

"I'll tell no one who the father is. I promise!"

"I can't trust you. The child must go. And you must go. I don't want either of you in my town."

Shock of what she was saying flooded across Rosalie's face.

"You can't just throw her out like garbage. I won't let you!" Rosalie tried to rise, but the pain from giving birth racked her body.

"She will be better off and so will you. You can have other children someday. But I will not have my good name run through the gutter because you couldn't keep your legs together. You will do as I say, or I will have you charged with prostitution and thrown in jail. You have until tomorrow. The baby goes tonight."

Mildred turned and left the room.

Rosalie felt the baby move and held her to her breast, kissing the angry mark on her face. She promised she would love her forever and asked God to protect this child. She noticed a piece of paper on the nightstand and wrote a quick note.

"I'm asking God to protect her and save her from evil. I am only seventeen and forced to surrender her. Her father is dead. Tell her I love her. Please forgive me." Rosalie Scherrer.

Folding it quickly, she tucked the note next to the baby just as Mildred returned with Haven Carter.

Rosalie recognized him. He worked around the hotel sometimes and had always been nice to her. From the look on his face this wasn't something he wanted to do. Rosalie's tears flowed from her eyes.

"Did you bring the basket?" Mildred snapped at him.

Haven shook his head.

"I can't get you to do anything right. Stay here and don't move. I'll be right back." Mildred huffed as she waddled out the door.

Haven moved closer to the bed to see the baby. "She sure is pretty, Miss Rosalie. Please don't cry."

"Haven help me. Take the baby somewhere safe. Please don't kill her." She could barely say the words. She reached out and squeezed his hand. "Please Haven, I'm begging you."

Haven squeezed her hand back and nodded as if they had just signed a pact between them. He heard Mildred stomping down the hall and stepped back to where she had instructed him to stay. He gave Rosalie a brief nod and waited.

Mildred swept into the room and threw the basket on the bed. Reaching over, she yanked the baby from Rosalie's arms and dropped it in, covering the top so it looked like a lunch basket, then handed it to Haven.

"Get rid of this. I don't want to know where and you are never to speak of what happened here. Do you understand Haven?"

Haven stared at her.

She turned her back, waiting for him to leave.

Haven gave Rosalie a slight smile and tipped his hat. Then he was gone and so was her daughter. She never even got to name her. She turned her head into the pillow and screamed.

Mildred was standing over her, admonishing her to get over it and for her to be ready to leave in the morning. She had taken up too much of Mildred's time already.

***

Haven hurried from the hotel with his package. He couldn't think when people yelled at him, but he made a promise to Rosalie and he would keep it.

Retrieving his horse, he secured the basket in front of him and covered it with another small blanket he kept tied to the back of his saddle to keep it warm.

With a full moon to guide him, he took off across the high desert to the only place he knew the baby would be safe. A place he knew by heart.

***

Sister Mary heard the knock at the door and went to answer it. A young man was standing in front of her, holding a basket. He had his brown hat pulled down over his face and his clothes looked tattered.

"Can I help you my son?" she asked wondering what he wanted. He looked familiar to her. "Haven?"

He nodded.

She recalled he had been from a wagon train and lost his parents when he was six. He had lived at the orphanage until two years ago when he went to work in Shaniko, at the rail yards. She couldn't believe he was standing in front of her now.

***

Haven lifted his head and pulled the note from the basket, handing it to her without saying a word. He didn't know what it said, but he had promised Rosalie he would take the note and hid it before Mrs. Powell came in and told him to take the baby.

He liked Rosalie; she had always been nice to him, though he didn't understand why she didn't want to keep her baby.

Mrs. Powell was being so mean to Rosalie and when she shoved the basket with the baby in it at him and said to get rid of it, he knew he couldn't do that. He didn't know much about God, but he was sure he was doing something wrong and had hurried out into the night to bring her to the one place he knew she would be safe.

Now standing on the steps of the orphanage, his tiny package whimpered, and he held the basket for the nun to take it. As she took hold, he turned and ran down the steps to his horse, snapping the reins without a backward glance, he rode into the night.

***

Sister Mary opened the cloth and gasped. Not at the birthmark, but at the fact the child was so small. Hurrying inside, she summoned the Mother Superior and the other sisters to inspect the child who arrived cold and hungry on April 8, 1910. She was so tiny they were afraid she might not make it through the night. Wasting no time, everyone worked to save the infant. They heated a blanket, swaddling her, and prepared a bottle of warm milk. At first, she wouldn't take the nipple, but finally settled down and suckled as she warmed up.

Mother Superior read the note again, and her heart ached for the young mother. Folding it, she put it in her robe pocket to deal with later. Making the sign of the cross, she praised God for guiding the young man here as quickly as he did, for she feared the child would have died if left out in the cold much longer.

This was the youngest child ever brought to them in all the years she had been at Sisters of the Mountains Parrish. After checking her over and dressing her in a makeshift diaper, Sister Mary re-wrapped the baby in the blanket and held her close to her chest.

Mother Superior gathered them all together and said a prayer for the tiny child, asking God's blessing on the baby with the Angel wing on her face, then named her Kelly Turner. There was something special about this baby.

Sister Mary volunteered for the first shift and returned to her sleeping chamber, where she held the infant to her own body for warmth, and soon the baby fell asleep. Throughout the night she continued to hold the child, praising God for this tiny miracle.

In the morning, she brought the baby to Mother Superior, where she and the other Sister's agreed the baby looked much better, but they still worried about her small size. Wanting assurance herself, Mother Superior summoned the local doctor.

The sight of the baby shocked Dr. Mayfield. He figured she was barely a day old. When he learned where she had traveled from, he couldn't believe she had survived the trip. After examining the child, he declared her healthy and thought the birthmark on her face would fade as she grew older. Bidding the Nun's good day, he told them not to hesitate to ring if the baby became distressed in any way.

***

Haven returned to Shaniko by the next morning and informed Mildred he got rid of the baby.

Rosalie had packed and was preparing to leave on the train to Biggs Junction, then on to The Dalles to live with her brothers. Haven waited until she boarded the train and Mrs. Powell was nowhere in sight to let her know the baby was alive, but he wouldn't tell where he took her, for fear Mrs. Powell would go find her and hurt her.

"Thank you, Haven," Rosalie said. "Just knowing she's alive will help me go on."

Haven rolled the brim of his hat in his hands. "I'm really sorry, Miss Rosalie."

"You are a kind man, Haven, and I will be forever grateful." Rosalie gave him a kiss on the cheek before slipping through the door and finding a seat.

Touching his cheek, Haven smiled, jumped from the train, and waved as it pulled out of the station.

Returning to the stable, he waited until it was dark.

He had one more thing to do.

The fire started in the wood box next to the hotel's back door and flames crept slowly, finding their way into the dry, brittle siding.

From his vantage point at the end of the street, Haven watched the embers lifting into the sky and heard frightened voices screaming "FIRE!" through the night air.

Mrs. Powell came running from across the street right into the path of the horses pulling the fire wagon.

Though it wasn't nice to do, he couldn't help snicker at the thump, thump sound the wheels made when they bounced over her body.

A fitting end to a mean woman.

Grabbing his bedroll, Haven hurried towards the depot and made it on the last train out of town for the night. He gave a final salute when the flames engulfed the third floor and the train lurched forward to The Dalles and Rosalie.

***

Lou closed the book and set it on the table. Engrossed in the story; she hadn't noticed Grandmother retreat to her bed and was napping. There had to be more to this story, but Lou didn't want to wake her.

Retrieving a quilt from the chair in the corner, Lou gently covered her. She would come back tomorrow to find out the ending.

For now, her own mind was overflowing with so many images and emotions, she couldn't process them as she tiptoed out of the room.

Chapter Nineteen

Karol returned Monday morning to find Lou's car in the driveway and Lou still in bed. This wasn't like Lou, and it worried her. After getting her mother settled in the kitchen, Karol tapped gently on Lou's door but got no answer.

Cracking the door open, she saw Lou sprawled across her bed with pictures of Jason scattered all around her. She panicked until she heard Lou give out a little moan and turn over. Karol relaxed and closed the door. Returning to the kitchen, she let her mother know everything was all right.

Karol had picked up the Sunday paper when they came back and for the next hour, mother and daughter scanned the want ads for apartments, making a list of places to look at.

She was still uneasy about leaving Lou, but it was time for her to start over with her mother. Karol prayed Jason would come home soon so Lou wouldn't be alone for long.

They had just finished their third cup of tea when Karol looked up and Lou was standing in the doorway.

"Well hello sleepyhead. Would you like a cup of tea?"

Lou yawned and shuffled towards the sink. "I can't believe I slept this long. When did you get back? Hello, Miriam."

Miriam smiled and waved, and Karol folded the paper.

"We got back three hours ago. Mom and I have been checking out apartments in the paper. I asked Brad for the day off unless you need me today."

***

Lou leaned against the counter, waiting for her coffee to brew. Tea would not cut it today.

"No, I think I've found everything I've been looking for. I just have to put it together."

The coffee maker finished sputtering and Lou poured a cup, savoring the rich aroma. She was amazed how calm she was staying under the circumstance. She was still in shock about Jason and then reading her great-great grandmother's life story. When had life become so complicated? It was like she stirred up a hornet's nest and this was the punishment for poking sticks where you shouldn't.

"So, did you girls find anything interesting the paper?"

Miriam gave Karol a gentle pat on the arm. "I think we found a couple in our budget. Hopefully, they will be habitable. Would you like to come with us?"

Lou shook her head. "I think I'll stay here and let you two have all the fun. Besides, I need a shower and have a lot of notes to tackle." She set her cup down and headed for her room. "If you find one, be sure and send me pictures." Her resolve to hold it together was melting rapidly. "Later," she called as she closed her door.

Karol shrugged and rinsed out their teacups. Picking up the list, they left the house, not seeing Lou peek out the crack of her door with tears streaming down her face.

***

Elizabeth woke to the chimes announcing breakfast, then realized she had slept in her clothes the night before. She didn't remember Lou leaving and worried about her mental state with all that had happened. Susan hadn't been able to fight off the demons of depression, Elizabeth feared, had been handed down from her own mother. She prayed fate would spare Lou and swore to do everything she could to help Lou through this challenging time in her life.

First, she needed a plan and placed a call to her brother. Next, she had the office look up George McClelland's address.

She felt it was time to meet her son-in-law. Changing her clothes, she called for a cab. It was time for action.

***

George had just returned from the market and was helping Mary put the groceries away when he noticed a cab pull up front and an elderly woman exited.

"Are you expecting company today Mary?" he asked motioning towards the driveway.

Mary moved to the window and looked out. "No, are you?"

George shook his head. "Well, someone is coming to the door, so I guess we better answer it."

Mary took the lead and George was behind her when the bell chimed. Opening the door an older version of Vivian stood in front of him. He thought he was seeing a ghost.

"Are you George McClelland?"

George nodded, unable to speak.

"My name is Elizabeth Johnson. I believe you are my son-in-law. May I come in?"

Mary gave George a little jab in the side, bringing him back to reality. "Yes, yes, of course. May I take your coat?"

Elizabeth entered the hallway. "I think I will keep it on if you don't mind. I seem a little chilled today, but I would like to sit down. My old feet aren't what they used to be."

George ushered Elizabeth into the kitchen and helped her get seated. "This is my wife, Mary."

Mary approached Elizabeth and held out her hand.

"It's nice to meet you Elizabeth. Lou mentioned you to us the other night. As you can expect, it was quite a shock to George."

Elizabeth returned the gesture. "I'm sure it was. Louise, or Lou as you call her, said the same. Please sit, so we can talk. I realize I may be overstepping my bounds, but I am extremely worried about her."

George and Mary took a seat across from Elizabeth.

"Why? What has she told you?" George asked.

Elizabeth placed her hands, on top of the table.

"Lou came to me yesterday and told me what happened with Jason. She was so distraught, she cried for hours. She feels God is punishing her, but I tried to make her understand that God loves her, that we all love her. It's life that gets in the way, and this has nothing to do with her. My biggest fear is that she will fall into the same depression that Susan, I mean Vivian, did after she lost the baby. It would kill me to lose Lou to the same fate."

George's face went white. "What do you know about the baby?"

"Vivian came to see me after she got out of the sanitorium. She looked like a shell of herself and said you were on the road. She had Lou with her, and we talked for quite a while. She said she didn't like the medication they had her on, that it made her feel dead inside. I tried to help her understand it was for her own good and to give it time to work. Vivian became agitated and wasn't making sense. I worried she might hurt herself, so I begged her to stay and let me try to call you, but she wouldn't have it. She said everything was my fault for the way her life had turned out and swore I was dead to her from then on." Elizabeth seemed to choke up and stopped for a moment until she regained her composure.

"Lou was in the kitchen with my brother Gene but came running when she heard Vivian yelling. The look on Lou's face was the saddest thing I ever saw. It was also the last time I ever saw her again. I saw Vivian years later. It was right before Lou had to put her in the care facility. She was having a very lucid moment and wanted to talk. She knew something was wrong with her and she was getting worse. She wanted me to know she was sorry for the things said so many years ago. She wanted me to tell Lou, if I ever saw her again, that she loved her and wished she could have been the mother she deserved. She wanted me to tell you she was sorry for blaming the baby's death on you and driving you away. Her last request was that I do not contact Lou until she was gone. It was hard, but I agreed. I held my daughter for the last time that day, and I think she had finally found peace with herself when she left."

George tried to force down the lump in his throat. Caught up in his own misery after losing their son, he had never looked at it from Vivian's side. He just saw her irrational behavior and took it as a sign she didn't love him anymore.

"I'm sorry Elizabeth, I had no idea. Vivian never talked about her life before we met. I asked if she had family and she said no. I had no reason to doubt her. I loved her very much. We had a good life until the baby died, then everything changed. I didn't know what to do to help her, and the more I tried, the more she pushed away. I thought if I stayed away, she would have time to heal, but I was wrong. I should have been there for her and Lou."

George buried his face in his hand and sobbed. Mary slid her arm over his shoulder and held him close to her.

Elizabeth shifted in her chair.

"George, I didn't come here to place blame. I've learned it does no good to anyone. Vivian had problems way before she met you, but that's not important anymore. My primary concern is Lou. She needs all the support and love we can give her to help her through this challenging time. I just want to know you will accept my help if she needs it."

George wiped his eyes. "Lou is my life and Mary's now. I already lost too many years without her, so whatever she needs we are with you, but you must know she's spent years building walls to protect herself. Sometimes it's hard to get through to her, even with the greatest of love."

Elizabeth nodded. "Yes, she comes from a lengthy line of hard-headed women, but she is also a survivor. She just has to remember her life is meaningful and that God and her great-great-aunt are watching over her." Elizabeth reached into her bag and pulled out a card, handing it to George.

"This is my brother's address. We feel it would be helpful for Lou to have her entire family around her and would like to have a luncheon a week from this Sunday, welcoming her, along with you and Mary, to the family. Also, if you know of her friends who would like to join, please let them know. I've planned it for 1pm."

George flipped the card over in his hand. "I wish I would have met you sooner, Elizabeth."

"We know each other now George, so let's not waste any more time. I look forward to seeing everyone." She rose. "I'll leave it up to you to get her there. In her state of mind, she might fight you, but I'm sure you can manage our girl. Another thing, would you mind calling me a cab?"

George chuckled and called the cab company. They made small talk until the cab arrived and he helped her to the car. She gave them a brief wave as she rode away, leaving them on the front porch.

Mary returned to the kitchen with George following behind.

"That was intense. Are you alright, George?"

George put his arms around her and held her tight.

"As long as you still love me after all you've heard."

Mary kissed him. "George, whatever happened with Vivian, has nothing to do with us. I love you. You're a good man who made bad choices. Now we just go forward and help Lou get through this sadness."

"How did I ever get so lucky to find you, Mary McClelland?"

"It's all in the cooking, George." She said with a big grin. "All in the cooking."

***

Lou sat at the kitchen table sipping her cold coffee. She let Brad know she would be working from home today if he needed to get ahold of her, managing to not let on about Jason. It was the only way she was keeping her sanity at this point.

After a long hot shower, she dressed and fixed something to eat, but nothing had any flavor, just like her life. Suddenly it had become bland, like vanilla pudding. She was becoming vanilla pudding. The drive that had been pushing her now seemed to have dissipated and doubted she had the strength to finish her story. Would people care? So, she found out who Kelly's mother was and discovered she was related. But in the grand scheme of things did it even matter?

Lou questioned if this was how her mother felt after losing the baby. Did life matter anymore?

Sure, other people needed her, but it was so exhausting trying to put on a smiling face and pretend you're not dying inside. It would be easy to crawl into a hole and stay there like her mother had. She felt a part of herself leaning that way, but her life's lessons of survival were keeping her from falling over the edge.

Pushing the coffee aside, she wondered if life would have been different if she had insisted, they get married after Jason had proposed to her. Maybe they would have gone back to New York City. Maybe life would have turned out different.

Lou knew all the maybe's in the world would not change the fact the man she loved with all her heart was gone, and maybe she could have prevented it.

One thing she knew, it would disappoint Jason the way she was behaving. It was time to put on her big girl panties and face reality. This would be something she would have to live with for the rest of her life.

Rinsing her coffee cup, Lou wanted to speak to Grandmother once more to get the ending of the story, then she would write the best follow-up piece of her career. After that, she might take off work and visit Julie for a change of scenery and to clear her head. She had her entire life ahead of her and suddenly didn't have a clue what to do with it. The pain from losing Jason bubbled close to the top, but she pushed it down for now. He would say she was overreacting, and life goes on. Lou knew the big hole in her heart may never heal, but the parts left would hold his memory forever.

***

Elizabeth returned to her room, content that she had conducted her mission. George seemed like a nice man and she was sure he had love Susan the best he could. His new wife, Mary, was very pleasant and Elizabeth liked her.

It felt invigorating to have new family. She was hanging up her coat when she heard a knock and went to answer.

"Good afternoon Lou, please come in."

Lou gave her a peck on the cheek as she entered.

"Sorry I left last night without waking you, but you looked so peaceful sleeping."

Elizabeth noticed she seemed nervous.

"That was alright. Though I missed you when I woke this morning. Shall we sit and visit awhile?" She motioned towards the couch.

Lou waited until Grandmother settled against the cushions, then sat next to her. "I finished the book before I left, but there are still a few questions I have."

"I'm sure you do. Go ahead, you can ask me anything."

Lou cleared her throat. "What happened after Haven set the hotel on fire and rode away on the train?"

Elizabeth sighed. "From what Grandmother Rosalie told me, Haven followed her to The Dalles and went to work for her brother Max, at the dairy the brothers had started here in town. Rosalie knew Haven would always protect her after what he did to save her daughter. They became close under the circumstances and eventually fell in love. My mother, Irene was born two years later. Irene was a troublesome child growing up, with bouts of melancholy, they called it back then, and a challenging time making friends. When she met my father, she jumped at the chance to marry, but soon discovered life as a wife and mother was harder than she thought. By the time I was seventeen, I, like you, had suffered from her outbursts. My father was a rail man, and stayed away for extended periods of time, like your father. Grandmother Rosalie had been my salvation. When I fell in love with Cliff and became pregnant, I feared she would no longer love me. Telling her was the hardest thing I ever had to do."

Lou sat forward, "What did she say? What did your mother do?"

Elizabeth reached out and took Lou's hands in her own.

"That was the night she told me about her first daughter. I was shocked and asked if Mother knew about this, but she said no. Only she and Haven knew the truth. She begged me to never give up my child no matter what the future held for us, and to never repeat what she had told me.

As for my mother, she went off the rails sputtering how I would tarnish their good name all over town if I carried this child to full term. She wouldn't listen when I told her Cliff, and I were in love and that he would marry me. She called me horrible names and told me to leave. I went to Grandmothers and stayed with her until Cliff and I got married two weeks later, the day after I turned eighteen.

Mother was still making threats to tell everyone in town I was pregnant, so the only thing Cliff and I could do was to move away. We left that night on the train for Yakima. Over the next three years, I wrote to Grandmother often. She kept me up on the news around town and how my parents were doing. Grandfather Haven had a heart attack and died that fall, so I made the trip back to town for the funeral. Cliff stayed home with Susan. Grandmother Rosalie had aged so much since I last saw her, and it broke my heart. Mother ignored the fact that I was even there, though my father said a quick hello, before throwing up his hands and walking away. I know this isn't the Christian thing to say, but at that moment, I hated my mother more than life itself. I swore I would never treat my child the way she treated me."

Lou pulled her hands back and picked at her fingernail.

"So, what happened to my mother?"

Elizabeth folded her hands in her lap. "I have to believe her depression was handed down from my mother, or possibly from Haven. He was always a little slow, but a good man. In his later years, he would have bouts where he couldn't get out of bed for days. Grandmother would say he was having a sad day.

Years after they had been married, she said he surprised her one day with a picture of a young woman who looked to be about eighteen. It was the graduation picture of Kelly, which was the name listed from the nursing school. Unbeknownst to Grandmother, Haven had been checking on her daughter over the years. He still wouldn't tell her where he had taken the baby that night, but assured Grandmother that she had grown up loved, despite the mark on her face. He just wanted her to know that. It was the greatest gift he ever gave her. Peace of mind. She had planned to try to find Kelly, but Irene had problems and she put the notion aside and left that part of her life behind."

Lou swiped a tear from her cheek, and Elizabeth noticed the worried look on her face.

"What is it, Lou?"

"Do you think I will be crazy like my mom and your mother?" The words choked in her throat.

Elizabeth pulled her into her arms. "Oh Lou, never say that. From what I understand about your life, you are the strongest one of all of us. If the chain had broken along the line, you would not be here today, and if great-great grandmother Rosalie were standing here she would tell you that herself. I hope you believe me that we love you, and always have. Your story is not over yet."

Lou couldn't hold it in any longer. "But without Jason, the story ends."

Elizabeth stroked Lou's hair. "No, the story begins again. You will just have to wait to see what God has written for you."

Chapter Twenty

Lou returned home to find the house empty and grateful Karol and her mother were still out apartment shopping. She wasn't in the mood for conversation and was exhausted from talking to Grandmother. It had helped, but it didn't ease the pain of a broken heart. She would just have to let time try to do that.

Checking her phone by habit for messages, she saw a text from Julie and knew she would have to call her back. It was time to be honest about what she was going through, and she needed to hear her friend's voice.

Lou grabbed a cup of coffee before placing the call, knowing once they started talking, she would need it.

"Hey momma, how's it going with that little boy of yours?"

"He is so adorable, and he's really growing. John said Daniel held his head up for a few minutes today."

"Well he should be, the kids almost three months old. Is he talking yet? Driving a car?"

Lou could hear Julie laughing. "You're so silly. I don't know if making you his Godmother was a clever idea. Have you read any of the baby books I sent you?"

"Um...sure," Lou coughed.

"Lou McClelland, I bet you haven't cracked one book open."

Lou threw her hands up as if Julie could see her.

"You got me. But when it comes time to do the Godmother thing, I promise I will be ready. And Julie?"

"Yes."

"That won't be until he is in his teens, right?"

Julie's hysterical laughter filled the airwaves and Lou had to back the phone away from her ear. This was what she needed and waited for Julie to catch her breath.

"Are you done laughing at me?"

"I'm not laughing at you, okay I am, but it's because I love you."

"I love you too. So, on to more serious news. Karol and her mother are looking for an apartment and plan to move in together. I found my grandmother and an uncle, living right here in town. She is cool, and you will have to meet her next time you are here. Jason is missing and presumed dead, and I think spring is coming early." Lou could feel the silence on the other end.

"What did you say?"

"I think Spring is coming early?"

"Lou! What did you say before that?" Julie's voice was rising.

Lou didn't know if she could say those words again, but she had to face the fact they were true.

"Jason is missing and presumed dead."

Julie gasped. "Oh my God, Lou. When? How? Is someone there with you? I better come now."

Lou could hear Julie calling for John.

"Julie? Julie, listen to me. Are you there?"

"Yes, I'm here. John will watch the baby and I will be on my way in an hour."

"No."

"What do you mean, no? You can't be there all by yourself. I need to be there for you."

Lou could hear the tears in her voice.

"Julie, listen. I'm okay. As much as I want to see you, you need to be with your son and husband. Karol will be home soon, and I have been spending time with my new grandmother. Dad and Mary are all over me, and you know how I get when everyone tries to smother me. I won't lie, this is hard, but I must go on. Jason would want me to. Though right now, I am furious at him, but it will pass. Give me a few more days to adjust as best I can, then we can set up a play date."

"Are you sure?" Julie was still sobbing.

"Please Julie, no more crying. I have cried enough for a lifetime. You give those men of yours a kiss for me and I will call later in the week."

Lou hung up before Julie could protest and turned the phone on silent. She just couldn't talk to anyone else even though she knew Julie would call Dad. He would just have to leave a message. Checking her watch, she noticed it was after four. She hadn't heard from Karol and Miriam all day and worried they weren't finding anything livable.

Feeling hungry, Lou checked the fridge. There were still cold cuts from Saturday and vegetables that looked edible. Grabbing a block of cheese, she sliced cubes and arranged them on a tray with crackers and the other goodies. She was just setting the tray on the table when she heard laughter coming through the front door.

"Hey, I'm in here," she called out as Karol and Miriam swayed into the kitchen arm in arm, like two schoolgirls back from a recent date. Lou envied them.

"Are you guys hungry?" She pointed towards the table. "Look, I made dinner."

Karol plopped down in the chair first, then Miriam followed. "Wow. That's impressive, Lou." Karol teased at her. "No really, that was very nice of you, since Mom and I are starved." Karol grabbed a plate and handed it to her mother. "Here Mom, dig in. Come on Lou, sit down and join us."

Lou settled into her chair and picked at the food on her plate. "So, did you find anything?"

Miriam shook her head. "You would never believe the apartments people are trying to rent out there. It's just disgraceful." She took a bite of cracker.

"Mom's right, Lou. I would rather live at the YWCA or in a barn, compared to what we saw today. And the prices they wanted for these dumps would blow your mind. There were a couple more, but it was getting late and I didn't want to leave you by yourself too long." Karol noticed the look Lou gave her. "What's going on Lou? You've been acting strange since this morning?"

Lou pushed her plate aside. She didn't know if she had the strength to repeat the sordid details one more time, but knew she owed it to Karol. They had been through too much together to keep secrets now.

"There's something I need to tell you. Please don't say a word until I'm done, or I'll never be able to get through it."

Karol made the motion of zipping her lips, as Lou recounted the events of yesterday, then wiped her eyes with her napkin.

"I'm so sorry, Lou, but are you sure he's dead? I mean, did they find his body?"

Lou dipped her head; she couldn't look Karol in the face.

"The only thing they found was his duffle bag. I don't think there's a body." The words cut even deeper into her heart. "From what his sister Joan told me, it will take months to identify the remains of everyone, but they believe the blast killed him."

Karol and Miriam were sobbing.

"So, there's no rush to move out now. I was even thinking, maybe if you wanted to, your mom could move in with us. I get my room back; she gets your room and you take the spare room." Lou couldn't believe the words coming from her mouth, but the thought of living alone terrified her.

"Don't you need time?" Miriam asked.

"Time for what? Jason is gone and life goes on." Lou stiffened in her chair. "You said there was nothing out there so stay here until you find the right place."

Karol stood and threw her arms around Lou's shoulders. "I love you, Lou," she whispered in her ear, then returned to her chair. "What do you think Mom? Would you like to live here with Lou and I?"

Miriam seemed at a loss for words. "I... are you sure about this Lou? I mean, you've been dealt a great tragedy."

"If I have learned anything over the last two years, life is full of tragedies, but it's how we deal with them that gets us through the hard days of our lives. Karol has shown me that. I would be grateful if you and Karol would stay, even for a while."

Karol grabbed Lou's hand and then her mothers. "To the three amigos!" she laughed, lifting them into the air.

Miriam chuckled, and Lou burst out laughing.

***

The next day Miriam and Karol set off to get the few things Miriam had at her sisters. Lou called Dad to inform him of the new living arrangements and to her surprise, he seemed happy for her and showed up to help. They spent the better part of the day moving everyone around. It felt good to be back in her old room. Not that she didn't like her mother's room, she never felt comfortable in it.

Lou poured two glasses of water and handed one to Dad.

"Whew, that was a lot of work," she said, taking a deep drink. "I'm exhausted. How about you?"

George held up his finger as he gulped down the cool liquid, then wiped his mouth with his sleeve.

"Let's sit for a spell. My back is killing me."

Lou looked alarmed.

"I'm fine Lou, just a little tired. Remember, I am older than you." He chuckled and brushed her cheek with a kiss. "How are you holding up, kiddo?"

Lou joined him at the table. "Honestly? Better than I thought I would. I have my moments but staying busy is helping. Grandmother has been an immense help too. She lets me talk or cry and seems to understand what I'm going through. Not that you and Mary don't, it's different. I hope you understand."

"You don't have to explain it to me Lou. I'm happy you have someone to help you deal with this. I know I wasn't particularly good with your mother."

"That's not true, Dad. You did the best you could. We all did." Lou sipped on her water. "I was wondering when you would like to meet Grandmother and Uncle Gene?"

Dad coughed. "Well, to tell you the truth, I already met your grandmother."

"Really? When?"

"She came to see Mary and I the other day. We had quite the visit. Bottom line, I like the woman. I wish I had known her when your mother was alive."

Lou sat dumbfounded. "So, what did she say?"

"She was expressing her concern about you and worried you might bury yourself in the pain of losing Jason, the way your mother did after the baby. I told her we were all supporting you and she needn't worry, but she wants to do more."

"Like what?" Lou couldn't believe they were having this conversation.

"She wants to have a luncheon at your Uncle Gene's house a week from this Sunday. I think she said 1pm. Anyway, she wants to bring the family together, a way to show you how much you're loved."

Lou sat back in her chair with a frown on her face.

"Hey look, I know this is probably a bad idea, but she insisted. How could I say no to such a nice old lady? Actually, my mother-in-law."

Lou couldn't help but grin. "Do you think I should go? It hasn't been that long since I got the news about...you know."

Dad stroked her hand. "You don't have to stay long, but I think it would do you good. You can bring Karol and her mother too, since they are now part of this extended family of ours."

"I don't know if I'm ready to face everyone with all their sad faces, telling me how wonderful he was and how life is unfair. I know all that stuff." Lou chewed on her bottom lip. "I'll have to think about it."

"Fair enough, but let your grandmother know by the middle of next week, so she doesn't go to a lot of fuss for nothing." Dad finished his water and stood, stretching his back. "Is there anything else we need to move before I head home? Please say no."

Lou cracked a smile and shook her head. "I think we've got it all. Karol can help her mother with whatever she brings back. My room is done, so I think you're good to go."

Dad gave her a kiss on the head. "You rest and I'll show myself out. One more thing, Mary and I expect to see you and your guests for dinner this Sunday. No excuses."

With that last word, he was out the door, leaving Lou to stew by herself. She was still mulling over their conversation and was no closer to deciding if she wanted to go to the party, when she heard a car door slam, and Karol's voice.

Her family was home.

***

Laughter filled the house like a girl's sorority dorm. They each had assigned jobs and the first week had run smoothly. Lou made sure she filled the cupboard with groceries, Miriam took over cooking their dinners and Karol helped with the laundry.

Lou was amazed how well they all got along and was rinsing her cup when her phone pinged with a reminder from

Dad about dinner tomorrow. She also knew she had to decide about Grandmother's party and was deep in thought when Karol and Miriam walked in the kitchen.

"Hey, why the sad face Lou?" Karol asked, snatching a fresh-baked cookie off the counter.

Miriam slapped at her hand.

"You quit eating those or you'll spoil your dinner."

The comment made everyone laugh, and Lou turned to face her roommates.

"No cooking for you tomorrow night Miriam. Our presence is requested, well it's demanded at Dad and Mary's at 4pm."

Miriam frowned. "Are you sure you want me to come?"

"Absolutely, they will love you. And don't be surprised if Mary gets you cornered on recipes. That's her favorite subject, which is lacking in my department. You two will have a great deal to talk about. As for Karol and me, we'll eat the desserts and keep Dad company. Sound good to everyone? Oh, wait, there's one more thing."

"You're so bossy, Lou." Karol gave her a wink. "So, what's the other thing?"

"Grandmother is having a luncheon next Sunday at 1pm at Uncle Gene's house. She wants to welcome the families together and thinks it would do me good to get out. She also insisted you both come, but if you don't feel comfortable, I would understand. Though I really would like you there, if I have to go."

Miriam had a look of panic on her face and touched her dress.

"What's wrong Momma?"

"I have nothing that would be nice enough to wear to a luncheon. Everything happened so quickly, I haven't had time to think about new clothes."

Karol hugged her mother. "That's okay, we'll think of something. I have a little money saved and we can buy you a new dress."

Lou could see Miriam was struggling to hold back the tears. Then it hit her. Her mother's clothes were out in the garage, in boxes marked for the Goodwill. Miriam was about Vivian's size, and surely there would be something she could wear. Even Karol might find a dress or two.

"I have a great idea." Lou turned and headed for the back door. "Come on you two, I want to show you something."

She was out the door before they could answer.

Following close behind, they found her pulling the tape off boxes and muttering to herself.

"What's all this Lou?"

Lou turned and handed Karol a box. "Here, take this one into the house and that one over there. Oh, and this one Miriam. Grab the little one next to it, too. I will bring these others. Go, go. This will be so much fun."

Karol and Miriam hustled their boxes into the living room, stacking them by the wall. Lou was dashing back and forth, tossing more boxes at them, until there wasn't room to move. Finally, she returned with one last box, added it to the pile and plopped onto the couch.

"That should do it." Lou said.

The two women stood in shock. "Lou, have you gone mad? What is all this?" Karol's curiosity was getting the better of her, as she lifted the lid off the smaller box closest to her, and gasped.

Lou jumped up and lifted the glittering purse out of the box. "This was my mom's stuff. I forgot about it until now. Isn't it pretty?" The purse glistened in the evening light. "All this was hers and I want you and your mom to go through every box. Try things on and if it fits and you like it, it's yours."

Karol pulled the tape from another box and lifted out a beautiful peach colored suit. "Oh Momma, this would look beautiful on you."

Miriam held the soft fabric to her body. "Do you think?" She looked at Lou.

Lou nodded. "Please Miriam, let me do this for you and Karol. Whatever clothes are left, I'll give to the ladies shelter in town."

Miriam dashed for the bedroom as Karol searched through the boxes, setting things aside she liked. She had just pulled out a yellow sundress when Miriam returned, glowing from head to toe. The suit fit perfectly.

Lou rifled through the shoe boxes and found a cream-colored pair of low heels and a small bag to complete the outfit. She felt a wondrous joy watching as they tried one thing after another, like she was the curator of her own fashion show. Most of the clothes worked, others did not, giving them all a great laugh. By the time they emptied the last box, everyone was exhausted and sprawled on the couch. Karol and Miriam had enough clothes to last years.

"That was fun." Lou rolled her head against the cushion and closed her eyes. For a moment she thought she could see her mother smiling, and it gave her a warm feeling. "Did you find everything you needed?"

Karol glanced over the stacks of clothing, shoes, and purses she had assembled and then at her mother's pile.

"I think we have everything covered except for our personal things, which we can take care of. Are you sure you want to do this, Lou? You could sell a lot of this and make money."

"Absolutely not. I mean, I want you to have them. I don't care about the money. And I think this would make my mom happy."

Miriam gently squeezed Lou's hand. "Your mother would be proud of you and your generosity. But what about you? What are you going to wear?"

"Me? Oh, I'll find something."

Karol rolled her eyes at her.

"What was that for?"

"I've seen your wardrobe."

"Karol, that's not a nice thing to say."

"Mom, believe me, I've seen her choice of clothes. So, tomorrow after we get back from dinner, the three of us, and Mary, if she wants to come, are going shopping to bring Lou into the 21st century, kicking and screaming if we have to!"

Lou couldn't help noticing the wicked look in Karol's eyes. Why not? It was time to start new. "Okay, but nothing flashy. You know, simple, white, and beige." She burst out laughing at the look on Karol's face. "Got you."

It took the three of them the rest of the evening to hang, pack and put away all their treasures and it was after ten, when she taped the last box and placed it back in the garage. Monday, she would take them to the women's shelter as a final salute to her mother. She was locking the back door when Miriam and Karol entered the kitchen.

"That was fun, Lou. It was like playing dress-up, but we got to keep the clothes. I can't thank you enough for helping us."

Lou set the plate of cookies on the table between them and grabbed the gallon of milk.

Karol retrieved the glasses and poured each one half full.

"I believe we need to celebrate all of our new beginnings."

Lou's hard shell crumbled, and she rushed from the room.

Karol rose to go after her, but Miriam pulled her back.

"Let her go. She's been trying so hard all day. I think the true reality of her situation is sinking in."

Karol had tears in her eyes. "But how do we help her?"

"We give her a little space and we just love her. It's an old saying, but time will heal."

Lou slammed the door and threw herself on her bed, screaming into her pillow. Exhausted, she rolled over and stared at the ceiling in the dark.

Reflections from the crystal angel that hung in the window danced across the walls. She felt small, all alone and afraid. Afraid that no matter how hard she tried; she would become her mother.

Lou closed her eyes and rocked herself. She swore she heard the voice calling to her again. *'It's time to leave Lou. Find your own happiness.'* The words kept repeating in her head until she drifted off to sleep.

***

Worried, Karol checked on Lou throughout the night. Sometimes she could see Lou staring at the ceiling and others, she was softly snoring. It was after 4am when she settled down herself, only to be wide awake four hours later to the smell of coffee brewing.

Slipping on her new robe and slippers, she quietly shuffled out to join her mother. When she reached the kitchen, it surprised her to see Lou and Mom sitting at the table talking.

"Good morning, ladies. Here I was trying to be quiet and you're both up." Karol poured herself a cup and joined the table. Lou looked better and Karol relaxed.

"I was filling your mom in on my story about Kelly, and how with your help, we located her family, who turned out to be my family too."

"That is such an amazing story. God works in mysterious ways."

Lou gave a deep sigh.

"I'm sorry, Lou."

"It's okay, Miriam. As much as this hurts me, I wouldn't have missed it for the world. Jason was a good man... no... he was a great man. He taught me how to love and laugh, and for that I will be forever grateful. Today is a new day and I promise to cherish each one in his memory, from now on."

Lou took the last drink of her coffee. "So, ladies, we have a lot to do today. First, I must call my grandmother and tell her lunch is on, second, we pig out at Dad and Mary's, and third, Lord help me, we go shopping. Are you up for all that?"

Karol clapped her hands. "This will be so much fun. And Lou?"

"Yes, Karol."

"No white or beige. Understood?"

Lou gave her a pouty face before going to her room.

Karol shook her head and knew this would be the mother of all challenges.

Chapter Twenty-One

Lou called Grandmother and assured her she would be at the luncheon. She called Julie next, filled her in on the latest news about Karol and her mother living with her, then asked if she would come to the party, before she dropped the bomb, she was going shopping for some new clothes and maybe a dress to wear. Lou swore she could hear Julie choking in the background.

"Okay, you can quit with the gagging routine. I said maybe a dress."

"Are you sure this is my best friend? Is Karol there? I need to talk to her." She was still trying to compose herself.

"Very funny Julie."

"I'm sorry Lou, but you caught me off guard. I think that's wonderful and yes, I would love to be there." She paused. "Do you think Karol would mind if John and Daniel came too? I don't want to cause any trouble, but I really want you to see him. Will you ask her for me?"

"Hang on a minute." Lou walked down the hall and knocked on Karol's door, opening it.

"What's up Lou?" She noticed Lou had her cell phone in her hand.

"Someone wants to talk to you. Bring me the phone when you are done." Lou tossed the phone to her and walked away.

"Hello?"

"Karol?"

"Julie? Oh my God, it's so good to talk to you. How's my... your son? Are you guys happy?" Karol couldn't hold the tears from cascading down her face.

"He's growing like a little weed and he brings us so much joy every day. How are you doing? I hear your mother is living with you and Lou. I'm so happy for you."

Karol sniffled. "I'm doing okay, it really helps to have my mom here. I haven't decided were to go to college yet if you're wondering."

"No. You take all the time you need. The reason—I mean—Lou just told me about the party, and I want to come. I know you said you didn't want to see the baby again, and I don't want to cause you pain, but I really want to bring Daniel and John if you will allow me to."

"Julie, I have no right to tell you what to do. Lou is your best friend. You're his parents. I know I said I never wanted to see him again, but if you come, maybe my mom could meet you and see it was the best thing for him."

"I would like that very much." Julie choked back the words. "Thank you, Karol."

"Your welcome," was all she could say, as she dashed down the hall and tossed the phone back at Lou.

Lou could hear Julie calling Karol's name on the other end.

"Hey Julie, it's me. So, what did she say?"

"She said she would like her mother to meet us, and Daniel."

Lou could hear the quiver in her voice. "What are you worried about now?"

"You don't think after she sees Daniel, she would try to take him away from us, would she?"

"Oh, for heaven's sakes. Karol is an adult; she gave him to you. The courts signed off, and he is yours, so stop worrying. Frown lines don't look good on that pretty face of yours."

She could hear the sigh in Julie's voice.

"I love you so much Lou. And I can't wait to see you in a dress."

"I said, maybe a dress. Anyway, I must go, it's dinner at Dad's. You drive safe and I'll see you next Sunday."

Dinner was fabulous as usual. Miriam and Mary spent their time in the kitchen going over old recipes, as if they had known each other forever. Lou kept Dad and Karol busy with the latest jigsaw puzzle set up in the den while everyone enjoyed Mary's peach cobbler with ice cream.

Lou felt like she was breathing again until they brought up the shopping trip.

Mary agreed to join them and after two hours of trying clothes on, Lou was getting cranky. She thought the new styles looked silly on her, and she didn't like the weird colors that were supposed to be in fashion.

She did find a couple of nice pastel sweaters and chose navy slacks instead of khaki-colored ones, to which Karol rolled her eyes at her.

The hardest part of the trip was finding a dress. Lou conceded that she needed to clean up a little, since Grandmother was going to all the trouble with this luncheon, but nothing compared to the lavender floral print dress she had stuffed in the back of her closet.

Jason had told her she looked beautiful that night and it was the first time he kissed her. The memory choked her up.

"I think I've had enough shopping for one day. How about you ladies?" Lou hung the last dress back on the hanger.

Mary saw the look in her eyes and nodded in agreement

"Your right Lou. Besides, my feet are killing me and its almost closing time."

Karol carried the items Lou had chosen to the register.

"You got a few things, Lou. And I love the navy slacks with the color blocked sweater. You looked so hip."

Lou smiled. Karol could do that with her crazy comments.

"So, I looked real hip, as in big hips your saying?"

Karol frowned, then laughed. "Oh Lou, you know what I mean."

Lou gave her a wink and payed for her purchase. They were all laughing as they exited the store.

After dropping Mary off and thanking her for her help, Lou was ready for bed by the time she pulled into the driveway.

"I don't know about you two, but I can't keep my eyes open. So, I will say goodnight and go to bed as soon as we get inside. And Karol?"

Karol popped her head up from the back seat.

"What?"

"I looked hip, as you say, in that outfit. Thanks for helping, and you too, Miriam."

"It was our pleasure," they chimed in and followed Lou to the house.

Lou went straight to her room, set her new clothes on the bed, and closed the door. She heard Karol and Miriam pass by on the way to their rooms and waited for the sound of doors closing.

Walking to her closet, she slid the doors open. Yes, she was boring, but now, according to Karol, she was hip. Whatever that meant, it made her smile for a moment as her eyes scanned the contents, until they rested on the floral dress and her breath caught in her throat.

Carefully she moved the other clothes aside and pulled it out, holding it against her body. She thought for a moment she could smell Jason's after shave as a wayward tear escaped the rim of her eye.

This was the dress she would wear to the party.

***

Elizabeth had spent the week putting the last changes on the party and so far, everything was going as planned. Thursday evening, she invited George and Mary over to the farmhouse to meet Gene, as she had something to discuss. When she finished talking, George was shocked, and Mary teared up.

"Elizabeth, that's quite a gift, but I don't think she could afford the upkeep, or the taxes on her salary." George said.

"All that has been considered. This house and the land are listed with the National Historical Society, thus freezing all taxes if she keeps it in the family. We had planned on giving it to her mother and feel this is her birthright. There is a maintenance fund set up to take care of any repairs the house may need now, or in the future. The only requirement, she would have to have an open house once a year to keep it registered."

"Where are you going to live, Gene?" Mary asked. "Or will you stay here?"

Gene looked around the kitchen. "As much as I love this house, it's getting too much for me to take care of. I think it's time I turn the keys over to the next generation. Elizabeth has suggested I move to the retirement home she's at. They have a nice unit a few doors down from hers."

George frowned. "What are you going to do is she says no?"

Elizabeth smiled. "I'm not sure, but we can cross that bridge when we get there. I feel this would give her something of her own to focus on."

Mary patted his arm. "Give Lou a chance, George, she may surprise you."

"You're right. I guess I never thought of her leaving the house. I know that sounds silly, but she's been there her whole life. Maybe it's time to start her own memories."

George felt his cell phone buzzing. Pulling it out of his pocket, he recognized the number.

"I need to take this, if you don't mind." He got up and walked down the hall, listening. When he returned to the table, he was white as a ghost.

Mary gasped. "George? What's wrong?"

"You will never believe this."

By the time he finished with his story, everyone agreed on an alternative plan. It would take a little doing, with only three days until the party, but everyone believed they could pull it off.

Chapter Twenty-Two

The Sunday morning dawn pushed through the mini blinds straight into Lou's face and for a moment she thought someone was shining a light in her eyes. Pulling the blanket over her head, she moaned. She could say she was sick and skip this whole party thing, but that would hurt Grandmother's feelings and she never wanted to disappoint her.

"Time to be a big girl, Lou," she muttered to herself and threw the covers back. It wouldn't be too bad. Julie was coming and she would get to see Daniel, and John. And she wanted to have them meet her new family. Springing up with a new resolve, she headed for the shower.

***

Karol paced back and forth in the kitchen. "I don't know if I can keep my mouth shut, Mom. What if I slip up and say something?"

Miriam sipped her coffee. "Calm down, before Lou comes in here. George wouldn't have told you if he didn't think you could manage this. So, put on a smile and try to act natural. Here she comes now. Good morning Lou, would you like a cup of coffee?"

"Stay seated. I can get it myself." Lou poured a larger cup than usual and set it on the table next to Miriam. "Morning Karol."

"Morning Lou." Karol was fidgeting with the buttons on her bathrobe.

"Okay, what's wrong? Are you nervous about seeing Danial today? I can call Julie and ask her not to come."

Karol plopped in the chair next to her mother.

"A little, but I want her to come. This is your party and she should be here."

Lou took a long drink of coffee. "Okay then, I guess we have a party to get ready for."

Miriam took her cup to the sink. "Have you decided on what to wear? We never went back and look for a dress."

"I'm wearing a dress I have. The only one I have, but it means something special to me."

"Then that's what you should do. If you two will excuse me, I'm going to get in the shower before Karol does, and uses up all the hot water."

Karol stuck out her tongue as her mother hurried down the hall. "So, are you excited about today?"

"Honestly, I would like to hide in my room, but I can't disappoint everyone who is trying to be so nice."

"It will be a wonderful day Lou. You just wait and see."

"Really? You know something I don't?"

"I mean, it will be great to see all your friends." She jumped up. "We better get ready. It'll be time to leave before you know."

***

Lou pulled her robe tight around her and emptied her cup. Something was up with Karol, but she couldn't put her finger on it. Probably just the jitters about seeing the baby and the fact her mother would see her only grandchild for the first time too. She was sure it would be an emotional day for everyone.

***

George had been over at the house since dawn, helping set up the tent in the garden. For the end of February, it amazed him the weather was so warm. It would be perfect.

Elizabeth agreed to let him hire a catering company for the food, along with tables, chairs, and anything else he could think of. Mary wanted to help, so she took charge of the dessert and had been in the kitchen all morning.

George was adjusting the last row of chairs when Gene and Elizabeth walked into the tent an hour before the party was to start.

"It looks lovely, George. Especially the yellow roses."

"Do you think she'll get suspicious when she sees all this?"

"I don't know how she would, unless someone tips her off."

Gene shook his head. "Not me."

George's eyes grew misty. "Is the special delivery still set for 3pm?"

"So far everything is on schedule. Has Mary finished the secret dessert?"

"Yes, I had her put it in the parlor like you said, and we locked the door."

Elizabeth smiled. "Well then, I guess you better get cleaned up. We have a party starting in thirty minutes and, from the cars pulling into the driveway, people are already arriving."

Gene held out his arm. "Shall we greet our guests?"

Elizabeth encircled her arm in his and headed for the front door.

George dashed upstairs to change, grateful Mary had brought his clothes with her, and was waiting for him.

"Do you think she'll be mad at us when she finds out?" He was pacing back and forth across the room, shaking his head.

Mary stopped in front of him. "George, take a deep breath before you pass out. She might be for a moment, but it will pass."

George hugged his wife and glanced out the window in amazement. People were lining the sidewalk waiting to get into the garden. He smiled when he recognized the Bakeoven group.

"Your right, Mary. The means justify the end." He held out his arm. "Ready?"

Mary nodded, and together they descended the stairs to greet everyone who came for this special day.

***

Lou looked around at all the cars parked up and down the street. "What in the world are all these people doing here? I thought Grandmother said it was just a few friends and family."

Karol shrugged. "I guess you have more friends than you think. Oh, look. There's Pastor Bill. Come on Momma, I want you to meet him." She pulled at her mother's arm. "You go ahead Lou; we'll see you inside."

Lou stood on the sidewalk, flustered. Pulling her coat tighter, she had a mind to just turn around and go home and would have, if she hadn't heard Julie calling her name.

"Lou. Lou, over here." Julie was waving from the porch.

Lou waved back. "Hi, I'll be right there."

Darn, now she would have to stay. Pasting on a smile, she marched up the steps and gave Julie a hug. John was standing next to her, holding the most adorable baby she had ever seen.

"He's so cute. Have you seen Karol or her mother yet?" Julie gave her a worried look. "Everything will be fine, so relax."

Julie shrugged her shoulders. "You're right. I'm over thinking this. So, let me see the dress. Is it new?"

"No, I couldn't find anything at the store, so I wore one I had."

Julie was motioning for her to unbutton her coat.

"Okay, okay, give me a minute." Releasing the last button, she held it open. "See, it's nothing special."

John let out a low whistle. "You look hot."

Lou closed her coat and shook her head. "You are a depraved man."

"I think you look beautiful, Lou. Shall we go in? I'm sure everyone is waiting for the guest of honor."

Lou frowned. "Do I have to?"

Julie was about to say something when the door opened, and Grandmother was standing there.

"Lou, my darling. We were worrying about you." She gave her a kiss on the cheek. "And who is this beautiful child, with his parents?"

"Grandmother, this is Julie, John and their son Daniel. The ones I told you about."

John held out his hand. "It's nice to meet you, Mrs. Johnson."

Elizabeth clasped his hand with hers. "Oh, please call me Elizabeth. Mrs. Johnson sounds so old." Her smile relaxed them all. "Now that you are here, let's get this party started."

Wrapping her arm in Lou's, she guided her towards the garden.

Dad and Mary were waiting to greet her and had a look of relief when she entered.

"About time, young lady." Dad kissed her cheek. "Let me take your coat."

Lou grudgingly shed her garment.

"You look beautiful, Lou."

"Thanks, Mary. And Dad, it's not my fault. I had to park a block away. Who are all these people?" She scanned the room, looking for familiar faces.

Mary smiled. "I'm not sure, but your grandmother invited them. Oh look, there's Lydia from the Historical Society. If you'll excuse me, I would like to talk to her." She hurried away, leaving them standing at the edge of the tent.

"I know this is awkward for you Lou but try to have a wonderful time." Dad gave her a hug and walked away to say hello to someone he recognized.

Lou chewed on her lip. She could do this; she just had to smile and say hello.

An hour and a half later she had made the rounds and greeted her guests. It had pleased her to see her friends from the Bakeoven story and catch up on how they were doing. Julie and Karol came face to face, and though there were tears in the beginning, everyone including Miriam, were taking turns holding the baby and laughing. Dad was in his glory, making sure the food kept flowing and Mary and Grandmother were keeping a close eye on her.

She was standing at the edge of the garden when Pastor Bill approached.

"How are you doing, Lou?"

Lou continued to gaze across the river. "I don't know. This isn't how I thought my life would be. If you asked me a year ago, I thought I'd be planning my wedding by now, not standing here without him."

Pastor Bill sighed. "It's hard to understand God's wisdom sometimes but try to believe he is watching over you."

Lou turned to face him. "I want to believe God has been on this journey from the beginning, guiding me, but does he have to make it so hard? When do I get to be happy? Look at Julie and Karol and Dad. Even Grandmother and Uncle Gene. I know I'm being childish with all the good I have in my life, but when is it my turn?" She felt her voice crack and was on the verge of tears. "I'm sorry, this is just too much."

Lou dashed for the ladies' room and Pastor Bill went to find George.

***

Elizabeth saw Lou rush by and checked her watch. She wanted to end the charade now, but she had made a promise. If everything went as planned, this would be over in thirty minutes. Until then, she just had to keep Lou from imploding. Following her, she tapped on the door.

"Lou? It's Grandmother. May I come in?" She waited, then tapped again. "Please, Lou."

The door lock clicked and opened slightly. Lou was standing over the sink, staring blindly in the mirror. It broke her heart. "Are you all right, dear?"

Lou lowered her eyes. "I really appreciate what you and the rest of the family and friends are trying to do for me, but I don't think I can stay Grandmother."

Elizabeth put her arms around her. "Just a bit longer. Will you do that for me?"

Lou leaned back against Grandmother's shoulder. "If it means that much to you."

"Thank you and you won't regret this. Now, dry your eyes. We wouldn't want your guests to think you aren't enjoying your party." She handed her a tissue. "That's my girl. Come with me." Elizabeth guided Lou out the door and back to the garden tent.

George and Mary were standing to the side with worried looks on their faces. Elizabeth mouthed, 'it's time' and ushered Lou towards the front, with them following. She signaled to George, and he lifted a glass and tapped on it with a knife to get everyone's attention. The room quieted and Elizabeth stepped forward.

"I would like to thank everyone for coming today to honor my granddaughter Lou, and her family. This reunion has been a long time in the making. The home we are standing in has been in our family for generations, and for a while we feared it might not go on. Fortunately, that won't be the case." She turned to Lou.

"My darling granddaughter, as the rightful heir, Gene and I would like to present this house to you." Gasping voices filled the room. "As our only living relative, we hope you will accept this piece of your history and cherish it as much as we have."

***

Lou glanced over at Dad and Mary, who were nodding at her.

"I don't know what to say."

"Say yes!" A voice yelled from the back of the room.

She knew that voice and jerked her head, trying to see where it had come from. She could feel her heart pounding in her chest when the room parted, and he walked towards her.

"Say yes, Lou, and say you'll marry me here in front of our friends and family."

Lou blinked her eyes. This couldn't be true. She must be having a nervous breakdown, but Jason was standing in front of her, with Joan and Fred behind him. She closed her eyes and could smell his cologne, and when his lips touched hers; she felt like lightning had struck her. She leaned into his arms and whispered. "I thought you were dead. Joan said—"

Jason held her closer. "I'm so sorry, Lou. It was a huge mix up. But I'm here and I'll never leave you again. I love you. Marry me, Lou. Marry me now. Let's not waste another moment apart."

Lou felt her soul take flight. "Yes, I'll marry you."

Jason turned to the crowd and threw up his fist. "She said yes!"

The room erupted in cheers and whistles.

Lou frowned. "How can we get married? We don't have a marriage license."

Dad was standing next to them. He reached in his jacket and pulled out an envelope and handed it to her. "We have taken care of everything Lou."

She looked at him warily. Had he been keeping this from her all day? Had everyone? She looked around the room, full of people she loved and people who loved her and realized it didn't matter. Jason was here, and they were getting married.

Total chaos erupted while, everyone helped move tables out of the way and lined the chairs on each side of the room to form an aisle.

Jason stayed with her dad and Pastor Bill, as Julie and Karol whisked Lou off to the bedroom to give her time to breathe.

"I'm not dreaming this, am I?" Lou stared at herself in the mirror. She turned to Julie, and Karol was shaking her head.

"When did you find out he was alive? Who else knew?"

"Your dad called me this morning. We wanted to tell you, but Jason made everyone promise not to. He's waiting out there and, in a few minutes, my best friend will get married." Julie was fighting back the tears.

Lou threw her arms around Julie and Karol. "I don't know if I should be mad at the two of you or not. I know this is the happiest day of my life."

Karol wrapped her arm in Lou's, Julie did the same.

Dad was waiting in the hall when they came out of the bedroom.

"I'm sorry I kept this from you, but I didn't want to ruin this moment if something had happened and he couldn't get here. I hope you can forgive me."

Lou kissed his cheek. "It's okay, Dad. I know you did it out of love. All of you."

Music began to play in the garden, and that was their cue it was time.

Karol and Julie led the way, and Lou followed, clutching her father's arm. As they entered the garden, Jason stood at the end of the aisle, with Fred next to him. Mary and Joan were waiting in the front row, and Joan handed her a bouquet of yellow roses and dandelion wishes when she got to the front. It was perfect.

Lou could see Dad fighting back tears when he gave her hand to Jason and stepped back. Everything she ever dream of was coming true when Pastor Bill pronounced them husband and wife.

Jason wasted no time kissing his bride to the excitement of the crowd.

When they walked back down the aisle, a beautiful wedding cake was sitting on the table next to the door. Mary beamed and Lou knew she had to have made it. Yellow roses cascaded down the side of the white buttercream frosting and two carved hearts, a gift she knew came from Dad, rested on top. Her emotions were bubbling to the top.

Jason must have felt them too, and he pulled her closer to him. "Are you okay?" he asked, as they stood for pictures before cutting the cake.

Lou could only nod, but the smile on her face said it all.

An hour later most guests had left, and they were standing at the edge of the garden looking out at the river. Lou had pulled two dandelion wishes from her bouquet and was holding them in her hands.

"Do you believe in wishes, Jason?"

"Yes, I do. From the first day I met you, I wished that my heart would heal, and I could love again. Then the accident happened, and I wished you could love me the way I loved you. When I became lost, I wished God would bring me home to you. If it hadn't been for your story about Bakeoven Road, none of my wishes would have come true." He turned to face her. "What about you? What are your wishes?"

Lou tilted her head. "I wished to find a story that would change the way the world saw me, to prove that I mattered. I wished to find Kelly's family and found more than I could have imagined. I wished for love, but I was too scared to accept it and when I finally did, you were gone. I wished to find peace, only to discover God had a plan of his own when you walked into the room."

Lou handed the dandelion to Jason. "Will you make a last wish with me?"

Jason held the stem in his hand. "And what are we wishing for?"

"How about everlasting love?" Lou lifted the puff to her lips.

Jason followed her lead. "I think that's a perfect wish. Are you ready?"

Lou nodded.

The dandelion seed puffs burst upward, dancing on the breeze, lifting them high into the evening sky. Jason and Lou watched until they disappeared, then hand in hand, walked back to the house, to the beginning of a new wish.

The End

Acknowledgements

I hope you have enjoyed the final journey of Lou and Jason in their quest for happiness.

I want to thank my readers, family and friends who continue to encourage me on this journey.

Coming 2021

A new two book series:

Book one:
"Life of a Lie"

Book two:
"Lies Never Die"

Check out information at sandycereghino.com